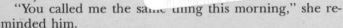

"What was the meani   r-lier?" Shannon asked.

Hunter did not answ   r closely.

"You called me the same thing this morning," she reminded him.

"Peta Wicahpi." Hunter spoke the name as he would a gentle caress. "It means Morning Star. I call you this because your beauty rivals that of the star that rises over mother earth each day."

He reached out and pulled the pins from the top of her head. Her thick copper rope of hair fell down her back. "Your hair shimmers with the gold of the Morning Star," he went on. "I would see it free, hanging down your body."

She pulled her eyes away from his intense regard and jumped to her feet, breathless, speechless, embarrassed. "I . . . I should be leaving," she said.

Hunter's smile was tender, his voice husky as he asked, "Will you return to me tomorrow?"

Some inner sense of caution told Shannon that she should run for her horse and never look back. But instead, she promised to return, then rushed out of the cabin. For a few trembling moments she leaned against the frame of the door.

What kind of strange power did this man hold over her? she asked herself. How was it possible that she could feel herself melting from within by the simple sound of his voice? Why, she had almost reached out and run her hand over the bronze flesh above his heart!

BOOK YOUR PLACE ON OUR WEBSITE AND MAKE THE READING CONNECTION!

We've created a customized website just for our very special readers, where you can get the inside scoop on everything that's going on with Zebra, Pinnacle and Kensington books.

When you come online, you'll have the exciting opportunity to:

- View covers of upcoming books
- Read sample chapters
- Learn about our future publishing schedule (listed by publication month *and author*)
- Find out when your favorite authors will be visiting a city near you
- Search for and order backlist books from our online catalog
- Check out author bios and background information
- Send e-mail to your favorite authors
- Meet the Kensington staff online
- Join us in weekly chats with authors, readers and other guests
- Get writing guidelines
- AND MUCH MORE!

Visit our website at
http://www.zebrabooks.com

BLAZE OF
DESIRE

KATHLEEN
DRYMON

Zebra Books
Kensington Publishing Corp.

http://www.zebrabooks.com

PROLOGUE

The Great Plains.

It was during the season when the snowmaker places his blanket of white over the face of grandmother earth that the army soldier coats attacked Spotted Pelt's Lakota village and took his wife, Hinhan Ska, Snowy Owl, and their two sons far away.

Hinhan Ska was known among the people as She-With-The-Pale-Hair, and Spotted Pelt loved her beyond all life had to offer. The war chief knew it was not the Great Spirit's will that his family be taken away from their people. He went far from his village in his search for his family, but he never found them.

Three years later, during the time when game is scarce, Spotted Pelt crossed over to join the sky people. His father, Two Owls, never forgot the family that had been taken from his son.

Two years after Spotted Pelt went on to join the spirits of his ancestors, a young warrior of fourteen summers rode into Two Owls's village. The young man's slate-gray eyes were hard, his features strained with knowledge that one his age should not have had.

The young warrior was known as Hunter, one of the children of spotted Pelt and Hinhan Ska. In his hand he clutched a small box close to his heart.

Hunter was solemn. There was none of the rejoicing among the villagers as is expected when a lost son returns

among the Sioux. As he rode his war horse through the
village, he acknowledged none of the greetings of welcome
called out to his name. He halted his mount outside his
grandfather's tepee. Entering the lodge, he greeted Two
Owls before the old warrior's central fire pit.

Silent tears escaped his silver eyes as he held out the
box as though presenting Two Owls with a great treasure.
"Grandfather, I have brought my mother's and my
brother's heart home. Their spirits will at last be able to
rest now that they are returned to the sacred mountains
of the people."

Lifting the lid, and drawing away the piece of hide cover,
the old warrior began to sing the death chant that he had
been taught long ago by his father. Setting the box down
next to his fire, he pulled forth his sacred pipe, the stem
made from the leg bone of a buffalo, the bowl from red
pipe stone.

As Two Owls continued to chant, at intervals he drew
upon the pipe stem and blew smoke toward the box, the
swirling gray clouds caressed the contents before traveling
up the lodge's smoke hole, and carrying on to the land
of the spirits.

ONE

Sleep this evening was proving far too hard to win. Try as she might, Shannon Stone was finding it impossible to get comfortable. Once again her copper curls rose up from the pillow and she beat a slender fist upon the satin pillowcase. Laying her head back down upon the soft indentation, she could not chase away the memories of having been caught eavesdropping outside her uncle Graylin's study door.

"Blaze and damnation!" Why should she feel like the one who had done something wrong? Her uncle and his business partner had been talking about her, after all! If Uncle Graylin had not spoken her name so loudly, he would not have drawn her attention as she was passing the room.

In the darkness of the chamber she could feel the flush of heat that stained her delicate cheekbones. Her big mistake had been in forgetting Ralph, uncle Graylin's manservant, and ever-watchful spy! It had been the despicable little man who had grabbed hold of her elbow and pulled her through the study door after he had spied her lingering in the hallway. It had been Ralph who had forced her to stand before Graylin Stone's wrath.

Throughout Shannon's eighteen years she had rarely backed down from anything, and shielding herself with her own anger at overhearing her uncle planning her future as though she were no more to him than another parcel of property, she had braved the lion in his den with as much courage as she could muster.

It had been plainly revealed on Graylin Stone's features that he was furious with his niece. Shannon had easily viewed his ill humor as he ordered her upstairs and demanded she remain in her room until such time as he wished to speak to her. Uncle Graylin was not used to being caught unaware, and that evening his anger was revealed, not only because of the embarrassment suffered him in front of his partner, but also because his intentions toward his brother's daughter had been so boldly found out.

Shannon had overheard her uncle claim he had every intention of marrying her off to the highest bidder as soon as possible. As he revealed his plans to Zack Majors, Shannon heard him mention that the man he intended to choose as husband for his niece would be a man under his own control, one whom he would be able to manipulate when his niece came of age and received her inheritance. Graylin Stone held every intention of keeping tight control over his dead brother's properties and money.

Shannon's own anger had been highly inflated after hearing her uncle's intentions for her future. Standing there in front of him as he sat so smugly behind his desk, she would have told him exactly what she thought of his plans, and in fact would have assured him that he would not find a willing accomplice in his niece. But Ralph's fingers were digging into her upper arm, and before she could get the words out that would condemn Graylin Stone for the foulest kind of kin, Ralph was dragging her from the study and up the stairs to her room. The heated words that surged out of her mouth were shouted upon the manservant's head as he had closed the chamber door after shoving her into the bedchamber.

Shannon was wise enough to know that come tomorrow she would be confronted by her uncle's full wrath. Graylin Stone was a man who could be very cruel to those he deemed deserving of his harshness, and now that a few hours had passed since the incident downstairs in the study had taken place, and Shannon had had time to calm her own anger, she held no doubt that in Graylin's mind he considered his niece fully deserving of any cruelty he might inflict.

The upstairs portion of the house was quiet at this late hour. Sighing out a soft breath, Shannon sat upright on the bed, knowing that sleep would delude her throughout most of this night. She was much too worried about what would take place tomorrow to be able to sleep.

Pulling a satin wrapper over her shoulders and tying it at the waist, she made up her mind to go downstairs in search of a book. Tomorrow would come soon enough, and she held every intention of telling her uncle exactly what she thought of his plans for her future. Graylin Stone would soon enough realize she was no weak-kneed child who would easily do his bidding!

Leaving the bedchamber, Shannon found the lower portion of her uncle's mansion held in dark shadows. Fortunately she found a fire still burning in the grate in Graylin's study.

By firelight she searched the rows of expensive books that lined the spacious walls. Choosing a novel on an upper shelf, its rich red leather binding catching her attention, Shannon turned to leave her uncle's private domain, when from the corner of her eye she noticed the double doors standing slightly ajar.

The evening air held a damp chill. Approaching the door, Shannon shivered beneath the silk wrap. Uncle Graylin and the servants must have overlooked the open doors. Reaching for the knob, a noise from outside drew Shannon's full attention.

Aided by moonlight, Shannon was able to easily make out her uncle's features where he stood outside on the patio. He appeared to be arguing with man of smaller statue. Graylin's voice was loud and hard.

Before Shannon could attempt to turn and leave the two men to their privacy, she noticed her uncle raise his arm out and in an upward position. In the next instant the sharp report of gunfire filled the air. Sparks and acrid smoke circled the patio.

The man before Graylin slumped to the terra-cotta tile floor in a dead weight.

A sharp gasp of shocked denial left Shannon's parted lips. The hand holding the book opened in reflex to grab the door for support, and the book fell to the study floor. Disbelief over what she had just witnessed paled Shannon's features. Her wide blue-green eyes lifted slowly from the still form at her uncle's feet, and as they did, her gaze met and locked with Graylin Stone's.

His attention drawn by the noise coming from the study doorway, Graylin's gaze shifted from the man he had just killed to his niece standing pale and trembling beneath the moonlight. Instant rage fired anew. What the hell was the girl doing in his study at this late hour? Was she spying on him? Was there more going on here than met the eye? Perhaps one of his enemies had gotten to her, and she had agreed to report to them his dealings here at Stoneridge. This thought quickly tempered his caution. *Don't do anything rash. Take care of one problem at a time!*

Turning to confront his niece fully, Graylin lifted the hand that still clutched the pistol. Pointing the weapon directly at her, he ordered through gritted teeth, "Take yourself to your chamber. You and I will talk later!"

Shannon did not wait around to see what next her uncle might do. His voice broke the spell of disbelief that had overtaken her. The blood returned to her face in a heated rush as her heartbeat hammered wildly in her chest. Without a backward glance to see what her uncle would do with the man's body, or if he had begun to follow her into the study, she began to run through the lower portion of the house, up the stairs, to her bedchamber.

Slamming the door, she pressed her back against the wood frame as she drew in deep breaths of air. She relieved the scene of her uncle shooting the defenseless man until her head began to throb relentlessly.

What should she do now, she asked herself. At the moment she felt quite incapable of making a clear decision.

Get dressed, and go out into the streets in search of the authorities! that quicker portion of her mind cried out. But as soon as the thought struck, she reasoned it aside. By then her uncle was probably clearing away the little man's body and any disorder made by the senseless-appearing murder. By the time she could bring back the authorities, all evidence would be gone, and she would be left alone at Stoneridge to face her uncle's wrath.

Flee! The one word filled her brain. She had witnessed her uncle commit murder. She knew him to be far more ruthless and cunning of mind than any man she had ever known, and now she saw he could also be deadly!

He may well change his mind about marrying her off to a man who was held in his pocket. He might decide to do to her as he had done to the poor man on the patio! If she were to die, her entire inheritance would go to her uncle, he being her only living relative.

The horrible thought spurred Shannon into action. Hurrying over to the wardrobe, she pulled out a warm velvet traveling jacket, skirt, and a pair of kid boots. In short minutes she was dressed, and had finished throwing a few articles of clothing and personal belongings into her smallest carrying valise.

The coins she had in the bureau were few, but they would have to do until she could figure out where to go, and what she should do about the murder she had witnessed this night.

Right now she held no doubt that her life was in jeopardy as long as she remained at Stoneridge. If Uncle Graylin caught her in the act of fleeing, she could only imagine the repercussions her act would evoke.

Stepping to the chamber door, her hand hesitated as she reached out to turn the glass knob. Instead, she turned the key in the lock, then set the key on the vanity.

Going downstairs might well prove a grave mistake; her mind was thinking fast now. Surely, her uncle would be watching and listening for anyone on the stairway. More than likely, he had already engaged his trustworthy servant, Ralph, to help him dispose of the small man's body and clean up any sign of an altercation having taken place on the patio. They would hear her if she moved down into the lower portion of the house.

Racing across the Oriental carpet, Shannon pried the chamber window wide enough for her and her valise to slip without. There was a wooden trellis beneath the window. Shannon prayed that it would prove strong enough to hold up to her weight.

Daring to breathe in only short, erratic gasps of air, Shannon slowly climbed down the trellis. Her dark cloak was secured by the clasp at her throat, the handles of the valise strapped over her right shoulder.

An eternity passed before her booted foot touched the damp earth. Anxiously her turquoise eyes searched the manicured front lawns of Stoneridge, searching for any sign of a servant who might have been posted by her uncle, to keep watch.

Her eyes quickly adjusted to the darkness that enshrouded her. The patio was on the opposite side of the house from her chamber, and with any luck Uncle Graylin would be busy for a while longer before seeking her out in her chamber.

Shannon was wise enough to know that the locked door would be a barrier against him for only a short time. Knowing Graylin Stone as well she had come to know him over the past few months, she knew that a locked door would stand in his way for only a few minutes. Once he realized that his niece had fled him, he would be furious, and his fury would know no assuaging until he found her!

Such thoughts hurried her feet into motion. She did not have a spare minute to linger there beneath the chamber window. Tightening the dark cloak over her shoulders, she grasped the handle of the valise and began to run down the long, tree-shaded lane that lead up to Stoneridge.

The dark shadows cast by the trees intensified her fear of the night, and several times she made herself stand absolutely still. Clutching in her breath, she listened for any sign of her uncle or one of his servants giving chase.

Reaching St. Louis's main thoroughfare, Shannon directed her steps toward the dock area. She had been given little time to formulate a plan, but she did know that in order for her to survive, she had to get away from St. Louis. Her uncle was too powerful a man for her to remain in the city for long without him finding her.

The slim hope that filled her heart was that one of the riverboat captains might be persuaded to give her passage upriver. She vaguely held on to the thought that she would have enough coins in her valise to purchase a place on a riverboat, and be taken to Davenport Ohio.

Once she arrived in Davenport, she would send word to her father's solicitor, Homer Griswold. The elder man had always treated her kindly in the past while her father was alive. It had been Mr. Griswold who had soothed over the initial loss of her father, and the subsequent announcement that she would have to become the ward of her uncle. She felt sure that Mr. Griswold would know what actions she should take in order to insure her uncle Graylin pay for his crime of murder.

The waterfront district at this hour of night was teeming with life. The closer Shannon drew to the docks, the more the noise and activity appeared to intensify. On both sides of the street she viewed warehouses and shanties, and her unease of the area grew.

For safety's sake she cautioned herself to stay well away from the shadowed alleyways that appeared at short intervals along the street.

Attempting to keep away from any display of light caused by streetlamps, Shannon felt internal panic gripping her belly when she noticed two men up ahead crossing to the side of the street she was on.

Before the pair reached her, a small group of women left an establishment directly before her and passed her on the sidewalk. Their generous dousing of cologne mixed with the unpleasant odor of unwashed bodies was overpowering to her senses. Shannon was forced to step aside and allow them ease in which to pass her.

The women were a carefree group, their dress rather shabby in style, but they appeared dazzling beneath the dim gaslight, with their brightly colored dresses, feathers, and bows. The two men up ahead quickly took step with the group of women and amid laughter and catcalls the group went on their way, seeming not to take the slightest notice of the young woman wearing the expensive furlined cloak and holding a richly appointed valise tightly against her slender form.

Clutching the front of her cloak with a tight fist, aqua eyes wearily watched every movement along the street. The populace in this portion of St. Louis appeared much rougher than what Shannon was accustomed to associating with.

Her steps quickened. Now and then she looked over her shoulder to ensure she wasn't being followed by someone sent by her uncle.

Hurriedly, she passed the open door of an ale shop. Her breath stopped harshly in her lungs as the light from within spilled out onto the sidewalk and illuminated her presence. Her breath exhaled as she realized that no one within paid her any notice.

She had gone only a few steps farther down the sidewalk, when she was accosted by a drunken dock man.

"Over here, girlie. Come on over here and give Big Ben a wet kiss!"

Shannon jumped back in terror as the large, unkempt brute stumbled out of a dark alleyway next to the ale house. Dodging a beefy hand reaching out to grab her, she clutched her valise tightly to her breasts as she took off at a dead run down the sidewalk.

Big Ben's curses followed her footsteps. "Ye sprightly, little bitch! What harm be there in giving away a few kisses? In his state of inebriation Big Ben was in no shape to take off after the young woman. Instead, he turned back toward the alehouse. "I be finding me a bawd here in Johnny's den who will be appreciating Big Ben," he mumbled to himself.

Shannon ran until she feared her lungs would burst. When at last she dared to chance a backward glance over her shoulder and see if Big Ben was giving chase, she sagged against the side of a clapboard building. Relief filled her as she glimpsed no one giving chase, and drew in great gulps of reviving air.

Only a few seconds passed, which gave her time in which to gather herself, before Shannon heard a sharp whistle from across the street. Two men stood next to a brick building. Having watched the young woman taking flight down the sidewalk, they thought to try their own hand at capturing her attention.

"Hey, lass, ye appear to be in a right big hurry. Do ye be wanting some company on this lonely night? Me and me mate here have some coins to rent us a room. If'n ye be shy, and haven't been having two at a go a'fore, don't let that be a'scaring ye none. We have had us plenty of practice in the matter a'fore, and can be doing ye some fine justice! Ye'll be right pleased come morning, we promise!"

"No! Just stay away from me!" Shannon cried aloud as the full impact of the man's words settled upon her. Without waiting another second, once again she was racing down the sidewalk.

"Now, see what ye gone and done, Petty? Ye gone and chased her away. Ye always were one to be having a big mouth! Ye should have tried a little coaxing with such a dove."

Shannon rounded the street corner, her nostrils filling with the tangy odors of the waterfront as she slumped into a dark corner to the side of a building.

Fear and panic were a heady inducement for exhaustion, and realizing that it was far too dangerous for her to roam the streets alone at night, she began to look for a place in which to hide away for the rest of the evening.

Staring down into the dark alleyway next to the building she was leaning against, she shivered with inner terror as she remembered that Big Ben had stepped out of just such an passage. With indecision goading her every thought, Shannon turned from the alleyway, her blue-green eyes searching frantically for a small space in which to hide.

A few steps down the sidewalk an overhead swinging sign drew her attention. *Madame Lilly's Retreat For Young Ladies,* the wooden sign read.

A noise from behind her instantly made up Shannon's mind. She took the sign to mean that the establishment was some kind of school for young women. Though at the moment she did not question why such a school would be in this district of the city, she knew only that her chances of survival were far better inside this Madame Lilly's establishment than out alone on the streets!

Slipping through the front door undetected, Shannon found herself standing in a small gilt-and-red-wallpapered foyer; the tracings of the artful pattern illuminated by rose candlelight. Music and laughter assailed her from the room to the left. To the right of the foyer was a stairway that led upward to the second-floor landing.

Knowing her appearance was in severe disrepair after her flight through the St. Louis streets, Shannon could not force herself to take the necessary steps that would lead her into the room to her left.

Hesitating only a few seconds, she began to silently climb the red-carpeted stairway. If she could only find an empty space in which to rest until morning, she would be eternally grateful.

Silently, Shannon made her way down the long hallway on the upper floor. High-pitched feminine laughter, followed by a hoot of male glee, assaulted her from beyond the first chamber door and hurried her steps down the hall.

Her hand tightened on the handle of her valise as she

wondered what kind of school Madame Lilly was running. Nervously, she passed the next closed door, and then the next. At the very end of the hall she drew in a deep breath in order to steady her frayed nerves.

Reaching out a tentative hand, she lightly took hold of the brass doorknob. Cautiously, Shannon pulled the door open a few inches. Ready to dart back down the hallway at the slightest provocation, she peered into the dim interior.

A single candle was lit on a small table next to a net-draped bed. Shannon could barely make out the outline of a pale figure beneath a mound of lacy covers.

"Who is there?" A soft voice moaned out the question. "Violet, is that you? For a moment . . . I feared that Lilly had sent up a customer, but I should have known that even she could not be so cruel. I was hoping you would come before the end, Violet. I can no longer see clearly, dear, so you must come closer. Please hold my hand. I am so afraid of being alone when my time comes."

Standing frozen in her tracks, Shannon stared at the woman on the bed. Looking back down the hall, she was unsure if she should enter the room or flee the house and return to the streets.

"Madame Lilly won't know you are here in my room. Just sit with me for a few minutes. That is, if you're not too busy with a gentleman. I am so lonely." A racking cough took hold of the woman's frail form, the bedcovers shivering with her fit of coughing.

If, like the woman claimed, she could not see clearly, what harm could there be in spending some time in her chamber, Shannon asked herself. The woman's voice held a pleading quality that was hard for Shannon to turn away from.

Deciding that the chamber would be preferable to the dangers of the streets, Shannon eased the door shut and slowly made her way toward the side of the bed. At any second she expected the woman to call out that she was an impostor, and not the woman called Violet, who she believed her to be.

Anxiously, Shannon stood at the bedside, and as seconds passed, her gaze traveled around the room. The entire chamber was decorated in a gaudy display of red, pink, purple, and gold. On the far wall hung a large painting of a naked woman reclining upon a scarlet and gilt-edged sofa.

"Sit here in the chair next to the bed, Violet. You need not say anything. I only fear dying alone."

Now that Shannon was there in the chamber, she had to strain to hear the woman's softly spoken words. As the realization hit that the woman was dying, Shannon's gaze went back toward the chamber door. It might be wiser to find someplace else in which to pass the night. But even as she thought this, she did as the dying woman bid.

Placing her valise on the floor next to the chair, she sat down in the straight-back chair pulled up to the woman's bedside.

The woman sighed softly. For a minute or two she lay still against the red-satin-encased pillow beneath her auburn head.

Shannon studied the gray-tinged features, and for a few seconds wondered if indeed she had already died, so still was the woman, Shannon could not view any movement from her chest.

"Fate can rule one's destiny with a cruel hand, Violet. I have so painstakingly found this to be true. Only a few months past I believed I held the world in the palm of my hand."

Shannon heard the pain trembling in the straining voice and offered the little comfort she could to the dying woman. "Shh, there is no need for you to tell me this now. Try to rest, perhaps you will be able to regain your strength."

The woman attempted to laugh, and once again was thrown into a fit of coughing.

Noticing a bowl of water and rag on the small table next

to the bedside, Shannon dampened the cloth and pressed it against the woman's fevered brow, brushing aside the dull-red strands of hair.

"I will get all the rest I'll be needing soon enough." she whispered as the coughing spasms quieted.

"It is hard to believe now that the painting on the wall over there is me. The most famous artist in the city sought me out. Me, Honey Belle, he declared to be the most beautiful woman in all of St. Louis. I am told that hundreds of copies of the painting were made. They hang in saloons and dance halls all across the West. I guess I have had my few minutes of fame here in this lifetime."

How could Shannon respond to the dying woman's words? Her surprise at the woman's confessing to having been the model for such a lurid painting she kept to herself. It was apparent the woman needed someone to confide in before she passed from this life, and Shannon was the only one available to act the part of the dying woman's confessor.

"I had so many plans for the future. Now they are all for naught." Honey Belle sighed heavily, and silvery tears made a path down her sallow cheeks.

"I was to leave for Montana Territory tomorrow morning on the steamship *Missouri Lady.* This was my most guarded secret. I didn't wish for Madam Lilly to get wind of my plans. Once one becomes one of her girls one hardly ever gets away from her. But still, I had my hopes."

Shannon wasn't quite sure what the young woman was talking about, but she allowed her to ramble on without interruption. After all, the woman was dying, and she deserved at the least to be allowed to say her piece, even if she wasn't making sense.

"You see, Violet, I answered an ad in the St. Louis, Missouri, gazette, for a mail-order bride. The papers are all there in the top drawer of the nightstand, with my passage ticket, and money for stage fare. I married a gentleman called Alex Cordoba. Can you tell by his name that he is a gentleman?"

Taken by surprise at this new revelation, Shannon softly agreed. "Yes, Honey, he sounds very much like a gentleman."

"We were married by proxy. Oh, it's all legal. It was done in front of a lawyer. Honey Belle Cordoba, that's my name now. Only, you are the only one that will ever know my secret."

"It is a beautiful name." Shannon felt her throat beginning to tighten with sympathy for the woman.

"I had my dreams of going to Montana Territory and losing my past forever. I hoped to be able to have at least a dozen kids like my own mother did. Only I would have showered each and every one of them with lots of love. None of my daughters would be turned over to a whoremaster in order for their mother to buy a pint of gin."

Shannon was shocked by such a confession and could not imagine the hardship Honey Belle had endured in her lifetime. "Hold on to your dreams, Honey." Shannon soothed the fevered brow with the dampened cloth.

For another hour or so Honey Belle revealed her plans for a future she would never live to see. Twice during the conversation convulsive shuddering overtook her frail frame, and afterward she stilled, her breathing barely discernible. It was after the third such attack that Honey Belle Cordoba passed on to her maker.

Shannon wept softly at the young woman's bedside. In life and death a kinship had been formed between the two women, and Shannon knew she would always remember Honey Belle's dreams.

Straightening out the bedding around the young woman who now appeared to have at last found a measure of peace, Shannon noticed that the first traces of dawn were stealing over the city. "I hope you find the happiness you deserve, Honey." The woman's spirit was now free to travel the open spaces of the land she had believed she would have been able to lose her past in.

Shannon's glance went to the night table, and as it did, she asked herself if this Montana Territory could be far enough away for her to hide from a man like Graylin Stone.

Feeling like an intruder even though she had shared the most intimate part of Honey Belle's life, Shannon pulled the small drawer open and picked up the small packet within, tied with a piece of scarlet ribbon.

As the dying woman had claimed, there was a ticket to travel upriver on the *Missouri Lady*, a sum of cash, and legal documents stating that Honey Belle had indeed wed a gentleman by the name of Alex Cordoba six weeks prior.

Staring down at the papers in her hand, Shannon realized that she was looking at the means in which she could lose her own past, and the threat that her uncle posed, at least until she could claim her inheritance, and at the same time reveal to the authorities what she had witnessed that night outside Graylin Stone's study.

TWO

"This will be the first and the last such appearance that you will make here at Stoneridge, Mr. Ivey. From here on out, we will conduct business only through A. D. Armstrong, our mutual contact."

Not by so much as a flicker of an eyelash did the man sitting across from Graylin Stone indicate that he was put out by the abrupt instruction. Nathaniel Ivey was used to dealing with men such as Graylin Stone. There was little difference in this rich man sitting before him and the others who had crossed Ivey's path. Money and power bought them the right to give orders and have said orders carried out.

"Here is the packet that I told Armstrong I would have ready for you. Inside you will find a description of my niece. Also, I wrote down a few of her peculiarities. Perhaps something in there will give you a lead to her whereabouts." Graylin slid a large envelope across his desk toward Ivey.

Ivey's dark gaze never left Graylin's ruddy features. "Armstrong said she has been missing for two days." It wasn't a question but a statement to verify that the information he had already received about this case was correct. Nathaniel Ivey was a man who made few mistakes in his line of work, this due to the fact that he was meticulous in his searching out every detail regarding his quarry.

If not for the fact that he had been assured Ivey was the

best in his profession, Graylin would have held doubts about the slender man with the soft, gravely voice. *Deadly* did not seem to be an accurate description of the man sitting so at ease across from his desk.

"It would appear, Mr. Ivey, that my niece has simply vanished. My men have combed the city for her without much luck. As far as I know, she has little money. I would suggest you start your search along the wharf area in the city. She might have decided to return to Ohio, where she was living before my brother died and she came here to Stoneridge as my ward."

It didn't matter to Ivey one way or the other about Graylin Stone's reasons for wanting his niece silenced. "Armstrong told you my fee?"

"The money, as well, is in the packet. Wire Armstrong if you need anything else. An account has been set up. I will expect an updated report of your progress at reasonable intervals, Mr. Ivey. It is important to me that you take care of this matter in a timely fashion." If Shannon told anyone what she had witnessed, everything Graylin had built up over the years would be destroyed; his reputation as well as his freedom were at stake here!

"Leave the matter to me, Mr. Stone. Your niece's fate need not concern you again." Ivey gazed down at the envelope on the desk, his piercing eyes were fanatical as they looked back toward Graylin.

"I am considered by some to be the right hand of the Lord. This Jezebel will be banished before His kingdom, and placed within that resting place where she will be unable to do any more harm."

Graylin appeared somewhat taken back by the man's words but did not question his strange form of speech. What did it matter to him if the bloke thought himself the right hand of the Lord? All that mattered was the job be taken care of before it became a problem too large for Graylin to see its finish. "Don't disappoint me, Mr. Ivey." Graylin rose to his feet, dismissing the man from his study.

"You won't be disappointed, Mr. Stone." Ivey's slim fingers reached out and picked up the packet before he turned and walked through the study door.

Graylin Stone held no remorse for what he had set into motion. It was either him or his niece. He was not a man who would allow anything to stand in his way.

"Here now, watch your step, miss." The first mate of the *Missouri Lady* reached out a steadying hand to assist Shannon's descent down the gangplank, the board stretching from riverboat to dock.

"Please allow me to help you with your bag, Miss Belle." Robert Vale appeared at Shannon's side, and with an easy grace maneuvered the handle of her valise from her hand into his own even before her copper head nodded in agreement.

Shannon bestowed a gracious smile upon the first mate of the *Missouri Lady,* who had been kind to her throughout the voyage upriver. As he went back to his work, she turned her attention upon Robert Vale, who, she had learned aboard the riverboat, was a gambler having come west to explore the possibilities of enriching the wealth in his pockets.

The first day aboard the *Missouri Lady* Shannon had remained isolated in her cabin. Her worry over being signaled out for an impostor had kept her on constant guard.

As the days passed aboard the *Missouri Lady* and no one appeared to be aware that she had taken over another's identity, her charade became easier to play out. Strangely, Shannon found herself feeling carefree and at ease around people now that she had taking over Honey Belle's identity. With her burnt-copper curls flowing down her back and resting against her waist, and her flashing turquoise eyes, Shannon had been too hard for most of the males aboard the *Missouri Lady* to resist. She had been entertained and praised for her rare beauty, and slowly she had stepped into the role of another's character.

As she gaily laughed at some sally a young man quoted

for her ears alone, she could easily imagine Honey Belle
flirting in a like fashion in the days before she had taken
ill.

Shannon had always been a tad overly reserved; her father had devoted much of his time to teaching her to relax
and enjoy life, but Shannon had always held a measure of
distrust about other people's motives.

Charles Stone had spoiled his only child outrageously,
taking her with him on long business trips, and on holidays
to Paris, London, and occasionally New York. She had always had the best that life had to offer, and lived a well-
guarded life. But now, as she posed as Honey Belle, she
was finding it easier for her to trust people, and to relax
her guard, and forget the fact that she was heiress to a vast
fortune.

"Will you be going straight on to Montana Territory,
Miss Belle? Or will you perhaps be staying on here in Great
Falls for a few days?" Robert Vale prided himself as being
a gentleman of the first form. A good hand of poker, a
smooth glass of brandy, and a beautiful woman dangling
on his arm lent him all the necessities that life had to offer.
If time allowed, he would be more than pleased to be the
gentleman that would escort Miss Honey Belle through
the town of Great Falls.

"I'm afraid I will be going straight way to the stage depot, Mr. Vale." Shannon glanced up and down the street,
wondering in what direction she might find the stage office.

"Allow, me, my dear. I have been to this fair town on a
past occasion. It will be my pleasure, even though my disappointment, to escort you to Mr. Bragg's stage line."

"You are very kind, Mr. Vale." The morning Shannon
had left Madame Lilly's school for young ladies in search
of the *Missouri Lady*, she had been consumed with fear
that she would be seen by her uncle or one of his servants,
but her fear had lessened considerably with each mile she
had put between herself and St. Louis. Her fears now were
those of the unknown. This was the first time in her life

she had been forced to depend totally on herself. Any offered assistance by such a kind gentleman, she would certainly not turn aside.

The stagecoach was due to depart the station shortly after Shannon arrived at the depot. Her valise was quickly taken and strapped atop the concord as soon as she handed over the ticket agent the required cash for her ticket.

Standing on the sidewalk, her blue-green gaze showing amazement as she noticed the number of men sitting atop the vehicle. The driver and guard were already in position upon the wooden seat atop the coach, and at least five other men were sitting on the large concord and clutching any available strapping in order to keep their seat.

Never having traveled by such means in the past, Shannon looked to Robert Vale for information. "Is this usual?" As well, the interior of the vehicle looked overly crowded with travelers sitting on both seats.

"I'm afraid so, Miss Belle. Transportation in these parts is hard to come by, and everyone takes advantage of the stage." Robert Vale's dark eyes held some sympathy for her plight. He had traveled by stage in the past, and did not envy her the few days' travel she still had before reaching her destination.

If not for the fact that Shannon still held some worry over her uncle tracking her down, she might have made the decision to stay on in Great Falls after looking at the stagecoach.

Attempting to hold forth a brave front, she drew in a deep breath before smiling in a reassuring manner at the gentleman at her side. "I'm sure I will be very comfortable within the vehicle. I was just somewhat surprised to see so many passengers, that's all."

Robert Vale did not respond by words, his concerned smile said it all. Soon enough the young woman would learn that there was little comfort to be had in a concord of this size. The best she would be hoping for at the start of each new day would be for the day to end quickly and the stagecoach to arrive without mishap at the designated stop for the night.

Shannon waved fondly at Robert Vale from her position on one of the interior seats, where she had been forced to squeeze in next to the window and a very large elderly woman. This was the second leg of her journey, and she told herself that even cramped within the vehicle as she was, she would not allow her spirits to become disheartened.

By midafternoon Shannon was all but ready to scream. The stagecoach was a shuddering vehicle of torture! Starting with the first lurch of the concord, her spine had been jarred down hard upon the spring-worn seat, and from there on things only worsened.

Perhaps she would have borne up to these hardships of travel somewhat better if the fat lady sitting next to her did not smell of perspiration with a liberal amount of flowery perfume dosed over foul odor. The heat within the cramped space trapped the woman's stench and circled it back in forth among the travelers.

On the other side of the fat lady was a slender man of middle age, who held a small birdcage on his lap. The bird was a gift for his daughter and his wife, who had stayed on at their farm while he had gone alone to handle business matters in Great Falls.

On the opposite seat sat a family consisting of a farmer, his wife, and three small children. The baby on his mother's lap whined without letup, and the two other children miserably bemoaned their discomfort.

The combination of passengers, dust, and body odor was enough to give any person a splitting headache, and by the finish of the day, Shannon's head indeed throbbed with a piercing numbness.

By the time the concord pulled up in front of the Thompson farmhouse shortly after dusk, the passengers had to be assisted from the vehicle in order not to fall over in their tracks from total exhaustion.

The Thompson farm was the first such station the concord would stop at. Here at the farm, the driver would rest the horses overnight and change any of the animals that appeared lacking from his team.

Stella Thompson, the stationmaster's kindly wife, had a pot of bubbling stew on her crude hearth awaiting the weary travelers, and crusty bread came hot from the oven to sop out the last remains in the tin plates she offered at her table.

Shannon was simply too tired to appreciate the tasty cuisine, and after barely nibbling at the fare in front of her, she beckoned to Mrs. Thompson to be shown to her sleeping quarters.

Unfortunately for Shannon, Mistress Mott, the fat lady who had pressed Shannon tightly into the corner of the vehicle throughout the long day, was also to share the sparse space that the Thompsons had partitioned off from the rest of the main room for the single women travelers spending the night in their home.

Unused to such extreme discomfort, Shannon found the straw mattress as hard and unyielding as she had found the stagecoach seat, and Mistress Mott's ample snoring did little to allow peaceful slumber.

Awakened in the middle of the night by an unusually loud snort, gurgle, and wheeze coming from the opposite bed from her, Shannon bent the thin pillow around her head in an attempt to close out the intruding noise. She was unsure how much of this torment she could take, and could only count herself lucky that Mistress Mott would be departing the stage at the first stop this second day of travel.

Morning came early for the weary travelers, Mr. Bracket the stagecoach driver, declaring that they had to put as many miles behind them before evening as possible. It was still dark when Stella Thompson awoke the women behind the curtain. Setting down a fresh pitcher of water for the women to wash with, she hurried them from their beds with the promise of a hearty breakfast.

Shannon could have easily forgone breakfast for a few more minutes' rest, but the ever-persistent Stella Thompson would not hear of such a thing.

"Why, young lady, you barely touched your food last night. I won't have it being said that Stella Thompson sent one of her customers from her home without a full belly. Now, you just freshen yourself up here behind the curtain, and then come on out with the rest."

Mistress Mott decided against using any portion of the water in the pitcher; instead, she splashed just a touch more perfume over her stout frame, and with a morning greeting thrown toward Shannon, Mistress Mott's large girth disappeared around the partition.

Shannon yawned tiredly, going to the bowl and pitcher of water on the small table between the pair of uncomfortable beds. She could easily hear the rest of her traveling companions on the other side of the curtain as they stirred and began to sit around Mrs. Thompson's wood table.

Wearing the same traveling skirt and jacket she had on the day before, Shannon did her best to swipe away the dust that clung to her clothing. Wisely, she pinned her lush curls atop her head, hoping the arrangement would prove to lend her a measure of coolness within the stifling stagecoach.

Stepping around the partition with her valise in hand, Shannon was greeted warmly by most of the male population in the stationmaster's house.

"Ye look right fetching this morning, Miss Belle." Henry Coker, the stage-line guard, welcomed Shannon with a nod of his beaver-capped head. He indicated that he would be right pleased if she took the vacant seat to his right.

"Indeed, my dear, you are a rare breath of beauty out here in the wilderness." Avery Hampton, a gentleman who held the same destination as Shannon, quickly rose to his feet, and taking it upon himself, he lightly took hold of

Shannon's elbow. "Sit yourself down right here, my dear, in my place."

"Oh, no, I wouldn't want to take your chair, Mr. Hampton." Shannon was overwhelmed with the solicitousness she was receiving from the gentlemen, and looking around the table she felt her features turn warm as she felt every male eye, including the farmer's, resting upon her.

"Nonsense, my dear, I will stand close and finish what is left of my meal." Avery Hampton would love nothing better than to stand nearby and watch the lovely Miss Belle break her fast.

A noisy grunt of disapproval escaped Mistress Mott's full lips. "In my day, a young woman did not allow such a great deal of neck to show. Enticement is the devil's handiwork, you know."

Taking the seat Avery Hampton pulled out for her, Shannon's hand automatically encircled her bare throat. "I thought because of the heat, I would wear my hair up today." Feeling somewhat uneasy with everyone looking at her, she stilled the testy remark she would have liked to have returned to Mistress Mott about her being sure that in the good lady's day, as today, it was best for her to cover all the plump flesh that she was able!

"Your hair is lovely, miss." Surprisingly, it was the farmer's tight-lipped wife who spoke out. Seeing her husband staring at Shannon, as were the rest of the men around the table, she kicked the side of his leg with her pointed, too-tight shoe. "Some men will stare for reason or not, and some women are downright jealous, and only wish that in their day they had a neckline to show off!"

The farmer's features turned bright scarlet, his gaze immediately turning back to his plate. Mistress Mott, having been soundly put in her place, hissed through the open space between her front teeth but kept any more opinions to herself.

The last thing in the world Shannon wanted to do was create friction within the group of travelers. Looking at the farmer's wife dressed entirely in black, from the little scarf tied over the crown of her head to the narrow shoes on her feet, Shannon smiled in gratitude that someone had spoken her same thoughts aloud, and was surprised when she received a shy smile in return from the farmer's wife.

The stagecoach pulled away from the Thompson farm a short time later, the travelers grateful for the cool morning breezes coming down from the mountains.

By midmorning the heat began to stir within the vehicle as the dust filtered through the air. Shannon was forced to clutch a handkerchief over her nose because of Mistress Mott's liberal dousing of perfume instead of using the water in the pitcher during her morning toilet.

Everyone within the vehicle was pleased with the fat lady's departure at the afternoon stop. Gladys Sims, the farmer's wife, was relieved that her five-year-old daughter could sit on the opposite seat from her quarrelsome seven-year-old brother, and there was more room for Mr. Sims and herself to share the responsibility of the infant that was passed from one lap to the other.

It was not until that evening that Shannon and Gladys Sims had a chance to talk privately. Shannon had stepped out on the porch of the stationmaster's small house and had found Gladys sitting in a rocker, singing the baby in her arms to sleep.

"I thought I would take a breath of air before retiring." Shannon explained, sitting in the wood rocker next to Gladys.

"I know what you mean." Gladys sighed aloud. "Ralph is getting the two older children to bed. I thought to take the opportunity for a few minutes of quiet."

During the time Shannon had spent within the stagecoach she had observed how Ralph Sims helped his wife with their three children, and had decided that the farmer was a man a cut above many she had seen before. He was quiet, and kind and loving to his family.

"We'll be leaving the stage in the morning. I hope the rest of your journey will be as pleasant as possible." Gladys was happy to have a moment alone with the young woman. It seemed like ages since she had had a woman near her own age to spend even a short time with.

"As long as we don't pick up any newcomers like Mistress Mott, I will be happy enough." Shannon laughed in response.

Gladys shared in the humor for a few minutes before turning serious. "We are going to visit with Ralph's parents for a couple of weeks. This will be the first time that the children and I have met them."

Shannon heard the worry in the other woman's voice, and was quick to try and reassure her. "I am sure they will love you, Gladys, and certainly they will adore their grandchildren." Looking down at the baby with his golden head resting peacefully against his mother's breast, Shannon wondered how Gladys could think otherwise.

"Oh, the children aren't Ralph's." Gladys's blue eyes lit upon Shannon's features as though trying to gauge her response. "Ralph and I have been married only a little over two months."

Shannon was more than a little surprised at the confession. "I'm still sure his parents will love you all." What else could she say?

"Ralph was married before. His wife died last year during childbirth. The way he tells it, his parents loved Amy as though she were their own daughter."

"I'm sure they will love you and the children the same."

"Ralph is a hard worker, and is fond of the children. I guess I could have done a lot worse for myself."

"Did your husband, the children's father, also pass away in an untimely manner?" Shannon realized that Gladys's husband would have had to have also died recently. The baby in her arms could only be a few months old. Though she didn't mean to pry, Gladys seemed willing enough to talk about her life, and Shannon was curious.

"The children's father ran away to the gold fields in California." Gladys's eyes held a haunted appearance as she revealed this.

Shannon was too stunned by the other woman's statement to say anything.

"You see, the children are not truly mine." Gladys looked searchingly around, as though fearing someone might be listening in on their conversation. "They are mine now, of course. But they belonged to my sister, Cassey."

Shannon recognized the pain in Gladys's voice; she also recognized a young woman who had a lot on her mind, and needed someone to share her thoughts with. "Where is your sister now, Gladys? You say the children's father went off to California. Did Cassey leave to go in search of him?" Shannon had heard of foolish young women who had thrown away everything to chase after a man. She had never heard of one throwing away their children, but it didn't seem impossible.

Gladys's thin arm tightened around little William in her arms, and the babe squirmed uncomfortably in his sleep. "William had been only a few days old when Adam announced to Cassey that he was leaving her. She begged him not to go, for all the good her pleading did her." Gladys drew in a ragged breath, as though bracing herself to go on with the rest of her story.

"It was sweet little Mary who found Cassey swinging by the rope she had fashioned on a crossbeam in her bedroom."

"Oh, my God!" Shannon never would have expected to hear such a horrible revelation.

"Yes, the poor little dear still has nightmares of finding her mother."

"I imagine so! How horrible it must have been for the little girl to find her mother hanging from the ceiling."

"Cassey's death still was not enough to change Adam's plans about going to the gold fields. He was going to send the children to an orphanage. The only choice I had was to marry Ralph and take the children on as my own."

Shannon's respect for Gladys Sims grew tenfold. "You

are an amazing woman, Gladys. Not every young woman would marry and take on three children."

"I loved Cassey very much, and I have always adored her children. I care for Ralph, and am sure that in time, I will learn to love him as he deserves. He is a wonderful man, and already loves the children."

"I'm sure you will do just fine, Gladys. Ralph's parents are going to love you and the children. Once they get to know you, they won't be able to help caring for you."

"Ralph says the same thing, but I just can't help worrying sometimes. That's why I thought I would talk to you, Miss Belle. You seem to be so self-assured, and not afraid of anything. Why, I would have never thought to travel alone, as you are doing."

"Oh, Gladys, you are much braver than I." Shannon stated softly, she alone knowing the truth, that she was running for her life.

THREE

Lemuel Bracket's snakelike whip whistled over the backs of the team of six horses, the crack of the rawhide braid lashing the air and claiming more speed as the concord swiveled and swerved, racing down the main thoroughfare of Last Chance Gulch.

Shannon's slender fingers clutched the window frame in order to steady her seat within the careening vehicle. A whoosh of breath escaped her as the coach came to a skidding halt in front of the dry goods store.

Looking as pale and shaken as Shannon did at the moment, Bonny Ingram sighed loudly, her one hand clutching her hat atop her vermilion-dyed hair, the other hand holding on to the threadbare bag resting on the seat next to her.

"Thank the Lord and the saints above that we made it in one piece! I swear, this dust is enough to force a refined woman to drink! And thank God I never have been a woman anyone has considered refined! I aim to find me the nearest drinking hole and wash away some of this infernal dust, and while I'm at it, I just might find me a paying job."

Shannon was no longer shocked by Bonny Ingram's forward manner. In fact, she rather enjoyed the young woman's hearty appetite for life. Yesterday, when the Simses had departed the stagecoach, Bonny had boarded, and right from the first she had made it known that she was a

woman who made her own way, and she didn't give a
tinker's damn if the other passengers liked her and her
actions or not!

Henry Coker climbed down from his seat atop the vehicle, and opening the coach door, he began to help the
passengers descend. The first one out of the stagecoach
was Abigail Primer, Last Chance Gulch's new schoolteacher. With a steadying hand, the stagecoach guard
helped the slender-framed woman to the wooden plank
sidewalk in front of Cliff Beamford's dry goods store.

As Bonny Ingram was handed down from the coach, a
tall, lanky cowpuncher called out from where he and a few
other men were sitting in front of the dry goods store,
"What ye got there, Henry?"

Henry Coker ignored the man's remark as he cautioned
the flame-haired young woman to have a care about her
footing.

"It 'pears like our little ol' town done hit it big this day!"
The same cowboy shouted out as Shannon was next to exit
the vehicle. "I swear I ain't never seen such radiance in
all my born days!"

Shannon gave little thought to the group of men in front
of the mercantile, but Bonny Ingram thought to put her
best foot forward in this new town. "Maybe you will be the
one hitting it big, cowboy! You just look me up when I get
myself settled, you hear?" Bonny opened her lacy scarlet
parasol and twirled it with an expert hand before turning
away from the dry goods store, and, the men staring after
her, she started down the plank sidewalk to the saloon
several yards down the dusty street.

"Whooo-weeee . . ." the cowboy shouted, and smacked
his dusty hat against his knee. This time a chorus of voices
joined in agreement with him.

"Hmpppp!" Abigail Primer snorted, her bony chin rising several notches. "Of all the nerve! Some people have
no decency about them at all!" She glared her ill humor
at Bonny's trim backside.

"No, ma'am, they sure don't." It was the same cowboy

once again who spoke up, and two men standing in the doorway of the mercantile snickered at the cowboy's attempt to cover all his bases.

Stepping away from the wood chair he had been sitting in while leaning against the building, the cowboy placed his hat back on his head and offered, "Can I be of some assistance to you, ma'am?" His friendly gaze lingered on Shannon's glorious copper curls flowing freely down her back, but something told him this woman would not easily be persuaded into allowing him the pleasure of walking her to the hotel.

"Why, I am not sure, sir." Abigail Primer felt her cheeks blushing, because she was unused to a man's attention. Back east she had been considered plain and too prim. It had been her hope that the move to Montana would change not only her future career, but she also hoped to find herself a husband. She had been told that there were many more men than women in the West, and already she was seeing her opportunities change.

"Well, ma'am, why don't you just take hold of my arm and tell me where you wish to go. It ain't safe in this town for a respectable woman to go about the streets alone."

"You are certainly very kind, sir." Abigail's voice squeaked with nervousness as she reached out for the extended arm.

"I'll get your bags, ma'am." The cowboy reached down and hefted her valise up in his free hand. No one ever said that Tom Davis wasn't a man to reach out and take what fate set before him. There were few enough women in Last Chance, for a fellow like himself to let a chance slip on by.

"Now, where is it that you wish to be going? We have a fine hotel just down the way."

"Oh, I do believe that I am to report to Marshal Taylor as soon as I arrive. He made the arrangements for me to come to Last Chance Gulch. I believe there was mention of a small house for me, near the new school."

"Yes, ma'am, I'm sure you're right as rain." The cowboy

heard a few more snickers coming from behind him but ignored them as best he was able. He had heard tell that a new schoolmarm was coming to Last Chance Gulch, and though she weren't much to look at, she might be able to teach him a lesson or two before moving on to greener pastures.

Shannon watched the interaction between the cowboy and schoolteacher with some quiet amusement. It was simply uncanny that such a plain-featured woman could step off a stagecoach and within minutes be swept away on the arm of a man she had only just met.

"Will you be needing some help, Miss Belle?" Henry Coker would be more than pleased himself to have this beauty place her slender fingers upon his arm. All the men standing in front of Beamford's store appeared to be holding their breath awaiting her answer.

"No, thank you, Mr. Coker. You have been kind enough already. I thank you for all your help, but I believe I will just make my way over to the hotel." Shannon lifted her valise from the sidewalk, and without hesitation started to make her way across the street toward the Last Chance Hotel.

Shannon was unsure if Honey Belle's husband by proxy was suppose to meet her upon the arrival of the stage, but since no one had stepped forward and presented himself as Alex Cordoba, she assumed that she would have to await him at the hotel.

She had been allowed several days' time in which to plan what she would do once she arrived in Last Chance Gulch, and the first step was to meet her supposed husband, then beg out of the marriage. She should be able to find herself some work; after all, she was well educated, and very capable of cooking or sewing if it came to that.

She could not imagine Graylin Stone discovering her whereabouts here in Last Chance Gulch. This rough, uncouth, mining town would definitely not be a place her uncle would search for her.

Looking about, she noticed that the streets were occupied for the most part by sluice boxes and gravel heaps. Miners wearing red plaid shirts and top boots crowded the streets and sidewalks, among the variety of men here at Last Chance. Indians, long-haired Missourians, ranchers standing by their loaded wagons, all had come to Montana Territory with the hope of improving their lot in life. No one would ever expect Shannon Stone to have traveled so far to this congested, dingy little town.

Distracted by her thoughts, Shannon all but stumbled headfirst in the middle of the street as a large man wearing tight-fitting leather breeches and a dark duster swept closely past her.

"Excuse me, ma'am." The man reached out and steadied her with a hand upon her elbow, and at the same time lightly touched the brim of his wide black hat.

Strange reactions swept over Shannon in those few passing seconds. Her arm tingled where the man touched her, the husky tremor of his voice setting off a trail of gooseflesh racing down her spine as her heartbeat stilled within her breast, even though his cool gray gaze barely glanced at her.

"Are ye the one they call Hunter, mister?" Another man, down the road somewhat but appearing menacing in the center of the street, called out in a challenging tone. As Shannon glanced in his direction, she noticed the man's right hand resting on the butt of his pistol.

Shannon stood stock-still there in the middle of the street, her wide aqua eyes looking at the scene before her with total disbelief.

The large man with the silver eyes was standing only a few feet away from her when he halted. "You have the name right."

"I've been told yer looking fer me, half breed."

"If your name is Mike Snyder, you've been told right." Hunter did not allow the man's taunting of his lineage to affect him one way or the other. He had been called worst names in his lifetime than half breed.

"Before I kill ya, why don't ya tell me what yer nosing into my business fer?"

The other man was large, but not as big as the one standing directly in front of Shannon. For a few insane moments, as she felt herself drowning in the huskiness of his voice, Shannon could only stare at the long, inky-black hair hanging down the man's broad back.

It was Henry Coker who at last came to Shannon's rescue. Seeing her standing there in the middle of a gunfight, the stagecoach guard ran to her side. "Here now, Miss Belle, this ain't no place for you to be. Come on back over here, where you won't be getting yourself hurt."

Shannon had no strength to resist the arm that drew her back the way she had just moments before come. Feeling totally out of her element, she could only murmur, "He certainly is a big man."

"Yeah, they grow them that way here in Montana Territory, ma'am." Coker laughed softly as he stood next to her on the sidewalk.

Shannon could not resist looking back at the large man wearing the duster. He looked very dangerous as he pushed aside the duster, revealing his .45 Peacemaker, housed in a Slim Jim holster, which was strapped against his muscled thigh.

Pulling her handkerchief from her skirt pocket, Shannon attempted to fan the rush of heat that had traveled up her face. *What on earth is the matter with me?* she wondered, unable to pull her eyes away from the life-and-death affair that was taking place in the middle of the street.

With his left hand Hunter pulled forth a scrap of paper. "It says here that you're wanted for murder and robbery, Snyder. Didn't your mama ever teach you not to rob trains? Especially those owned by the Walker Railroad?" Strong fingers released the flyer, and it floated upon the afternoon breeze, settling on the dusty street.

"I heard tell yer a Pinkerton man, I reckon that's the truth. Now there's only one more thing I heard and be wondering if'n there be any truth in the telling."

"What's that, Snyder?"

"I heard tell yer better than any man alive with that Peacemaker strapped at yer side."

"Why don't you just find out the answer to that for yourself?" Hunter had a deadly look in his slate-colored eyes as he watched for the slightest flicker of movement from his opponent.

"I might jest do—" Before Snyder finished his sentence, his hand reached down for his Colt revolver, but before he could clear leather, Hunter pulled his Peacemaker and fired.

Snyder fell to the ground, screaming for all he was worth that his shooting hand had been blown to bits, and he would never be able to shoot again.

"What kind of man are ye, half breed, to do another like this?" Snyder rolled on the ground, clutching his hand as Hunter strode to where he lay and stood over him.

"You won't have long to worry about that hand, Snyder. Once you stand before the circuit judge, and your sentencing is carried out, you won't be thinking a second thought about your shooting hand."

Marshal John Taylor heard the gunfire from his office, where he was explaining to Abigail Primer about the job she was expected to perform here in Last Chance. Leaving Miss Primer in the capable hands of his deputy, he left his office and hurried to the center of town, where the gunfight had moments earlier taken place.

"What the hells going on here, Hunter?" Marshal Taylor demanded as he looked from Hunter to the man moaning and writhing on the ground.

"Here's one for your jail, Marshal. I'll come by later this afternoon to pick him up. Hanging judge Harry is in Billings another week or two. Old Hanging Harry will be pleased to see Snyder here. He killed his son-in-law."

Marshal Taylor reacted immediately. "Jim, you go and fetch Doc Martin." He instructed a bystander, and then, bending down, picked up Snyder's Colt before grabbing him under the arm and yanking him to his feet.

"Yer going to get what's coming to ya, Hunter. Ya jest wait, my brother Billy will track ya down, and get ya when ya least expect it!"

"And your brother Billy will get a taste of what you just got, Snyder. Send him on," Hunter replied easily before turning away from the scene.

Shannon watched the happenings in the center of town with a sense of excited amazement. Back in Ohio, matters were not settled in the middle of a busy street; things were much more civilized.

Wiping the perspiration from her brow, she was as caught up in the excitement as the men standing on the sidewalk around her. She had never witnessed a gunfight before, and was stunned by how quickly the man called Hunter had drawn his weapon as well as impressed by how cool and collected the large man had remained.

Caught up in the excitement, Shannon did not resist as she was pushed along with the male citizens of Last Chance as they headed for the Red Dog Saloon. In fact, Shannon thought that a drink might be exactly what she needed at the moment. She could wash away the travel dust from her throat as Bonny Ingram had suggested, and also take a moment to steady her frayed nerves.

Often while growing up her father had taken her along with him to his clubs, and at a reasonable age she had begun to partake of light spirits. Shannon saw no reason why she shouldn't join the group and have a drink before going to the hotel for her meeting with Alex Cordoba. Yes, indeed, a drink was exactly what she was in need of!

Having never been in such an establishment like the Red Dog Saloon before, Shannon stared around in wide-eyed wonder. The imposing interior of the building had clean wood-plank floors, several windows having been thrown wide to allow fresh air and light into the front of the structure. Toward the back of the saloon, tables had been set up, the lighting appearing somewhat dimmer in this area.

Shannon glimpsed Bonny Ingram sitting at one of these

tables, talking to a gentleman who appeared to be the owner of the establishment. On the opposite wall from the swinging double doors, a large, well-tended bar ran half the length of the room, and it was toward this bar that the group entering the Red Dog pushed their way.

Encircled by the group of men, Shannon was shoved along. The excitement over the gunfight still lingered as the men talked and jostled one another as they bellied up to the bar.

"What will it be for you, little lady?" Sporting a waxed handlebar moustache, the bartender gave Shannon the once-over with a critical eye. It wasn't usual that a woman stepped off the streets and entered the Red Dog. But Bailey Jones had already been told that the schoolmarm had arrived at Last Chance, and another woman beside the one the boss was talking to now in the back of the building had gotten off the stage. Perhaps this one wanted a job, too, and with her looks she would do right well here in the Red Dog Saloon.

Most of the noise around Shannon stilled with Bailey's question. Several of the men around the bar seemed to realize for the first time that a woman had entered the Red Dog among their group.

As all eyes rested on her, Shannon nervously looked around behind the bar, her pale reflection staring back at her from the length of mirror that covered much of the back wall. "Brandy." she fought to keep her voice steady. Moments earlier she had thought nothing wrong with entering the saloon; now, with so many men staring at her, she was afraid she might have made an unwise decision. Well, she would have her drink and then be on her way, she told herself.

"I'll pay for her drink, Bailey." A short, squat man wearing a derby and a pinstripe suit spoke up.

"No, Bailey, here's the coin, right here in front of me, for the little lady's drink." Another man volunteered.

Before Shannon could explain that she would be paying for her own drink, a broad-shouldered man in his early

twenties shoved the little man wearing the derby away from
the bar.

"If'n anyone is going to buy a drink fer this here lovely
lady, it's going to be me." The man plunked his mug dawn
on the bar, some of the contents spilling on the front of
his plaid shirt, but he paid it no mind.

"Maybe after we share us a drink, ye would like to be
going on upstairs with me, little lady? Bailey will be letting
us have a room fer the afternoon fer two bits."

Shannon gasped aloud as she was taken by surprise at
the man's invitation. Backing away from the bar only a
foot, she felt her back press against another man's chest.

Perhaps at another time Shannon would have felt a little
more intimidated, but as the man stood there grinning at
her, she felt her temper beginning to build. Did none of
these men have any manners? Did they all think that just
because a woman entered a saloon, she was fair game to
them all? "No, thank you, sir, for the offer." Her voice
could be heard to harden with each word spoken.

Turning her gaze from the man who had bestowed the
vile invitation of a drink and more upstairs, her cool blue-
green gaze looked directly at the bartender. "I am per-
fectly capable of purchasing my own brandy, sir." Her
fingers began to pluck at the drawstrings at the top of her
purse.

"There ain't no need fer that now." The man was per-
sistent and took a step closer, his green eyes looking Shannon over closer with a hungry regard. Damn if'n this one
weren't a looker, he thought to himself, and with the
thought he felt the blood rush with a fierce intensity in
his loins. He would hurry her with the drink. He couldn't
wait to get a better look at her without all those clothes
on.

"I believe the lady already told you she wasn't interested." Having entered the Red Dog Saloon without much
notice because of the activity at the bar, Hunter had drawn
closer, and chose that moment to make his presence known.

The man standing close to Shannon didn't hesitate, but

quickly stepped aside, unwilling to go up against the gun-slinger, who had only moments before shot down Mike Snyder. "I . . . I didn't mean no harm, mister. I jest wanted to buy her a drink."

"And the lady refused your offer. Now, take your drink and go find someone willing to bide your company."

Hunter didn't have to tell the man another time. Lifting his mug back up from the bar, he hurriedly made his way back toward the back of the saloon.

"Thank you." Shannon sighed as she watched the man walk away from the bar, but now her gaze warily held this newcomer.

Hunter appeared not to pay any more notice to her as he ordered himself a mug of beer.

The rest of the men who had entered the bar at the same time as Shannon silently took themselves away from the bar, preferring to partake of their libations from a distance, in order not to give the slightest offense to the dangerous-looking man who was known in Last Chance Gulch as a man not to be toyed with.

Often in the past Shannon had enjoyed a glass of brandy with her father over a game of chess, but the potent liquor in the glass before her was a far cry from the mild amber liquid she was used to. Taking a gulp of the dark brew, she gasped out aloud, clutching her throat. For a moment she was unable to catch her breath.

A few moments passed before her coughing seizure passed and she was able to breath easily once again.

"Are you new to these here parts?" A small smile twisted Hunter's lips as his silver gaze lightly traced the delicate features that were slowly resuming their natural color.

"Yes . . . I mean no . . ." Shannon gasped out. Pulling forth her handkerchief, she furiously began to fan her overheated face. The so-called brandy had settled in the pit of her stomach and left her feeling overly heated.

"You are new to Last Chance or you're not." The smile never left Hunter's handsome face.

"I mean to say that I have come to Last Chance Gulch

to meet my husband." There, now maybe the man would just leave her alone. Knowing she had a husband, he should give her a few minutes to regain her senses.

"And who is the lucky man?" Hunter didn't know why he was bothering with the woman, but he rather liked looking at her. Right away he had noticed her out in the street, and had felt her standing behind him, even though he had attempted to put all his concentration on Snyder. Knowing that she was a married woman didn't seem to dampen his interest in her at all.

For a few seconds Shannon thought to ignore the man. Perhaps she should just turn her back on him and let him know that she didn't wish his company. But his very demeaner goaded her into making some kind of response. It could have been that liquid-silver stare that was holding upon her, or perhaps those earlier feelings when he had touched her arm. "My husband is Alex Cordoba, sir. Do you happen to know the gentleman?"

Laughter from the men standing around the bar exploded all about with the reply. Shannon glared at the men, not understanding their response, but never having been a person to abide being laughed at, she held her gaze steady, and soon they fell silent, one after the other.

She had not wanted to announce to the entire town that she was wed to Alex Cordoba. In fact, she had hoped to beg out of the marriage before anyone but the man who had married Honey Belle knew her reason for being in Last Chance Gulch. Now the entire town was privy to her business, and by the response of the male patrons in the Red Dog Saloon, her marriage, or her husband, appeared to be the subject of much amusement.

"I have heard of the gentleman, ma'am. I believe he is one of the owners of the Five Star Ranch." Hunter appeared to pay no heed to the men, who had drawn closer once again to the bar in order to hear more of their conversation.

Nervously, Shannon twisted the hanky in her hand. Looking at the glass of brandy, she declined lifting it once again to her lips. Without having to ponder the subject, she knew that it would be the wisest thing for her to leave the Red Dog Saloon and cross the street to the hotel.

Just as she was about to turn away from the bar, her attention was caught and held by the gilt-framed painting residing atop the mirrors behind the bar. There in all her naked splendor was a copy of the painting that had hung in Honey Belle's bedchamber.

Shannon's heartbeat accelerated. It just couldn't be possible that the painting of Honey Belle Cordoba was here in Last Chance Gulch! But unable to take her eyes away from painting, she knew there was no mistaking it.

"Are you all right, ma'am?" Hunter noticed her features turning pale, and as she swayed against the bar, he reached out a hand to steady her. Remembering that he had done the same thing out in the middle of a gunfight, his husky voice lowered as he stated for her ears alone, "It would appear that you are in frequent need of a strong man at your side, ma'am."

"I . . . I have to get out of here," Shannon stammered, as she was overwhelmed with the reasons that had brought her to Montana Territory. Swinging around, she ran out of the Red Dog saloon. Passing through the double swinging doors and out into the street, she drew in large gulps of fresh air and tried to put from her mind the image of Honey Belle lying on her deathbed.

Hunter's cool stare held the power to stay the men within the bar in silence. Reaching down, he picked up the valise the young woman had forgotten in her haste.

Shannon was already in the center of the street before Hunter caught up with her. "I think you forgot something, ma'am."

"Can't you just leave me alone?" Shannon lashed out as his husky voice flowed over her and halted her progress. She was in need of a few minutes in which to pull herself together. She had hoped to secure a room at the hotel, and behind closed doors she would be able to put her thoughts into some kind of order.

"You forgot your bag, ma'am." Hunter held the valise up in order for her to take notice.

Shannon had always considered herself a tall woman, but standing next to this man she felt as fragile as a piece of fine china. Reaching out for her valise, her hand became entangled with his, and for a few seconds her blue-green eyes sparkled with enchanting lights of excitement as they locked with those of silver fire.

In those few breathless seconds Shannon's entire world stood still. But as suddenly as she lost her soul to the cool depths of twining silver, an open buckboard passed the couple, and Hunter dropped his hand and took a step backward.

"I believe your husbands have come for you, ma'am." There was a trace of humor in the depths of his husky voice.

For a few seconds, standing there in the center of the street, Shannon felt light-headed, her knees feeling wobbly. Husbands? The single word left her lips in a confused question.

As Hunter stared down at the incredible beauty of her upturned face, he desired nothing more than to pull her against his chest and sample her soft pink lips. He had had little time in his life for women, but something about this one could have easily changed his mind.

Husky laughter spilled from his chest. He must be insane! Reaching out, his large hand gently turned her chin in the direction of the hotel. "Right there, ma'am. There's your husbands, the owners of the Five Star."

FOUR

Disembarking from the buckboard and dressed in their Sunday best, the owners of the Five Star stood before the Last Chance Hotel. Lucas Atwater, the oldest of the group at fifty-five, and usually the one to step forward and approach a problem, was the first to take notice of the young woman standing in the middle of the street with Hunter, looking in their direction.

Knowing Hunter's reputation as a loner, Lucas thought it reasonable to address the young woman. "Excuse me, my dear, but might you be called Miss Honey Belle?" As he spoke, his hand reached up and salt-and-pepper hair was revealed beneath the brown felt hat removed from atop his head.

For a few seconds Shannon seemed unable to recover her voice. She stared at the men standing before the buckboard, feeling all male eyes directed fully upon her.

With an ease that displayed him to be a man able to put forth his best no matter the circumstances, Hunter pushed Shannon forward with a slight pressure upon the small of her back. "Quite an appropriate name, ma'am, I mean Honey." He spoke softly, the words seeming to slide over Shannon with a smooth, seductive quality.

The underlying humor in his tone," though, was not lost on Shannon. Bracing herself for the ordeal she had to face with the owners of the Five Star, Shannon took a deep breath before turning and facing the man that seemed bent on tormenting her. "Thank you, Mr. Hunter, for your assistance." With a huff of released breath she turned around and with determined stops approached the buckboard.

Hunter stood in the center of the street, watching the sway of her graceful hips, and realized that her flowery scent seemed to linger long after she had stepped away from him.

Shannon had every intention of setting this situation concerning Honey Belle's marriage aright as quickly as possible. She would confront Mr. Cordoba, and as she had planned, would sway him from forcing her compliance to a marriage she did not desire. Mr. Hunter was surely a man with a twisted sense of horror to imply that she had more than one husband to worry about.

Approaching Lucas Atwater, Shannon stood only a few feet distance when she held out her hand and stated in as strong a voice as possible under the circumstances, "I am called Honey Belle, sir. I presume you to be Alex Cordoba?"

Two of the men standing a few feet behind Lucas stepped forward to flank Atwater. Taking the slender fingers within his large hand, Lucas smiled warmly. "I am Lucas Atwater, my dear Honey. This fellow here at my right is Alex, and to my left Logan Barrett."

Before Shannon could respond, he turned with a quick, easy grace and introduced the two men waiting next to the wagon. "This is Jackson Tulane, and standing next to him is the youngest of our group. He prefers to be called just Cookie."

At fifty-two years of age, Cookie was a small man with a warm affection for a pretty woman. His brown eyes twinkled with warm golden lights as he quickly stepped forward and waited for Lucas to drop the hand he was holding, allowing him the chance to linger over the slender fingers.

Shannon was instantly overwhelmed as the five men circled her, and in their own fashion welcomed her to Last Chance Gulch.

Alex Cordoba in a fatherly affection wrapped one large arm over her shoulder and pulled her up tightly for a hug. "I bet you didn't think you would survive the stagecoach ride from Great Falls to Last Chance, but I can already see that you're made out of tough material. You won't be one to turn tail and run at the slightest upset. The Five Star needs a woman like you, Miss Honey." Alex's teeth flashed beneath a full gray moustache, his green eyes taking in every asset that the woman before him had to offer.

Shannon's head was swimming as she was passed from man to man, and each offered her a compliment, and a thought to how they believed she would fare in Montana.

"Mr. Cordoba, I believe that we should speak alone for a few minutes." Shannon felt a flush of heat staining her cheeks as the men all peered at her intently.

"Ain't she got the sweetest voice, Lucas?" Cookie asked in his gravely voice, and each man nodded his head as though the little man had repeated their very own thought.

"Sounds like the voice of an angel," Jackson put in.

"I remember my mother's voice being just that soft," Logan added.

"Mr. Cordoba, please. We must talk. In private." Shannon was beginning to feel uneasy standing before these five ranchers who were hanging on her every syllable.

"We will be much more comfortable out at the ranch." Lucas spoke up, appearing to come to his senses first. None of them had expected Alex's bride to be such a rare beauty. The woman had the ability to keep them all flustered and stammering, but glimpsing the frustration crossing her delicate features, he willingly interceded and took charge of the situation.

"Yes . . . yes, we should go out to the Five Star, and once there we will talk everything out." Alex reached out and took hold of Shannon's bag, her resistance not bothering him in the least. A little tug, and a few seconds later the valise was sitting in the back of the buckboard.

"To the ranch, then," Logan took one of Shannon's

elbows, and Cookie took the other, both men leading her toward the front of the vehicle.

Surrounded by the ranchers, Shannon was lifted onto the seat of the buckboard before she was capable of resisting. "Why can't we talk here? I had hoped we could talk about this . . . this marriage, here at the hotel."

"Nonsense, my dear. There is no sense in going into the hotel to talk. The ride out to the ranch is not long. Once there, Cookie will fix refreshments, and we will all have a nice, long talk." It was Lucas who once again took charge.

Shannon looked toward the back of the wagon and found her supposed husband making himself comfortable on the plank seat that had been fashioned to stretch across the length of the back of the flatbed wagon. "I don't understand any of this." She tried to protest, but the horses were already set into motion, Cookie driving the team with an expert hand at the reins.

"Don't you worry, my dear Honey, you are in very capable company. You will understand everything soon enough, I promise," Lucas assured her.

"I hope you like ranches." Jackson's voice held a touch of worry. "I don't remember if Alex wrote to you about the ranch."

"No, he didn't, Jackson, don't you remember? We thought it best for her to see the Five Star for herself. A letter can't hardly explain a ranch and cattle and a bunkhouse," Logan reminded his pal.

A ranch, cattle, and a bunkhouse? What on earth had she gotten herself into this time? Shannon wondered as the wagon pulled out of Last Chance Gulch.

As Shannon glanced over her shoulder, she glimpsed Mr. Hunter standing before Marshal Taylor's office. Several men grouped around him, all appearing to be watching the buckboard leave town. Shannon felt the heat from those silver eyes even at such a distance, and with the firming of her chin she turned away from his penetrating stare. Surely she would be safe enough with these gentlemen until she could explain that she must be returned to the hotel, she told herself, trying to put thoughts of Mr. Hunter out of her mind.

"Are you comfortable, Honey darlin'?" Cookie asked in a solicitous manner, and set off a barrage of questions centered around her comfort.

"I am fine, thank you all." Shannon gasped. Not quite sure how to handle the situation, she opted for a reasonable avenue of conversation that would not center upon herself. "How long have you gentlemen been here in Montana Territory?"

This was a subject that each one of the men delighted in the telling of. For over an hour Shannon heard different versions of how the five came to be the owners of the Five Star.

Lucas was the last to say his piece, adding several details the others had left out. "The five of us grew up hard on the streets of New York, and oven when we were youngsters we all had a hankering for something more than city life could offer."

"I was seventeen, Cookie was the youngest at fourteen, when we left the city by train and headed west. We split up a time or two, each of us going his own way. Fifteen years ago we caught up with one another again, and came here to Montana Territory to start up a ranch. Life's been real good here at the Five Star. We've fought off Indians, wranglers, rattlesnakes, and grizzly bears, but we got a home we're proud of, and there ain't a one of us willing to go back to New York."

As the wagon meandered slowly over the dusty trail leading into a beautiful fertile valley, all talk ceased. Shannon stared in amazement as she viewed the splendor laid out before her.

Sloping off into the horizon as far as the eye could see, rich green grass fanned knee-high over the valley floor. Horses grazed leisurely along the basin, and several colts spying the wagon and team began to stretch out their spindly legs as they ran alongside.

To the west the Rockies glistened beneath the midday sun, the snow-capped peaks reaching heavenward in a display of breathtaking splendor.

From a distance, appearing to rise up from the foot of the mountains, the two-story ranch house caught and held the eye. The large house had been built from Montana granite, quarried outside of Last Chance, and boasted red sandstone trimmings, which had come from Bayfield, on Lake Superior. An inviting open porch graced the house, and wrapped around both sides.

"It is a very beautiful sight." Shannon was charmed by the picturesque view as her wide eyes roamed over a trout-filled stream swollen by mountain runoff, and flowing down to the valley floor, where it cascaded into a pristine pond.

Relief erupted from the men in the wagon. The first step accomplished, they were delighted by her reaction to the ranch house and surrounding valley.

"You ain't seen nothing yet, Miss Honey." Logan Barrett grinned widely.

"Just wait till you see the rest of the Five Star. We have three thousand acres of prime land that lies out past the entrance of the valley." Jackson informed her.

Shannon was impressed by all she viewed. She never would have imagined that she would find such wealth in Montana Territory. Everywhere she looked she was greeted by the richness of her surroundings. From the fine animals to the outer buildings, and ranch hands that tipped their hats and called out greetings to the men in the wagon as they drew nearer to the house, everything openly displayed a ranch that was profitable and well run.

Shannon had had little time at Last Chance to consider the danger to herself by leaving town with these ranchers and coming out to the Five Star. After the hour's ride to the ranch she realized she had little to fear from these men. She could only hope she would not hurt them too badly with her refusal to stay married to Alex Cordoba, and remain at the ranch.

As the men rushed around the wagon, taking her valise from the back, and each in turn offering a hand down from the seat, once again she was overwhelmed by the solicitous manner each of the men bestowed upon her. One would never guess it was Alex whom Honey Belle had married. Each of the five treated her as though she were the most precious thing in their life.

"Watch your step now, my dear Honey," Lucas warned as Jackson and Logan took her elbow and helped her from the wagon.

"That's right, Honey darlin, you can't be too careful. A twist of your ankle in just the right spot, and you could be laid up for a week or more," Cookie added, carrying her valise and trailing not far behind the small group making their way along the granite steps leading up to the front porch.

"Not that it wouldn't be our pleasure to take care of you if you were to twist your ankle and be laid up for a time," Alex was quick to assure.

"It would be a delight to take care of you, Honey darlin," Cookie added as though wishing to assure her he meant nothing out of place with his warning.

"I am fine, gentlemen." This group of men was worse than a hens fussing over her chick!

"Here we are, my dear Honey. This is our humble abode. We hope you are comfortable and feel welcome here at Five Star," Lucas declared as the group stepped up on the porch.

"Oh, indeed, Honey darlin, you only have to say what you would like and it will be our pleasure to see that you receive it," Cookie was quick to add.

"I am fine, gentlemen. You really don't have to fuss over me so much." Shannon glimpsed the crestfallen look that instantly came over Cookie's elfin features, and quickly regretted she had not softened her words. "I only mean to explain, I am used to taking care of myself. There is really no need for you gentlemen to worry over me so much."

The smile instantly returned to Cookie's lips as her sing-song voice filled his ears. "We have little else to do besides worry over your needs, Honey darlin'. We've been waiting for this day for some time, and have set aside everything here at the ranch in order to make sure you feel right at home."

"That's right, Honey," Jackson backed Cookie up.

"Whatever makes you happy will make us happy!" Alex underlined everything the other men said.

Shannon gave up, realizing she was getting nowhere by trying to explain that she was not in need of their pampering. She would leave the men to their fussing for a little while longer, and then she would break the news that she had to be returned to the hotel at Last Chance Gulch, because she could not honor the marriage agreement made between Honey Belle and Alex Cordoba.

The ranch house on the Five Star was anything but a humble abode. The interior was spacious and decorated in a wealth of expensive furnishings. Rich tapestries and gilt-framed paintings hung upon several walls. Works of priceless figurines and treasures from all parts of the world were viewed upon tables and within glass display cabinets.

The group of men encircling Shannon led her through the foyer and farther into the house to the great room, with its polished stone floors and dark-wood-paneled walls.

"Here you are, my dear, sit yourself down. I am sure that you are exhausted after your travel to Last Chance, and then the ride out here to the ranch." Lucas led her to the most comfortable chair in the room.

Jackson pulled up a footstool, and, as Alex reached out to prop up her feet, Shannon quickly did the task herself.

"Would you care for a wrap or lap blanket?" Jackson questioned in a concerned tone.

"No . . . no, that won't be necessary." The great room boasted large open windows and open French doors, allowing in the cool mountain breezes, which Shannon rather enjoyed after her days of dusty travel. "I am fine, gentlemen," she assured once again. "I believe that Mr. Cordoba and I have a few things to talk about in private."

There was no sense in wasting any more of these kind gentlemen's time, she told herself. The sooner she explained she was no longer interested in being married, the sooner she could got back to the hotel at Last Chance Gulch, and these men could get back to their daily routine.

"Cookie will first bring us some refreshments, and then we can have this little talk, my dear," Lucas said, the rest of the men appearing rather nervous by her wish to speak alone with Alex.

Shannon would have argued that she had no desire to talk to anyone except the man Honey Belle had wed by proxy, but she was not given the opportunity. Cookie and Alex, as though glad for any reason to escape the room, jumped at the chance to go out to the kitchen and retrieve the refreshments Cookie had readied earlier that morning before the ranchers had left Five Star for Last Chance.

Shannon was unsure about Alex Cordoba's reasons for avoiding the talk they would eventually have to have, but she was just as determined she would have her say, and leave Five Star as soon as possible. Leaning back in the wing chair, she was entertained by Jackson, Lucas, and Logan as they pointed out interesting objects in the room and told her some history about each piece.

"And that rope, over there, hanging in the corner?" she questioned, finding it odd that a rope fashioned into a noose would be from the ceiling.

"I'm sure you noticed that Cookie's voice is a bit rough-sounding to the ears?" Logan was the one who took this question, and with the slight nodding of Shannon's head. he continued.

"The way Cookie recalls, it was during the winter of 'thirty-six, I would argue the event occurred in thirty-seven, but I usually allow him his way. It was in the California gold fields when he was hung with that there same piece of rope."

"Oh, my!" Shannon's aquamarine eyes enlarged, and

she leaned forward somewhat in her chair. "However did he survive a hanging?" She realized that the little man's voice must have been permanently injured by the result of such a terrible ordeal.

"Cookie will skin us all when he hears we done told his story. He likes telling how he was hung for a crime he didn't commit." Jackson thought to caution his partner, but the young lady seemed so interested in the story, none of the men had the heart to wait for Cookie to come back into the room.

Shannon could only stare from one man to the other as she waited to hear more of the story.

"It seems as though one of the miners in the mining town had his cache of gold stolen while he was visiting a certain lady in one of the shanties down the way. Of course, you wouldn't be knowing anything about the goings-on in such a place, Honey." Unknown to the men, the real Honey Belle would have known exactly what they were talking about, but glimpsing the innocent appeal in Shannon's wide eyes, Logan continued. "Well, the next morning, the first person this here miner spied was Cookie going to his own claim. The miner right away swears that it was Cookie who stole his gold, and gets the rest of the miners all riled up. Me and Jackson were in camp at the time, and it was a good thing we were."

"Yeah, but I don't know how much help we were to Cookie." Jackson laughed in a deep-throated, good-natured manner. "That ill tempered miner incited everyone in camp so much, a rope was brought forth, and two miners overtook Cookie despite his cries that he was an innocent man."

Logan gave Jackson an impatient stare before continuing from where his partner left off. "They dragged Cookie up on the back of the oldest horse in camp, and wrapped the noose tight around his neck. The other end was slung over the branch of a tree."

"And a good thing that the tree limb was rotten! Logan

here ain't the best shot in the world." Jackson laughed loudly, ignoring another one of Logan's heated looks.

"Well, as I was saying, Honey, they were all for hanging Cookie, and it was the miner who claimed he stole his gold who slapped that old nag on the rump. It was a right smart slap, one aimed at setting that horse off a good mile or so, if'n she had that much run left in her. I pulled my gun at the same time the miner slapped the horse, and fired at the rope. There wasn't much else Jackson and I could do, the miners were in such an uproar, they wouldn't let us within ten feet of our friend."

"How did he get away?" By then Shannon was sitting on the edge of her seat. "Did your bullet hit the rope?"

"Well, like Jackson here said, it was a good thing the tree limb was ready to fall off anyway. My bullet somehow missed the mark." Logan gave Jackson a look that dared him to say anything on the matter of his skills with weapons.

"Cookie was in the air only a few seconds before he fell to the ground," Logan continued. "In the meantime, while everyone stood around staring at Cookie, having been saved from their first try at hanging him, one of the camp women confessed to seeing the miner's lady friend, hightailing it out of camp at first light. The camp woman revealed that the other woman had been bragging how she planned to rob the miner of his gold before she left."

"Thank goodness she came forward with the information when she did." Shannon sighed softly. If not for the woman, surely the little charming fellow would not be with the ranchers today.

"Yeah, Cookie was mad as Hades at first that she didn't come straight out with the information, but I reckon the woman was like the rest of the people there in that mining camp. Their days were so boring, a hanging was as good an entertainment as they could hope for, and a failed hanging suited just as well."

Shannon was astonished that these men could take such an affair so lightly. Shaking her head, she could not imagine anyone being so bored that they would enjoy a hanging! "Poor Cookie. I am glad everything turned out so well for him."

"So is he, Miss Honey, so is he." Logan laughed loudly.

Cookie and Alex entered the room to hear Logan's statement.

"I reckon you done told her, huh?" Cookie's brown eyes rested hard on Logan before they traveled around the room, and he directed his penetrating stare at the other two men.

"She asked about the rope, Cookie. We had to tell her something," Lucas responded, wishing to smooth the little banty's feathers before Cookie worked himself into a full-fledged lather.

"Here you go, Honey darlin." Cookie ignored the men. "I made these little tarts just for you." He set the tray containing his delicious jam tarts down on the table nearest Shannon. As he poured her a glass of lemonade, his eyes surveyed the room.

"I reckon as how they done told you my story, so it's only fair I tell you a little about each of them, Honey darlin'. I guess it's as good a time as any to tell about the time Lucas was playing at being a bounty hunter and he was tricked by an old man and his three sons into lending them his horse—and the cash in his pockets."

"Now, look here, Cookie." Lucas puffed out his chest. "How was I to know they were part of the Masters gang. The old man had tears in his eyes when he claimed his grandson was dying from a rattlesnake bite."

The room of men laughed uproariously while Lucas's face turned red. "Every time I hear that story, I can just see old Lucas here being double-crossed and left standing without his horse and cash." Jackson slapped his thighs with good humor at the other man's expense.

"But, Jackson, wasn't there a certain lady who played upon your good nature that time in Abilene, when you were the president of Cutter's Bank and Trust? From what I hear tell, she chawed you up and spit you out pretty good

before she left town in the middle of the night with a
sizable portion of the town's money." Cookie wasn't about
to let any of the men off the hook.

"That's the straight of it, Miss Honey. Jackson will fall
for a woman's tears or sweet smile every time." Lucas
grinned, feeling somewhat better now that another one of
his partner's past had been revealed.

"Now, about Logan here, I know a few good stories that
I might be willing to reveal, Honey darlin'." Cookie was
grinning from ear to ear. "For a time he fancied himself
a ship's captain. Sailed the world over he did, and there
are many tales that can be shared, such as the time he got
so drunk on some confiscated kegs of brandy, he fell over
the railing and the crew had to lower a small boat to fish
him out of the sea."

Logan's features turned beet red. "All right, Cookie,
I'm sorry I told your story. From here on out Honey will
have to learn everything on her own!" Logan gave up,
knowing Cookie knew too much about him and all the
other men for any of them to step on his toes. They had
known better than to tell about the botched hanging!

Shannon did not notice the discomfort the men were
experiencing. Each of the men in the room appeared to
have a very interesting background, and she was intrigued
by what next would be revealed.

"Now, Honey darlin', it will be my pleasure to tell you
all about the rope hanging from the ceiling." Cookie sat
in a chair near Shannon, and for the next fifteen minutes
repeated everything Logan and Jackson had already revealed.

Shannon was smart enough to appear surprised and interested in just the right places. She could easily sense how
much pleasure Cookie received from the telling of the
story. "Well, Cookie, you were certainly lucky to escape in
one piece." She responded at the finish, and Cookie
mopped at the sparse brown hair on the top of his balding
pate as he grinned at her reception of his adventure.

"I surely was lucky, Honey darlin'. Lucky to be alive this

day and able to look upon such loveliness sitting right here at Five Star."

The little fellow's words reminded Shannon that she had a need to straighten things out with Alex Cordoba and then be on her way back to Last Chance Gulch. "Listen, gentlemen, I appreciate your kindness toward me, and, Cookie, the tarts are just wonderful. But I really need to speak alone with Alex for just a few minutes." Glancing at the man who had wed Honey Belle, she saw him hurriedly look at Lucas. Was that desperation she saw upon his features? she wondered silently.

Clearing his throat, Lucas responded, "My dear Honey, I think that whatever you have to say to Alex can be said in front of us all."

It didn't seem quite right that Shannon should break the news to her supposed husband, in front of all his friends, that she did not want to be married to him, but it seemed there would be nothing else to do. These five men appeared to be thicker than thieves.

She searched her mind for words that wouldn't make her appear uncaring and hard. "Truly, Alex, what I am about to say has nothing to do with you personally." She hesitated as she felt all five pairs of eyes watching her intently. It is just that I believe I was a little too hasty in agreeing that I would become a bride."

"In what fashion were you, too hasty, Miss Honey?" It was Jackson who posed the question, not Alex.

"Why . . . why I . . ." Shannon had supposed she would have to make up an excuse in order to get herself out of a marriage she had no desire for, but she had never imagined she would be facing five men, and each would take a part of the confrontation. She was more than a little confused as she looked around the room, and all eyes steadily watched her.

As the men awaited her reply, she blurted out the first thing that came to mind. "I . . . I didn't have enough time to make a clear decision about this marriage."

"How can that be, when you had a whole year to think

about the arrangement before it took place?" Lucas probed.

"A year?" Honey had not revealed she had had an entire year in order to decide if she wished to marry Alex Cordoba. She had assumed Honey Belle had answered the ad for a mail-order bride, and everything after that had taken place post haste. "Well, a year can seem a very short time under trying circumstances." There, that answer sounded reasonable enough. "Now that I have had more time to think upon the matter, I fear I have made a terrible mistake." Her voice sounded firmer as she looked at Lucas without flinching from his questioning regard.

"Then why did you leave St. Louis for Montana Territory?" For the first time, Alex joined in on the questioning.

This interview was not going at all like Shannon had imagined. Drawing in a deep, steadying breath, she attempted to explain as well as she was able. "Well, when I first answered the ad, I believed I was ready to marry. Now I am sure that I am not ready. The trip to Montana from St. Louis helped me to make my decision." What else could she say? She certainly could not confess to these men that she had witnessed a murder, found herself in Madame Lilly's Retreat for Young Ladies, and there changed identities with one of Madame Lilly's girls, whose last words were of Montana Territory and Alex Cordoba.

"Then you did come to Montana to change your life?" Again it was Lucas who asked the question.

"Why, yes. I thought that after Alex and I had our talk, I would be able to find some work as a seamstress, or perhaps work in the hotel, or even in a boardinghouse in Last Chance Gulch, before I decide where I want to go from there."

Lucas glanced around the room at the rest of the men before speaking. "It appears there have been some misconceptions on both parts of this transaction."

Shannon didn't understand what he was talking about. Certainly Alex Cordoba, for all his shyness, was the one who had been wronged in this situation. "I promise I will repay you the money that was spent for the riverboat trip and stage fare."

"Honey is the last thing any of us have to worry about, Honey darlin'." Cookie attempted to ease the worry that creased her delicate brow.

"Cookie's quite right. There is no shortage of funds here at Five Star," Lucas assured Shannon.

"Then I don't understand. What is it that you want?" She could not have been more plain about not wanting to stay married to Alex Cordoba, but the five men watching her closely did not seem in the least distressed by her declaration.

"You see, my dear Honey, money is truly not the issue. Neither is the piece of paper you signed in front of the attorney in St. Louis. My partners as well as myself for some time have been feeling the lack of a woman's presence here at the ranch. And so we came up with the idea of placing an ad in the *St. Louis Gazette* for a bride."

Shannon's jaw dropped, her mouth parting in surprise as well her turquoise eyes enlarged. "But . . . but I thought Mr. Cordoba desired a bride for himself . . ."

"Alex volunteered to be the lucky groom only because he has had dealings in such affairs in the past. He is the only one among us who has ever been married."

"But why take out an ad for a wife? Why not just hire a housekeeper?" Shannon was caught by surprise by this revelation.

"A housekeeper? Here in Last Chance?" Logan laughed, and the rest of the men joined in the humor.

"I'm afraid that we desired a woman . . . well, let us say, with a little more graciousness than we would be able to find here in Last Chance, or in fact the type of woman who would reply to an ad for a housekeeper as far away as St. Louis." Lucas was patient, hoping that by calmly explaining their situation the young woman might still decide to stay on at Five Star.

Slowly, Shannon was able to piece together in her mind what the men were trying to tell her. "You mean . . . Alex never truly wanted a wife for himself? You all wanted a woman to come and live here at the ranch, and in order to get what you wanted you devised this plan for a mail-order bride?" For a few seconds Shannon's anger surfaced, not for herself, because her own part in this situation was not what it appeared, but for Honey Belle. The woman had believed she was coming to Montana Territory to start a new life—a fresh start with a husband, and one day children.

"Now, my dear Honey"—Lucas was quick to glimpse the spark of anger that filled Shannon's eyes, and was fast to attempt to soothe her—"It was settled from the start that if Alex and you hit it off, and wished to remain married, it would be all right with the rest of us."

"Oh, it would be all right, would it?" Shannon was only glad that Honey Belle had not come all this way to be confronted by this deceit.

"It is easy to see that you would not suit as Alex's bride, nor bride for any of us old men here at Five Star," Lucas was quick to assure her. "But perhaps you would consider staying on at the ranch as . . . as a daughter of sorts?"

"A daughter?" The image of Shannon's father came to the forefront of her mind, and she remembered how proud she had been to be Charles Stone's daughter. "To which one of you would I be a daughter?" Her tone was softly questioning. Confused, she looked around at the group of men.

"To all of us!" the five men stated in one voice.

FIVE

"We have a room all fixed up for you, Honey darlin'. You won't be expected to do any work here at the ranch. I do the cooking and housekeeping." The five men glimpsed the surprise on Shannon's features, and Cookie was first to attempt to smooth the way.

"Cookie's right. We have lived here at Five Star so long without a woman, we have almost forgot how pleasant it can be to sit in a room and hear a soft voice, or inhale the scent of fragrant perfume." Logan took a hand at attempting to convince her to stay on at the Five Star.

"But I don't know anything about ranch life." Shannon said the first thought that came to mind. She had been born in the city, and had no idea how a ranch this size was run. What would she do at the Five Star? She certainly could not sit around indulging these men with sweet words. She had always lived an active life. Would she be allowed to do so at the ranch?

"You don't need to know anything about ranching. All of us will teach you everything there is to keeping the Five Star running smoothly," Jackson was quick to say.

"I . . . I just don't think my staying here at the Five Star would appear proper." Shannon's head was swimming as the men argued each of her worries aside.

"Proper? Who is to say it won't be proper? You will be treated as a favorite daughter by all of us. And if'n one of the hands, or anyone else, suggests otherwise, they'll have the five of us to answer to!" Lucas, like the rest, would not allow her arguments to hold up.

"I'm not really sure what my plans are. I wasn't sure how long I would stay on in Last Chance, and if I stay out here at the ranch, I can't be sure how long I will wish to remain before I think it time to move on." Shannon was slowly being worn down, but wanted it clear that she would not be a permanent guest at the Five Star.

"We will make this promise to you, my dear Honey, that when you believe it time to move on to better things, we will not stand in your way." Lucas smiled, knowing she was giving in. Five Star would at last have a real lady sitting at its dinner table!

"Can you read a proper book, Honey darlin?" Cookie questioned in a hesitant manner. "My ma used to, of an evening, sit before the hearth and read to me and my brothers and sisters. I reckon as how that hearing a woman read is one of the things I miss most living here at the ranch with only these codgers for company."

"Why, yes, Cookie, I can read very well."

"And can you tell a passable story?" Logan remembered the long nights at sea when much of the entertainment was in the form of one of the sailors telling an entertaining story. The winter days and nights here in Montana were long, and it would be pleasant to sit by a warm fire and hear a woman's voice as she told an exciting tale.

"Aye, Logan, I have been known to make up a tale or two in the past." For the first time, Shannon found herself smiling. These men, who had tamed a wild portion of this beautiful territory, were more like children sitting before her plying her with questions. Looking at each in turn, she glimpsed the pleasure upon their features. Perhaps it wouldn't be so bad staying at the Five Star, she told herself, but as quickly was reminded of the reasons she was in Montana Territory. She could not afford to become settled here at the Five Star. She must be ready, when the time was right, to return to St. Louis and reveal her secret, and claim what rightfully belonged to her.

"Then it's settled. You'll stay here at the Five Star for the time being." Lucas grinned warmly, as the other men nodded their agreement.

"I'll take your bag upstairs and show you to your room, Honey darlin'."

"No, I'll do that, Cookie." Alex jumped to his feet, as well as Jackson.

"Why can't I show her to her room?" Jackson questioned. Already his hand was gripping the handle of the valise.

"Gentlemen." Shannon sighed with some exasperation. "I am well able to carry my own bag. You need only show me where my room is."

"We will all show you upstairs, my dear Honey. You might wish to refresh yourself and rest for a while before dinner." Lucas saw the tired look on Shannon features, and knew that his partners' catering to and pampering of her would soon diminish. If she could beae up to them for a couple of days, everything would get back to normal at the Five Star.

Dinner that evening was a gay affair. The moment Shannon entered the dining room, all five men jumped to their feet and rushed around the table to her side.

"Gentlemen, you look as handsome as ever." She noticed that each still wore the same suit as earlier in the day. But they appeared refreshed and refurbished.

"And you, Honey darlin', look as fine as a queen herself." Cookie blushed, and all eyes took Shannon in from head to slippers.

Shannon smiled warmly, and took a second to turn around for their full enjoyment. She had found a lovely teal gown in the wardrobe of the room she had been shown to, and assumed that it, as well as the rest of the numerous gowns had been put there for her use; well, actually, Honey Belle's use.

"It's one of the gowns I picked out, Honey," Jackson was quick to inform.

"I'm surprised you were accurate in guessing my size." Shannon laughed softly, noticing the pride that filled Jackson's gaze.

"But don't you remember, Honey darlin'? You wrote Alex all about yourself, and in the letter you told your dress size."

"We all took a hand in having the gowns fashioned for you. As well, you will find the bureau bursting with other apparel." Lucas, like the other men, was very proud of the stunning beauty standing in their dining room entryway. The lady was ravishing with her copper curls pulled atop her head and soft tendrils delicately touching her shoulders. The color of the gown set off the radiance of her hair to perfection.

Shannon had already found the frilly undergarments and stockings that filled the large bureau, and was more than a little surprised to find these men had such good taste in picking out women's clothing. It was just a stroke of luck that the real Honey Belle had been about her size. It would have been a disaster if they had filled the wardrobe and bureau with over- or undersized clothing.

"Let's not stand around here in the doorway. She must be starving." Alex took hold of one of Shannon's elbows, as Lucas took the other and the men ushered her to the table.

"Sit yourself here, my dear, so we can all enjoy your loveliness." Lucas stated at the head of the table as Cookie pulled out the chair and Jackson and Alex eased her into place.

Assured she was settled comfortably, the men took their seats, Lucas at the foot of the table, at the opposite end from Shannon.

The table glistened with expensive crystal and imported china, and as Shannon glanced around the room she was impressed by the rich furnishings and the comfort that was to be had at Five Star. Covered bowls had already been placed on the table, and as Cookie lifted the lids, the delicious aroma of honey baked ham, vegetables, fresh baked bread, and apple pie assailed the senses.

Earlier, when Shannon had awoken from her nap, she had been allowed some time to reflect over all that had happened to her since arriving in Last Chance Gulch. The bold image of Mr. Hunter was forced from her mind, but the kindly men who owned the Five Star were allowed to remain.

Going over all the details of that afternoon, she decided there could be no harm in remaining at the ranch for the time being. These men seemed eager for her to stay, no matter that she did not wish to be wed to Alex Cordoba. Coming to the conclusion that the ranch would be more comfortable than the mining town of Last Chance Gulch, she told herself it would also be safer, in case her uncle had sent someone in search of her. Coming to these conclusions, she had decided she would enjoy herself, and learn what she could of ranch life.

"Here, Honey darlin', try some of this ham." Cookie sliced off thin pieces of the meat and placed it on her plate.

Then Alex piled her plate with fresh, steaming vegetables.

Jackson poured a sparkling bouquet into her wineglass.

All that was left was for her to lift her fork and place the food upon her tongue, that was, unless one of the men would care to do the chore for her, she thought with a warm smile. There was no denying these men were quickly endearing themselves to her.

"To the lovely addition here at the Five Star." Lucas lifted his glass, and the other men did the same. As all eyes held upon Shannon, they toasted their houseguest.

Not to be outdone, each man in turn had a small praise to state about their guest's beauty, as again and again their wineglasses were lifted.

Shannon was overwhelmed, but thoroughly delighted, taking part in their toasting by lifting her own glass. By the finish of the toasting, Alex once again refilled everyone's glass.

The food was delicious and filling, the company lively, as the group sat around the dinner table and told Shannon about the Five Star.

"We own over five thousand head of prime cattle here on the Five Star," Alex stated proudly.

"We also have some fine horseflesh. Tomorrow we'll pick you out a mare so you will be able to ride over the ranch," Jackson added.

Shannon had done little riding in her lifetime. Telling the men her concerns, she was quickly assured they would have her riding a horse as well as any hand on the ranch in no time at all.

"The only bone of contention we have around these here parts is our neighbors," Cookie warned. "Until you're used to life here on the ranch, we don't want you going far without one of us at your side."

"We fear the Bar-K might be harboring some pretty mean fellows, but there ain't a thing for you to worry your little head about, my dear Honey." Lucas directed a dark look at Cookie, warning the little fellow not to tell too much. They didn't want to run the little lady off before she got settled in.

Shannon would have asked some questions about the neighboring ranch, but dinner having been finished, Lucas proposed they retire to the great room for a glass of brandy.

As the men sat back and relaxed, Shannon roamed the room, attempting to walk off the fullness that had settled over her from the meal. "Feel free to light up, gentlemen," she announced, glimpsing Alex looking in her direction as he reached for a cigar in a wood box sitting on a table.

"You're sure you don't mind, Honey darlin?" It was routine in the evening after dinner for the men to retire to the great room and enjoy a glass of brandy and a cigar. But with Shannon in the house, the men would not hesitate to forgo smoking if it bothered her in the least.

"I don't mind at all. Some of my fondest memories are of my father and myself sitting in the parlor after dinner, playing chess and sharing a glass of brandy. He would always smoke cigars during these times."

The men did not argue, and each in turn took up a cigar and lit it, inhaling deeply before releasing the fragrant scent of cherry around the room.

Shannon found the atmosphere in the great room comforting, and as she walked around the room she touched this object or that. As her hand lightly caressed the embossed floral lid of a delicately worked carved box, Logan requested she open the lid. Delightful music filled her ears and circled the room.

"That is one of the treasures I kept from my adventures at sea. I picked it up on one of my trips to China.

Another fond memory she shared from her past was that of her and her father making up outrageous stories for each other as they companionably spent their evenings. Remembering Logan's desire to be told stories, Shannon's voice flowed over the men like spun silk as she wove a tale to fit the beautiful box. "Her name was Ming Lee, and she was the only daughter of the House of the Lotus."

The men relaxed back in their chairs, allowing her soft voice to take them to a place far from the Five Star.

"The box was a gift from her father on her fifteen birthday. The day after her birthday, her father brought her the news that Ming Lee's betrothed had run away with another woman.

"The House of the Lotus had been shamed before all in their community, and Ming Lee could not hold her head up, nor could she look her own family in the face. In the still of the night, she took only the beautiful music box and left her father's house."

Reclining upon the Persian rug, her back resting against the couch, for over an hour Shannon told of Ming Lee's struggles on her own, of her loneliness and heartache, and the shame that forced her to pledge never return to the House of the Lotus.

"Eventually the beautiful Ming Lee found herself living along the waterfront above the Little Dragon herbal shop.

Staring out her chamber window to the street below, Ming Lee was well aware that the red light district was teeming with life at this early hour of the evening."

"Her karma had brought her to this sorry position in her life, and as Ming Lee heard the timid knocking at the door, she knew Hanshiro, the brute whom she had sold herself to, had brought another customer to share her bed."

"Ming Lee's slender hand slipped to the music box and gently eased the lid open. As the soft music filled the room, she slowly pushed the pane of window glass open, and leaned toward her fate. She had loved her family. She had had such a bright future, but fate had set her upon a path that had only one end.

"As Hanshiro kicked the door in, he found Ming Lee gone from the room. Only the music revealed that a short time ago there had been life, and hope. Now all was gone."

As Shannon's voice grew silent, the room seemed oddly still, then as the impact of the story settled over the men, they began to applaud the storyteller.

"Bravo . . . bravo," Lucas shouted.

Shannon blushed before offering, "My mother read stories to me that were somewhat unusual. She also had the talent of making up a fine tale. After her death, my father and I would make up tales for each other.

"You are better at storytelling than I ever could have hoped." Logan grinned.

Shannon set her glass of brandy aside and rose from the floor. "The story was the least I could do after such a delicious dinner. I believe I will retire now, gentlemen. I hope tomorrow won't be too soon to begin my riding lessons? I am not one to sit around and waste my time, and I would love to look over all of the Five Star."

"No, no, my dear Honey. Tomorrow will be fine with all of us." Lucas beamed. It had been his idea that they bring a woman to Five Star, and everything was working out better than he had imagined. Miss Honey Belle was a treasure that was worth all it had taken to get her to Montana Territory. He and his partners were lucky that this young woman answered their ad for a male-order bride. Lucky indeed, he thought as Shannon left the room and he rested back in his chair. The girl would bring life to the ranch, and into their old hearts!

Disrobing and readying for bed, Shannon smiled at the reflection in the dressing table mirror. Five Star certainly was a sight more comfortable than Stoneridge. And the owners of the ranch were by far more pleasant than her brooding uncle, she told herself. She had been right in her decision to stay on at the ranch. She would be safe until the time she made the decision that it was safe for her to return to St. Louis.

She didn't want to think about Uncle Graylin now. After slipping on the satin nightgown that she had retrieved from the wardrobe, she turned back the covers of the over-sized four-poster and slipped between silk sheets.

As her head rested upon the pillow, she wriggled her body to find a comfortable position, and, shutting her eyes, her vision immediately filled with the image of Mr. Hunter. For a second she attempted to push away the tall, powerfully built vision, but soon gave up the attempt, and allowed Hunter's silver eyes to lock with hers the same way they had for those breathless few minutes, as they had stood staring at each other in the middle of the street.

Something unreadable and stirring was there in the depths of those liquid-silver eyes, and Shannon lost her reason, imagining again the feelings that had stolen through her body as she stood so near him.

Having never been attracted to a man so keenly in the past, Shannon attempted to remain somewhat distant from the strong reaction her body had to Mr. Hunter, telling herself that it must have been the heat that had forced the shivers over her body's length, and it must have been the fact that the man was so powerful and large that her heart had beat as though it would burst within her chest.

As slumber slowly overtook her, she snuggled deeper beneath the covers, and with the friction of the sheer silk rasping softly against her body, she imagined a large body pressed fully against her own, strong hands slipping over every curve in a highly seductive manner.

Simmering heat flushed over her limbs, drawing her breath inward sharply as her lover's touch grew bolder. Lifting her nightgown slowly, but tenderly, his fingers slid along her inner thighs, traveling upward to the heart of her heat.

A small moan escaped her parted lips, no resistance coming as smoky eyes held her captured within their spell. All feelings centered upon the heart of her passion. She was aflame, and when he did not move closer to quench the fire, she moved erotically against him.

"Blaze and damnation!" Shannon gasped as she jerked herself upright on the bed. "Can I get no peace from those damn silver eyes?" Pulling herself from the bed, she went to the double-framed windows and pushed them wide, allowing cool mountain air into the chamber.

As the fresh air cleared her head, she told herself she was just overtired from her days of travel and the excitement of arriving at the Five Star. If it hadn't been Mr. Hunter in her dream, then it would have been some other imagined man. She would forget that damn silver-eyed gunfighter soon enough, and good riddance to the memory!

For a while she sat beside the windows, looking out over the moonlit countryside. There was no denying that Montana was beautiful, and Five Star land at night was a lovely sight to behold. She remembered what the ranchers had said about having fought off wranglers, rattlesnakes, and grizzly bears, and she wondered what would come up against her in the future. Could any of the threats in Montana be as dangerous as Graylin Stone?

TO A. D. ARMSTRONG

HAVE BEEN UNABLE TO LOCATE QUARRY STOP HAVE RECEIVED NEW LEAD STOP EN ROUTE TO MONTANA TERRITORY STOP

N. IVEY

SIX

Over the next few weeks Shannon acclimated herself to life on the ranch. There were few easy minutes in her days, as Cookie and Jackson taught her the proper way to handle a range horse and Jackson entertained her with lessons on how to use a whip. Lucas showed her how to draw and shoot a six-gun, Alex attempted to inspire some enthusiasm about throwing a rope around a calf's neck, and Logan taught her a few choice curse words she had never heard used except at the Five Star.

Her first day had been the worst. By midmorning she was hot and dusty, and ready to forget riding the large horse Cookie and Jackson had chosen for her. Every time she tried to mount the blasted beast, her skirts became entangled with her boots and the stirrups; she fell three times in the dust in her attempts.

The second day had been somewhat easier because Cookie had come to her chamber early in the morning and showed her where he had stashed several pairs of jeans.

"Lucas told me not to order 'em for you, Honey darlin'. He didn't believe a proper lady all the way from St. Louie, would wear jeans like a man. But I reckon I couldn't see you riding the range in a cut skirt."

As Shannon stared at the pants the little man was holding up for her regard, she was not too sure about wearing them either. But as soon as he left the room and she slipped them on, she knew they would be more comfortable for riding and roping than her riding skirts.

Lucas and the other ranchers had been somewhat taken aback by her entrance in the dining room that second morning.

Strolling into the room, Shannon wore a pair of the tight fitting jeans, and a silk blouse belonging to one of the riding outfits, which was tucked in at the waist. She had already made a mental note to tell Cookie she would need to go to town to purchase a few cotton shirts similar to those the men on the ranch wore. They would be more durable to ranch work than the silk blouses she had in her wardrobe.

Cookie was the only one who was not surprised by Shannon's outfit, and as soon as Lucas recovered his senses, his glance went to his partner before returning to the woman who was acting as though everything were as usual as she pulled out her chair and took her seat.

"Is something wrong, gentlemen?" Shannon smiled, noticing the men were still standing, and still wearing that same stunned look on their faces.

"No . . . no, my dear Honey." Lucas was first to gain speech. "It is just that we are surprised to see you dressed in jeans this morning." He held his tone on a level keel, not wanting to display his real feelings. This was only the second day Honey had been at the ranch, and he didn't wish to say anything that might make her want to return to Last Chance Gulch. But in all of his imaginings of a woman living at the Five Star, the picture in his mind was of a woman who would be feminine and charming at all times. He admitted that she had had it a bit hard the day before, but with more practice, he was sure she would have been able to mount a horse while wearing a riding skirt.

"Sit down, gentlemen. I don't know about you, but I'm starving." Shannon smiled around the room, her eyes twinkling gaily as they met Cookie's.

As the men sat, she added, "Oh, I want to thank you all for being so thoughtful as to put the jeans in my bureau.

It is surprising to find a house full of men who understand how cumbersome a woman's skirts can be. I promise I will take even more care with my toilet for dinner; after all, a lady does enjoy portraying herself as a lady when the occasion merits."

Her words had the affect of soothing over any hurt feelings the men were suffering. And within short minutes, talk around the table resumed as usual.

Shannon found her evenings much easier than her days. As promised, she took special care to present herself refreshed and gowned each evening at the dinner table. The ranchers forgot all about the clothes she wore during the day as she appeared all feminine and lace throughout the dinner hour, and then with the finish of the meal she entertained the men by reading aloud from a book of their choice. As a rare treat, as she had the first evening at the ranch, she made up her own entertaining stories.

As the days passed, it was a rare occurrence when Shannon found time to dwell on the image of Mr. Hunter. By the time she retired of an evening she was thoroughly exhausted from her busy day; too tired to dream of the handsome gunfighter, or anyone else, for that matter.

It was during her second week at the ranch that Cookie announced at the dinner table that he would be going into Last Chance the following morning.

A flashing image of Mr. Hunter unbiddenly stole within Shannon's mind with the announcement. But pushing such thoughts aside, she eagerly volunteered to go with Cookie into town. "I need to purchase a few things at the mercantile, and perhaps I will have a few minutes to say hello to Bonny ingram, the young woman who was in the stagecoach with me when I arrived in Last Chance Gulch." Living at the Five Star, Shannon keenly felt the lack of a woman's company. It would be pleasant, if only for a few minutes, to visit with another woman.

Lucas smiled fondly at the woman sitting at the head of the table. "Cookie will open a line of credit for you at

Beamford's store. You go ahead and order whatever you need."

"I think I'll go along, too." Jackson stated. "I want to see if Beamford got in those tack supplies I ordered a month or so back. Enough time should have passed by now. He only had to send to Billings for my order."

"I'll send along two of the hands just in case you run into some trouble," Alex added as a precaution. "I heard tell there was some trouble with a couple of the Bar-K boys a few days ago. Seems like they got theirselves shot trying to hold up the stage."

"Yeah, I heard about that. It was a good thing Bracket was riding shotgun that day. There was a large shipment of gold on the stage," Logan contributed to the conversation.

Shannon remained quietly interested in the talk around her. She had already learned that these men held a mind to try and protect her from the harsher side of life in Montana, but as they warmed to the conversation on the subject of their neighbors, she sipped her wine and appeared to be lost in her own thoughts.

"While you're in town, Jackson, you could pay Marshal Taylor a visit and see what he's doing about our neighbors," Lucas instructed. "I've got a feeling that them boys are up to no good out there on the Bar-K, and if Taylor's willing to help, it would ease my mind some."

"Ben Farley said he was shot at again up there at the lion shack on the north range."

"That's where most of our cattle have been disappearing from. I told Farley to bring down any steers he finds up there. For the time being, I think it best to keep our beef closer to home." Lucas wore a worried frown.

"I've been thinking we might want to consider hiring on a few more men. A regulator might be the type we're needing here at the Five Star. I heard tell that fellow called Hunter shot one of them no-accounts from the B-K in town a week or two back. Maybe we need a man like him." Alex's voice was dead serious.

"We've went over this before, Alex." Lucas was just as serious. "We bring in the wrong man, and we could start up a range war."

"So what do we do? Just sit back and let them thieves steal us blind?" Alex was in no mood to let the seriousness of the situation at the Five Star be passed over again. "Every day our cattle are disappearing, and more and more our men are being targeted for potshots. Sooner or later someone's going to get killed."

Alex's statement seemed to startle the men into remembering there was a woman at the table. "Oh, Miss Honey, I didn't mean to scare you with the bluntness of my words. It's just that I'm growing tired of turning the other cheek."

Shannon's aqua eyes roamed around the table before she volunteered, "For what it's worth, gentlemen, I'm with Alex. Why should you sit back and allow a bunch of ruffians to steal your cattle?" She had been surprised to hear Mr. Hunter's name mentioned, but perhaps the Five Star was in need of a man who was experienced at looking danger full in the face and not backing down.

"Now, Honey darlin', you don't need to be worrying yourself none about those varmints on the Bar-K. We'll be doing like Alex here is saying, and hire on some more men for a while."

"I don't think a regulator will be necessary though." Lucas still looked somewhat worried.

"What is a regulator?" Shannon questioned, having never heard the word applied to a person before.

"Usually a bounty hunter or a retired ranger. Anyone that he finds on the property he is hired to protect is subject to his gun. He's hired to shoot first and ask questions second. Many range wars have been started with just such actions." Lucas furnished this information.

"Oh," Shannon gasped, fully understanding why Lucas thought it too dangerous to have such a man here on the Five Star. She wasn't so sure that it would be a good idea for Mr. Hunter to work on the Five Star after all. Though she had spoken to him for only a few minutes at Last

Chance Gulch, she worried that such a job would be too dangerous even for a man of his skill with a six-gun.

"I think it time we retire to the great room for a glass of brandy, gentlemen, and you also, Honey," Logan interrupted. "All this talk of gunfights and regulators is not sitting well on my full stomach. Let's wait and see what Marshal Taylor has to say on the matter when Jackson pays him a visit. There's no reason to grab the bull by the horns, if'n the marshal already has things under control."

"Logan's right." Cookie spoke up, having seen Shannon's frightened reaction with all the talk about a regulator and a range war. "We should be calling it a night, if we want to get an early start in the morning." The little man smiled in a fatherly fashion at Shannon, hoping to put her mind at ease.

The next morning, wearing a comfortable, flower sprigged day dress, and a wide-brimmed straw hat, Shannon sat on the buckboard seat next to Cookie while he drove the team.

Jackson and three ranch hands rode alongside the wagon, their rifles and pistols within reach. The men appeared in high spirits, and their easy banter put Shannon at ease as they traveled the little-used road into Last Chance Gulch.

Cookie pulled the buckboard up in front of Beamford's dry goods store. Dismounting and tying his horse off at the hitching post, Jackson helped Shannon down from the buckboard.

"You go on in and pick out whatever you want, Honey. I got some errands for the boys here to run. Me and Cookie will be in directly." Jackson let go of Shannon's elbow after being assured she was steady on her feet.

Pulling off her hat, Shannon smiled fondly at the men. "I shouldn't be too long. I want to go over to the Red Dog to say hello to Bonny ingram."

"You plan to go inside the Red Dog Saloon?" Cookie's brown eyes enlarged at her statement.

"Why, of course. How else will I be able to speak to Bonny except visit the establishment she is working at?" For a second Shannon wondered if Bonny had obtained a position at the saloon, but quickly discarded the notion that the girl would be turned down. Bonny was the type of young woman who would be hard to resist if she set her mind on something she wanted.

"Well, maybe I could go on in the saloon and fetch the young woman for you when you're ready, Honey," Jackson offered.

"I don't understand why you're both acting like this." Shannon frowned. "The day I arrived in Last Chance Gulch I entered the Red Dog, and even ordered a drink."

She didn't explain that the liquor was so strong she almost choked on the bad-tasting brew. If these two men thought they could follow her around and tell her where she could and could not go, she had better set them straight right from the beginning. She was only a guest at their ranch, she didn't have to take their orders.

Looking at the flush of heat on her cheeks, Jackson grinned widely as he took into his regard her wayward copper curls that fanned around her face and fell down to her waist. She sure was a beauty when she was in a temper.

"It ain't that we're meaning to tell you what to do, Honey, it's just that some think it ain't proper for a young lady to go into an establishments like the Red Dog Saloon."

"Is that what you and Cookie think?" Shannon's bright eyes looked from one man to the other as she attempted to gauge their response to her question.

"No . . . no, not us, Honey darlin'. You do whatever you got a mind to do. Me and Jackson here will be nearby if we're needed. You just go right ahead and enjoy yourself." Cookie wasn't about to tell this young woman that she couldn't enter a saloon.

She was the best thing that had come to the Five Star since he and his partners had started the ranch, and he wasn't going to rile her up. He and Jackson and the ranch hands would stand aside and let her enter any building in Last Chance she wanted. Anyone who tried to insult or harm her would have them to answer to!

Slowly Shannon's bright smile returned. "Thank you, gentlemen. Now that that's settled, I will see to my shopping while you tend to whatever it is you have to do." With that, Shannon turned on her heel and stepped through Beamford's doorway.

Jackson let out a chuckle of laughter as his gaze went from the young woman's disappearing back to his partner. "I reckon we got us a handful there, Cookie. Having a daughter as beautiful as Honey might well land us in a bit of heated water."

"Yeah, but I guess we're of a mind that she's worth the little portion of trouble she can stir up." Cookie grinned back.

Shannon entered Beamford's store and without hesitation began to pick out the items she needed at the ranch. As she set a small pile of plaid cotton shirts on the counter, and two more pairs of sturdy jeans, Mr. Beamford began to tally up the cost.

"Just put that on the Five Star account, and anything else in the future Miss Honey wants," Jackson informed Cliff while Cookie went to look for a new hat.

"So this must be the new bride?" Cliff Beamford looked Honey over with a thoughtful eye. He had heard about the young lady strolling into the Red Dog and informing the town that she was Alex Cordoba's bride the day she arrived in town.

A small grin twisted his lips. He as well as most of the town had already been informed by an ex-employee of the Five Star's that the bride coming out to the ranch wasn't just for Alex, but for all the owners of the ranch. Well, the young woman appeared to be holding up pretty well under the circumstances, Cliff Beamford thought to himself, glimpsing the beauty and grace the woman on the other side of the counter portrayed.

"Nope, you heard wrong, Beamford. Miss Honey is a daughter, not a bride."

Shannon had wondered how she would be able to live down the fact that she had come to Montana Territory to be Alex Cordoba's bride, but Jackson had remedied the situation with those few, informative words.

"But I heard tell the young lady herself stated in the Red Dog how she was already married to Cordoba." As owner of the only mercantile in Last Chance, Cliff Beamford was privy to most of the happenings in town. He allowed that no good ever came out of gossiping, but on the other hand he did like to keep up with the latest goings-on. There had been some considerable discussion about the young woman's arrival in town, and her being swept out of Last Chance Gulch by the owners of the Five Star ranch.

"Don't matter much one way or the other what you were told happened in the Red Dog. Miss Honey here ain't a wife, she's a daughter, and if'n anyone don't like it, all they got to do is say so." Jackson's face flushed somewhat, his green eyes looking directly into Cliff Beamford's uneasy gaze.

Cookie heard the interchange at the counter and hurriedly made his way to Shannon's side. "If you have picked out what you're needing, Honey darlin', why don't you go on about your business now. Me and Jackson will be along directly."

Having heard the terse note in Jackson's tone, Shannon would rather at the moment have stayed in the dry goods store and see what next would happen, but with Cookie's arrival, the store owner appeared to be at a loss of words. He turned his attention back to the tallying he was doing before Jackson approached the counter.

As soon as Shannon turned to leave the store, Cookie nudged Jackson. "Go on down to the Red Dog, Jackson, I'll be along directly. I'll just take care of the rest of the ranch's supply order." Cookie had every intention of having a talk with Beamford, knowing that anything he said to Cliff would be passed around town before the day was through.

Jackson didn't argue with his partner, knowing that one of them should go and keep an eye on their houseguest.

With the ribbon from her straw hat tied over one arm, Shannon drew every male eye along the street as she made her way toward the Red Dog Saloon.

"Morning, ma'am." A miner tipped his hat in her direction.

"Watch yer step there, young lady." A cowboy pointed out a loose board in the sidewalk. Halting there on the sidewalk, he watched the young woman's trim backside as she stepped around the board and kept on with her destination.

Standing outside the saloon, several men watched Shannon's approach. One of the men was dressed in the guise of a reverend, with black jacket and breeches and a white collar tightly drawn against his skinny throat.

Looking at the group of hardened cowhands, Shannon was not intimidated, as all eyes were directed upon her. "Excuse me, gentlemen," she stated, waiting for them to remove themselves from the doorway of the Red Dog.

For a full minute or two the men openly stared, as though having never before seen such a vision of loveliness, but soon enough they were routed, as Jackson stepped to Honey's side.

"The lady said to stand aside." Jackson's hand rested on the butt of his six-gun.

"There ain't no need to take that tone, Tulane." It was the preacher who spoke up. "The boys here were just about to move on out of the way."

"You and your boys will be moving all right." Jackson took a step closer to the men, but before anything further could be said or done, a phaeton pulled by a single pony pulled up before the Red Dog, and Bonny ingram called out in a loud voice to Shannon.

"Why, Honey Belle, have you come to town today to stir

up another ruckus?" Bonny's laughter circled all those standing out on the sidewalk before the Red Dog Saloon.

Shannon grinned widely at Bonny. "No, I didn't have a ruckus in mind. We came for supplies, and I had hoped I would see you before going back to the ranch."

"Well, now you see me, what do you think?" Bonny was sitting in a brand-new carriage, which was pulled by a beautiful little mare. Her curls were arranged atop her head, and a saucy hat with a purple feather was perched at a daring angle. The expensive velvet dress she was wearing was the same bright purple in color as the hat. "I think you look just splendid, Bonny." Shannon laughed.

There were murmurs of agreement among the group of cowboys standing on the sidewalk. Even the skinny preacher's roving eye traveled a slow path over the red-haired woman in the carriage.

"I'm afraid you have picked a miserable day fora visit, Honey." Bonny called from the carriage. Sammy has been waiting for over an hour for me, upstairs in his room." She was referring to Samuel Sterling, the owner of the Red Dog Saloon. "Now that I have this little ol' pony and carriage, maybe I'll come on out to the Five Star and pay you a visit."

"Oh, Bonny, I would love that!" Shannon was delighted at the prospect of spending an afternoon catching up with Bonny Ingram.

"Then it's all settled. I'll be out to the ranch by the end of the week." Looking at the group of men still standing there and watching the interchange between the two women, Bonny lifted a purple gloved hand. "Why, Billy Snyder, is that you I see over there? I would have thought you would have manners enough to help a lady from her carriage."

Jackson pulled Shannon away as the group of men hurried over to the carriage to help Bonny ingram from within.

"I'm sure Cookie has gotten the supplies by now, Honey. If you're ready, we can be on our way."

Shannon knew no one else in Last Chance other than Bonny ingram, and though she had thought she would get another glimpse of Mr. Hunter before leaving town, as she was led back to the buckboard by Jackson she told herself she was just being foolish with her girlish fancies about such a dangerous man.

Before leaving Last Chance, Cookie pulled the buckboard up before the marshal's office, and Jackson went inside for a few minutes to see what Marshal Taylor was going to do about the boys who worked and lived out at the Bar-K. The same boys, Shannon was informed, who had been standing outside the Red Dog with the skinny preacher.

As the buckboard began to head back in the direction of the ranch, Shannon questioned, "Why on earth would a preacher take up with such men as those who live on the Bar-K?"

"They call him Preacher Rufus. As I hear tell, he's from the South somewhere. No one knows for sure if he ever was a preacher. More's the time I've seen him riding out to the Bar-K with a whiskey bottle lifted to his lips," Cookie informed her.

"For a while he was suspected of selling the Indians guns and whiskey, but Marshal Taylor couldn't catch him in the act," Jackson added.

"I reckon as how he's found his like kind out there at the Bar-K with Billy Snyder and Hector Bowden."

"Wasn't it this Billy Snyder's brother who got shot in a gunfight the day I arrived in Last Chance?" Shannon knew she had been somewhat disoriented that day as Mr. Hunter had stood nearby and the handsome gunfighter had faced the man called Mike Snyder, but if memory served, the wounded man had challenged that his brother would kill Mr. Hunter, and she was sure he had said his brother's name was Billy."

Worry creased Shannon's tender brow with the reminder. Had this Billy Snyder already found and murdered Mr. Hunter? Was that the reason she had not seen him in town today? For some strange reason the thought of Mr. Hunter being killed left her feeling somewhat disheartened.

"Yeah, Mike used to work out at the Bar-K, too." One of the ranch hands Shannon knew as Jeff Peters joined in the conversation. "Last Chance is well rid of a snake like Mike Snyder. He's in Billings, and I heard tell they already have built his gallows. Ol' Hanging Harry's already sentenced him."

"Mike and some of the Bar-K boys have been talking about going into Billings and busting Mike out of jail." Sam, another one of the ranch hands, added.

The ranch hands seemed pretty well informed, Shannon thought, wondering how they got their information.

"They say Sheriff Bates has posted extra guards around the jailhouse just in case there's an attempted break out." Jeff seemed to be warming to the conversation.

"He'll hang if Hanging Harry has anything to say about it." Jackson noted Shannon's interest in the conversation, and was pleased to see that she wasn't appearing faint of heart as so many ladies would when hearing such hard talk. "The only mistake Hunter made the day he shot Mike was he didn't shoot his brother, too."

"Just give him time," Jeff assured. "Hunter ain't a man to trifle with. I've heard stories about the half breed that could make even a man of stout heart tremble. Ya know his grandpappy is ol' Two Owls himself."

"It was Two Owls and his warriors who were terrorizing those settlers some years back. Why, I heard tell they rode into a town and killed everyone in it, women and children included." Sam seemed unaware that Shannon's features had paled with his words. "I wouldn't be surprised if Two Owls taught Hunter everything he knows about killing and torture."

"There's a story about Hunter being just like the old man even as a boy. Why, he killed his first white man while he was just a kid," Jeff supplied.

"I wonder why he started working for the Pinkerton Agency?" Sam questioned aloud.

"Don't rightly know, and don't think I'll be asking Hunter his reasons. He pretty well minds his own business, and doesn't take much to a man meddling into his affairs," Jeff answered.

The image Shannon carried in her mind of the handsome, silver-eyed gunfighter was now somewhat distorted with this information she was digesting. Mr. Hunter was far more dangerous than she had allowed herself to believe.

That same afternoon Hunter was meeting with Silas Applebaum, his contact man in Montana, and also one of Robert Pinkerton's top men.

"Have a seat here, Hunter. I have already ordered our food. I took the liberty of ordering us both steaks. Though, I'm sure a tough longhorn will be supplied." Applebaum pointed to the chair opposite him, having arrived early enough at the restaurant in Billings to be assured he was sitting facing the door of the establishment.

Hunter himself would have preferred sitting in Applebaum's chair, but instead of holding any ill feelings, he again reminded himself how aware of his surroundings the other man was at all times. He was not lost to the fact that Applebaum had probably arrived at the meeting place a good half hour early. Hunter would store this information away for the next time he met the older man. "Steak is fine with me." He positioned his chair so he could see who was entering the restaurant from the corner of his eye.

Silas Applebaum was not lost to Hunter's thoughts, and, laughingly, he poured both glasses full of wine. "I see that you are still in one piece, Hunter." Lifting his glass, he stated thoughtfully, "To you and your health, may you stay fit in the days ahead."

Hunter lifted his glass, and with a salute of the crystal in the other man's direction, he took a drink. "I'm fit enough." He smiled as he set down the glass. There was no need to tell Applebaum that he had killed two bush-whackers on his way out of Last Chance yesterday afternoon and before arriving here at Butte. No doubt they were friends of Billy Snyder's.

After the waitress set down two large platters of potatoes and steaks, Silas Applebaum stated, "Mr. Pinkerton sends his regards and asks how things are going around Last Chance Gulch. Have you found any more information about who is selling rifles to the Crow along the Yellowstone River?" The Pinkerton agency had been hired by the U.S. government to find out who was responsible for the robbery of a detail of wagons carrying U.S. rifles and ammunition that had been on their way to Fort Peck.

The agency had gained information that a portion of the weapons had been traded or sold to Red Hand's band of Crow along the Yellowstone. It was Hunter's mission to find out who was responsible for the theft, and once doing so to apprehend the outlaws and turn them over to the commander at Fort Peck.

"I have a few leads," Hunter answered as he ate.

As usual, Hunter was not given to talking too much, but Applebaum knew this mission was more than just a job to the other man. There was information in Robert Pinkerton's files about Hunter and his past that claimed Red Hand's band of Crow Indians were sworn enemies of Hunter's grandfather's people. No good could come out of Red Hand's people having army-regulated rifles and ammunition. It would only be a matter of time before they would attack Hunter's village, and Applebaum was well aware that Hunter knew all this without being told. "Let's hope your leads prove out."

"They will. I'll have more information for you by the end of the month."

"Well, Mr. Pinkerton wants you to devote your time to this project, and for now forget about Snyder's gang of stage robbers. The government is getting nervous. They want some answers. The sooner we can give them what they want, the better for everyone concerned. There's no telling what will happen if more of those guns show up in the wrong place."

"I think Snyder and his boys might have had some involvement in the robbery of the supply wagons going to Fort Peck. I'm playing out my hunches and leads. I'll send you word when I have something substantial to go on."

"So Snyder and his boys might have been in on this robbery, too? Well, I'm not surprised by any means. There a mean bunch, Hunter. Don't take any chances. If you need more men to back you up, you know how to get in touch with me. I'll be staying here at the hotel in Butte until I hear from you. Oh, by the way, I heard that Billy Snyder broke his brother out of jail last night. You had best double your guard. I'm sure you will be a prime target down the sighting of their guns. After all, you're the one who wounded Mike's shooting hand." Applebaum laughed as though he had made a joke.

By the time the two men finished their meal and Hunter was leaving the restaurant, plans were already turning over in his mind on how best to approach the Bar-K Ranch and find out exactly what Snyder and his boys were up to.

Stepping out on the sidewalk, Hunter bumped into a young woman with bright auburn hair, and for a few seconds he was reminded of another young woman, but as he made his apologies and watched the woman walk away from him, his thoughts reflected shimmering copper tresses and bright blue-green eyes. The Five Star Ranch wasn't too far from the Bar-K; maybe he might just pay a visit to the ranch, and to the woman who had upon occasion stolen into his thoughts during the last couple of weeks—Honey Belle.

Preoccupied by her thoughts of Tommy Lang, the cowboy who had offered her his arm the day she had stepped off the stagecoach in Last Chance Gulch, Abigail Primer did not hear the schoolroom door open, announcing she had a visitor.

It was the sharp click of shoes hitting against the wood

plank floor that pulled her attention from where she was sitting behind her desk.

"Oh, my, I'm sorry I didn't even notice you were there. If you will give me just a few minutes, I will finish erasing the chalkboard, and then we can have a few minutes."

Assuming the visitor to be a parent, Abigail stepped to the chalkboard, and erased the day's lessons. Each afternoon she did this same chore in order to have a fresh start in the morning.

Turning her back toward the room as she clutched the eraser and swiped at the board, again her thoughts went to dear Tommy.

As yet, he had not made an official proposal of marriage to her, but after last night she held no doubt that any day now, she would he agreeing to become his blushing bride.

The only thing was, she no longer could claim to be blushing. Last night she had given Tommy Lang what she had never given to any man—the gift of her body.

Her body tingled in remembrance of what she and Tommy had shared in her bed there in the back room of the schoolhouse.

With her thoughts so caught up with Tommy, Abigail was totally unaware as she felt someone standing close to her and something slip around her throat.

Instinct for survival overwhelmed her as she clawed at the silk stocking twined around her neck. Her eyes enlarged as she tried to face her attacker, but the schoolhouse visitor possessed much more strength than Abigail could have anticipated.

Within short moments Abigail Primer lay in a prone position before the chalkboard, the silk stocking still wrapped around her throat.

SEVEN

For the next several days Shannon left the ranch house early each morning with Alex and Logan. Twice a year all available hands on the ranch rounded up the cattle. This was when the Five Star calves were branded, and bulls, cows, and yearlings were sorted for sale or stock cattle.

Though it was hard, dusty work, Shannon found pleasure in the vast open territory, and in the camaraderie that went on between the men. She was treated as their equal, neither the ranchers nor the hands seeming to take exception to the fact that she was a woman.

When she found a calf strayed from its mother, it was up to her to lasso the lost animal and drag it behind her horse until she regained the rest of the herd. Twice during the long week, Shannon shot at rattlesnakes; once she hit the mark and killed the deadly creature, the other time the snake slithered off into the rocks.

Daily, Shannon was growing more confident in her abilities on the ranch. She could almost forget at times her reasons for being in Montana Territory. She could forget for a while that she was anyone other than Honey Belle, a young woman seeking a better life in this vast land of mountains and prairies.

Toward the end of the week a note from Bonny Ingram was delivered to Shannon by one of the ranch hands. She would be paying a visit to the Five Star the following afternoon, and she would be bringing along a woman who had

newly arrived in Last Chance, and was now employed at
the Red Dog Saloon.

With all the activity taking place at the ranch, Shannon
had forgotten Bonny's promise of a visit and guiltily she
wished she could put the young woman's visit off until a
later date. Scolding herself for being unsociable, Shannon
advised the ranchers that evening at the dinner table that
she would be having guests the next afternoon.

The men seemed delighted, and all planned to be
nearby to share a cup of tea with the ladies.

The following morning Shannon awoke earlier than
usual. After dressing in jeans and boots and one of the
plaid shirts she had purchased earlier in the week, she
made her way downstairs to the kitchen.

Cookie was already up and busy preparing the morning
meal. Shannon didn't linger, but grabbing up a warm roll,
she placed a small kiss upon the little man's cheek. "I'm
going to get an early start with the hands this morning,
Cookie. I should be back by the noon hour in order to
change before Bonny and her friend arrives."

Cookie's features flushed, not so much from the heat
of his cookstove, but due to the kiss the young woman had
bestowed upon him. "You be careful out their, Honey darlin'."

"I will, Cookie." Shannon patted the six-gun that was
secured in the holster strapped to her side. "I'm getting
to be a pretty good shot. Did Alex tell you about the rattler
I killed?"

Grinning, Cookie poured her a cup of strong coffee. He
handed her the mug before she could go out the door.
"Mind you, there's more than rattlesnakes out there on
the range. Keep in sight of the hands. I'll have something
extra special fixed up for your company this afternoon, so
don't be worrying yourself about nothing 'cepting getting
yourself back here on time."

Shannon laughed as she went through the kitchen door.
These dear men who owned the Five Star were easily taking

the place of the family she no longer had and yearned to
belong to.

A few of the ranch hands were still outside the bunkhouse after Shannon saddled her mare and left the barn.
Seeing Shannon, they waved, and called out that they
would be following along shortly.

Shannon enjoyed this time of day best, when everything
was fresh and quiet, the mountain breezes caressing her
flesh as the morning dew glistened over the vibrant beauty
of a meadow that was about a mile from the ranch. Portraying an impressionist painting, the meadow shimmered
with a blur of color. A heady collage of red, yellow, purple,
white, pink, and even black from the olive-shaped cone-
flower all simply displayed against a backdrop of resonant
green.

For a few minutes Shannon allowed herself the pleasure
of indulging the impulse just to sit upon her horse and
stare off into the vista of beauty displayed boldly before
her regard.

Her peaceful respite was short-lived, though, as the loud
mewling sounds made by a calf caught her attention. The
sounds were coming from a short distance away, from the
stream that ran through the meadow, and which made a
path through a woods of pine and cedar.

Setting her horse into motion, Shannon followed the
streambank as it purled its way through a colonnade of
towering red cedars. On the lush bank, dense with old
timber, dew spangled an emerald tapestry of oak ferns.

Startled for a moment, Shannon reined in her mare as
the morning mist softened the surrounding area, and she
glimpsed a bull elk drinking from the mountain stream.
Hearing the calf downstream a short distance, Shannon
lingered for an added few minutes, allowing the elk to
drink his fill as she soaked up the transcendent peace that
filled her.

Throwing his head back, the bull elk snorted loudly before turning from the water and disappearing among the
lodgepole pines and cedars.

Shannon kicked her mount's sides, setting the mare into motion once again. Before reaching the calf, she retrieved the rope twined over her saddle horn. This was becoming easier each time she endeavored to rope a calf. She held the rope so that it would fall in a neat circle over the calf's head with her first throw.

And there, standing in the middle of the stream, was the calf. He couldn't have been but a few days old, and had been separated from his mother. Shannon softly crooned to the animal as she approached.

The calf eyed her warily as he kept up his mewling for a mother that was nowhere in sight.

"Easy, little guy. You're going to be just fine." Her mare stepped into the rushing water of the stream, and she threw the rope.

"Blaze and damnation!" she cursed under her breath, the rope falling short of the calf and landing in the water.

"Practice makes perfect," she mumbled as she had repeatedly stated this past week. She began to pull the rope in, and ready it for another try.

Before she threw the rope the second time, a noise from the surrounding trees drew her attention. Shannon's first thought was to make a grab for her six-gun, but with a grunt of released breath she noticed a cow emerging out of the woods. With a bellow given in the direction of the calf, the little fellow gave out one more mewling sound before splashing through the water to his mother's side.

Shannon's laughter disturbed the quiet sounds of nature as calf and cow started back upstream to join the rest of the herd.

It was just as Shannon turned her mare's head back toward the direction she had come that she glimpsed something lying in the underbrush a short distance from the water.

This time she did pull her gun from her holster, remembering Cookie's warning that there was more to fear than a rattler out here on the range. Her first thought went to the grizzly bears she had been warned were prevalent in

Montana, but whatever was under the brush appeared not to be moving. Perhaps an animal had come downstream and died. She slowly directed her mount closer for a better view.

The first thing Shannon detected was a pair of boots sticking out from under some thick brush. What should she do, she wondered, holding tightly to the hand of her gun. Was the man dead? Or was this some kind of trap, in the hopes of luring and overtaking an unsuspecting cowhand? As the quiet of the place was broken by a soft moan, Shannon wearily climbed down from the mare's back.

Keeping her gun ready, she silently approached the brush. There, lying pale and lifeless, was Mr. Hunter. Remembering the stories the ranch hands had told her about this man the day they had traveled back from town, Shannon did not hurriedly replace her gun into its holster. Instead, she bent down and touched his shoulder, as though verifying that he was still alive, and it had been he who had moaned a few seconds earlier.

With the slight brush of her fingers against his shoulder, Hunter's eyes flew open. He stared directly at Shannon with distrust burning in his pale regard.

"What happened?" Shannon glimpsed the pain in his sterling eyes, and quickly put away her gun.

"I was bushwhacked, over there by the stream," Hunter got out on an indrawn breath.

"Where are you wounded? What were you doing here on the Five Star?" So many questions filled her mind, but first things first, she told herself. She leaned over him, looking for a wound, and then saw a bright red stain on the shoulder nearest the ground. "Are you hurt badly? Where is your horse? We'll have to get you to a doctor." She gazed around the area for any sign of Hunter's horse.

"I'll be all right. You get on back to the ranch before someone comes back her and finds you with me." Hunter had lost a lot of blood, and weakness made his voice sound distant.

"I can't leave you here like this! You'll die if you don't get some help for that shoulder!"

"No doctor." Hunter attempted to pull himself upright.

Shannon hurriedly assisted him in his effort, noticing the pain the slightest movement was causing. "I could take you to the ranch. I'm sure Cookie could help you."

"No. I already checked, the bullet went clear through my shoulder. Nothing's broken. I only need a couple of days to heal up some."

"So what do you think to do? Stay here in the underbrush for any wild animal to come along and do you more harm?" Shannon had known stubborn men in her lifetime, but this Mr. Hunter took the prize for being the most bullheaded!

Husky laughter settled over her as Hunter unleashed the last of his waning strength. As the pain lacing through his shoulder intensified, he leaned back against a tree trunk. His argent gaze traveled over her, glimpsing the flush staining her cheeks, and he thought her even more beautiful than he remembered.

Her fiery hair was plaited down her back in a plump braid reaching her waist, her hat, having been thrown back over her shoulders, dangling by a tie around her neck. Dressed in jeans, shirt, and boots, she was a vision that even a dying man could fully appreciate. Why, hell, he had thought her a spirit from the other side when he had opened his eyes to find her leaning over him.

Drawing in a steadying breath, Hunter explained, "There are some men who would like to see me dead, and they will do anything to see that end. If I go to the ranch house on the Five Star, I would be bringing my troubles with me."

"But Lucas and the others would be more than willing to help you."

Hunter would have laughed again if he had had the strength. He had learned early in life not to trust the *wasichu*, the white man. This young woman didn't know how things were in Montana, or, in fact, anywhere there were Indians. The white man called him a half breed; they saw no further than his Indian blood. "My troubles are my own." He didn't have the strength left in him to argue with her.

"Well, at least let me help you." Shannon bent closer to get a better look at the gunshot wound. Pushing away his shirt, she grimaced as she peered at the gaping hole in his shoulder.

Hunter leaned back and shut his eyes while Shannon tore the bottom of her own shirt and dampened it at the stream. Forcing herself not to tremble, she washed the wound as best she could.

"You still need to get to a doctor. You could easily take fever and die from a wound like that." Frantically, she tried to come up with an idea that might appeal to this stubborn man; an idea that would save his foolish life. "I guess I could go back to the ranch and get some medicines, and something to bind your wound."

Hunter's eyes reopened as he studied her intently. No white person had ever offered him so much for nothing in return.

"But it's still dangerous for you to stay here. What if those men, those bushwhackers, return to finish the job?"

"They shot me farther downstream. I made my way here and hid under the brush while they were looking for me. They think I'm dead already. They won't be back."

Shannon doubted he really believed this. Why else would he have told her to leave in case they returned? "There's a lion shack that's not being used not too far from here. I guess you could stay there until you mend up." Shannon knew she was taking a lot on herself by inviting this man to use the Five Star lion shack, but she saw no alternative. She certainly couldn't leave him to lie out in the open and face whatever danger came his way. He was as weak as a kitten, and he would be defenseless.

Hunter would have argued that she should leave him and forget she ever found him by the stream, but he was too tired and weak from the loss of blood to put up any kind of effort to resist her as she went and brought her mount up close and helped him to his feet.

"Just try and pull yourself up." Shannon held Hunter around the waist and helped him mount as best as she was able. With some effort, he at last was sitting in the saddle, and Shannon mounted behind him. As he leaned back against her in order not to fall, she wrapped one hand around his chest and took the reins up with the other.

Thank God the lion shack was only a half-mile from the stream. Shannon doubted she could have held the man upright in the saddle for much longer. As it was, when they arrived at the lion shack and she climbed down from the mare's back, Hunter slipped into a heap at her feet.

She was not sure how long he had lain under the brush bleeding, but as she helped him into the small cabin, she felt heat radiating from his flesh. She directed him to the bed in the corner of the single room with both her hands encircled around his waist.

Hunter's breathing was somewhat shallow as she pulled his shirt off and once again studied the wound. She had washed away most of the blood earlier, but the move to the shack had produced a renewed flow. As he lay still upon the cot, she attempted to stem the blood loss.

When she was satisfied that the bleeding had been stanched, she grabbed up a bucket near the door and went out back to get some fresh water.

Silently Shannon washed away the sticky blood from Hunter's upper torso, her eyes marveling over the bronze, muscle-rippled flesh as her fingers tenderly traced a path from his neck to his waist.

Hunter appeared to have lost consciousness, so still was he during Shannon's ministrations. But as she stood up and away from the bed, realizing the necessity of hurrying back to the ranch and bringing supplies in order to attempt to save his life, Hunter's eyes opened once again.

"Tell no one I am here, Péta Wicáhpi, Morning Star."

* * *

Leaving the lion shack, Shannon held but one thought in mind, that of securing the medicine that would help Mr. Hunter have a fighting chance at survival. She pushed from mind all thoughts of how she had trembled slightly as she had taken off his shirt and her fingers had traced over the power of his broad chest. He was a man who was hurt, and needed her help. She would do whatever she could to save his life, the same as she would do for any other man, she told herself as she tried to ignore the strange attraction that overwhelmed her each time she was in the man's presence.

The ride back to the ranch seemed to take forever, and by the time she arrived, it was already noon. Cookie met her at the front door with a wide grin.

"Your company is waiting in the great room, Honey darlin'. Lucas and Alex are entertaining them for the time being. You have time to run on upstairs and change, if you have a mind to."

Her company? Thunderation, she had forgotten all about Bonny and her friend coming out to the ranch today! Shannon looked at Cookie with some desperation in her aqua eyes. Mr. Hunter was lying wounded in the lion shack. How on earth could she act as though everything were normal and take tea with the ladies?

"I was just going to take the ladies some lemonade. If you're not feeling well, I could make your excuses." Cookie was not lost to her distracted appearance, and worried that the heat had overtaken her.

"No . . . no, Cookie. I guess I just lost track of time out there on the range. I'll be only a few minutes." She turned and hurried up the stairway.

Even though her concern was for Mr. Hunter lying wounded in the lion shack, she could not be so rude as to send Cookie into the great room with some fabricated excuse for her not appearing. What would Cookie then think when she left the house again with medicine and supplies?

No, it was best that she change and visit with Bonny and

her friend for a short time. She would attempt to hurry the visit, and then be free to focus her attention back on Mr. Hunter.

Shannon hurriedly dressed in a teal gown with ecru lace edging. She took little time with her hair, wrapping the thick braid around the crown of her head and securing it with a few ornate pins. Within just a short span of time she was hurrying back down the stairs.

In the hall outside the great room she drew in a deep, steadying breath. You can do this, she told herself, even as her mind filled with the image of Mr. Hunter wounded and bleeding, lying there on the cot in the lion shack. Forcing a smile over her lips, she entered the room and greeted Bonny with a fond hello.

"Oh, Honey, we thought you would never get here." Bonny welcomed Shannon into the room with an exuberance that held the men sitting nearby entranced.

"I'm sorry I'm late. I trust Lucas and Alex have been keeping you well occupied?"

"Indeed, they have. I envy you living out here on the Five Star and having such wonderful gentlemen all to yourself." Bonny's sparkling blue eyes traveled over both men in a provocative fashion.

It was not until Shannon was fully in the room that she noticed Bonny's friend sitting quietly in a chair across from the settee. She was a striking woman with wheat-blond hair curled atop her head.

"Oh, Honey, I guess I must introduce Nancy once again. Nancy Inverness, Honey Belle. Nancy is working at the Red Dog, and has a beautiful voice. Though it pains me to admit, she is becoming the rage of Last Chance in a very short time."

Nancy Inverness smiled warmly at Bonny before turning her full regard upon Shannon. "You see, my mother loved to sing, and at an early age she held small soirees in order for me to entertain her friends by following in her vocation.

"I'm sure your singing is beautiful," Shannon responded. Bonny was one of those women who said anything that came to mind, and Shannon was well aware that this Nancy Inverness felt some kind of response was necessary because of the other woman's statement. The woman did, in fact, have an unusual speaking voice, and Shannon could well imagine that she was able to capture the attention of an audience when she sang. Her words were flavored with a husky mixture of feminine charm and erotic depth.

"I do hope we shall all be friends." Nancy's dark gaze held directly upon Shannon. "Bonny told me that you arrived in Last Chance the same day she did aboard the same stagecoach."

"Oh, my, yes, that was a miserable trip!" Bonny supplied. "By the way, I don't know if you have heard yet, but Abigail Primer, the new schoolteacher, was murdered the night before last."

"Murdered?" Shannon paled as she remembered the woman who had arrived in Last Chance the same day she and Bonny had. "Did they find the person who killed her?"

"There is a suspect. One of those cowboys who are forever hanging around Last Chance, but I heard he has an alibi. He claims he was with one of the girls from the Silver Garter dance hall. She swears she was with him all night, so they haven't arrested anyone yet."

"This is terrible." Shannon was shocked by the news. "How was she murdered?" Though she desired none of the grizzly details, for some reason she had to ask the question.

"She was strangled right there in the schoolhouse, and they say the killer left a silk stocking wrapped around her throat," Bonny willingly related.

Nancy did not join in the conversation about Abigail Primer's murder, but instead sat back in her chair and silently studied Shannon.

"I hope you don't think too unkindly of Last Chance

because of what happened to the schoolteacher." Lucas looked over at the newcomer to Last Chance Gulch.

"My goodness, by no means, Mr. Atwater. Besides the love of music, my mother also gave me a love for travel. Footloose and fancy free, I have visited more towns than I care to recall, and I have heard more stories about death than I would ever relate."

"Lucas. Call me Lucas, my dear." Lucas found the woman very attractive, and wished to keep this afternoon's visit as informal as possible.

Nancy Inverness visibly blushed, and responded in a throaty tone that was alluring to the male ear. "It will be my pleasure to call you Lucas as long as you call me Nancy."

News about Abigail Primer's death, combined with the worry Shannon harbored for Mr. Hunter, left her feeling that she was unpleasant company for her guests.

The ladies, though, seemed not to notice her distracted mood as they were entertained by the gentlemen; Logan and Jackson shortly joined the group. Shannon was relieved when Bonny announced that it was time for their departure.

It was still early afternoon when Shannon stood on the front porch and waved Bonny and her friend off. Turning back into the house as soon as the pony-pulled phaeton made its way down the long drive, Shannon started upstairs to change back into her working clothes.

"Why don't we all just call the rest of the day a holiday?" Lucas looked around at the men and Shannon, where she was standing upon the first step of the stairway.

"That's a good idea, Lucas. Honey here has been working as hard as any one of the hands and deserves a rest." Alex was quick to agree that they spend a pleasant afternoon together relaxing in the great room.

"I'm afraid that I promised Sam and the boys I would be back to help with the branding." Shannon hated to lie to these kind men, and she silently prayed that the ranch hands wouldn't relate that they hadn't seen her all morning, but she had to get back to the lion shack with the medicine for Mr. Hunter's shoulder.

She wished now that he hadn't made her promise not to tell anyone he was injured. It would be much easier if she could tell these men what had happened to Mr. Hunter, and enlist their help in making sure he survive his wound.

"You go on up and change, then, Honey darlin'. These old codgers can make do without your company until dinnertime." Cookie was quick to come to Shannon's aid.

Shannon smiled fondly at the little man be fore turning and hurrying up the stairs. Quickly dressing back into her jeans and a clean shirt, Shannon worried that she would return to the lion shack and find Mr. Hunter in worse condition than she had left him that morning.

Once again downstairs, she silently made her way to the kitchen area. With some relief she found the large kitchen empty. Cookie must be in the great room with the rest of the men, she thought as she took up a small sack and placed some food within, knowing Mr. Hunter would need nourishment to build up his strength.

Stepping out onto the back porch, she opened the small cabinet that had been tacked to the wall. She had seen Cookie take out some bandages from the cabinet one day when Alex had cut his finger.

She removed a bottle of antiseptic and some bandages, then hurriedly shoved them into the sack. With her heartbeat dashing harshly against her ribcage, she resaddled her mare and left the barn.

TO A. D. ARMSTRONG.

HAVE ARRIVED IN LAST CHANCE GULCH STOP HAVE ALREADY BEGUN TO TAKE MATTERS INTO HAND STOP WILL WIRE YOU WHEN JOB IS COMPLETED STOP

N. IVEY

EIGHT

Shannon opened the door to the lion shack and was greeted with the barrel of Hunter's Peacemaker. Gasping back a breath, her eyes widened, her hand freezing on the door latch.

Realizing who his visitor was, Hunter sagged back down on the bed and replaced his gun next to his side, under the blanket.

"I . . . I brought some food, and medicines." Shannon pulled her wits back about her and entered the cabin, shutting the door silently.

Setting the sack on the table near the woodburning stove, Shannon approached the bed tentatively. She couldn't forget everything she had heard about this man. Though lying there on the bed, he didn't look dangerous, she had seen the hostile glint in his smoky eyes when she had opened the cabin door.

Hunter could remember having worse wounds in his life than the one he was now suffering, but the loss of blood had left him weak and in need of a day or two of rest.

If the girl hadn't come along and found him, he would have eventually crawled down to the stream and washed the bullet hole, and found some medicine plant to halt the bleeding. By the next afternoon he would have regained enough strength to search for his horse.

More than likely, those back shooters had taken his mount or killed him. He had had the horse for a year now, and the stallion had always been faithful. He would be very unhappy if he couldn't recover him.

Feeling the woman's cool, slender fingers trace a tentative path over his forehead, Hunter held his eyes shut as he enjoyed her attentions.

Finding his brow only slight warm, Shannon sighed out her relief. Turning away from the bed with thoughts of getting the bandages and antiseptic from the sack, Shannon was caught by surprise when her wrist was captured in a strong grip.

The silver eyes looked at her with a penetrating stare. "Did you tell anyone that I am here?"

"Why, no. You told me not to, so I didn't." Shannon attempted to jerk her hand out of his grip, but surprisingly, she found him much stronger than she would have thought possible for a man who had lost so much blood.

"What took you so long to return?" Hunter rather enjoyed having her close. He could smell her womanly scent—jasmine, and a musk essence that was all her own.

"You can let loose of my hand." Shannon's temper was beginning to simmer. She wasn't about to answer any more of his questions until he released her.

Hunter's thumb grazed the soft indentation of her palm before he let her go. The action unwillingly triggered Shannon's heartbeat to race irregularly in her breast.

Putting some distance between them, Shannon went to the small table across the room and began to pull out the things that would be needed to tend his wound.

Going back over to the bed, Shannon laid out the necessary supplies on the blanket. "I had visitors at the ranch."

Her softly spoken words interrupted Hunter's silent appraisal of the crown of burnt-copper hair that was wound around her head, and the heart-shaped face that appeared intent upon not looking directly at him. "What?" he questioned in confusion.

"I was answering your question. Why it took me so long to return here to the lion shack. When I arrived back at the ranch, I had visitors. I had forgotten that Bonny Ingram and her friend, were coming out to the Five Star today." Shannon felt her face warm as Hunter's bright gaze held upon her lips as she was speaking.

Hunter, did not respond to her explanation. Instead, he warmed to the project of watching her. She was flawless, he thought as he saw her slender fingers pluck at the bandages and ready them for his shoulder.

As she pushed aside the blanket to reveal his entire chest, Hunter noticed the slight rush of heat that stained her creamy-smooth cheeks. With an effort he controlled the wish that overcame him to draw a finger over her high cheekbone and trace a tender path down her throat to the valley where her buttoned shirt revealed an outline of swollen breasts.

Shannon noticed that the wound had not started to bleed again, and picking up the bottle of antiseptic, her gaze rose to meet his. "I'm sure that this is going to hurt some." She waited for his response before pouring the liquid into the wound.

"Your tender care of me cannot bring me more pain than I can bear." Hunter prepared himself for the rush of searing pain he knew would shortly be gifted upon him.

Shannon put all her concentration on taking care not to hurt Mr. Hunter any more than necessary. Pouring a generous amount of the antiseptic into the bullet hole, she glanced up quickly to see his reaction.

She exhaled her pent-up breath when she saw his features were only slightly strained, his eyes holding upon her face. "I will have to do the same to the other side of your shoulder." she could feel drops of perspiration beading her own forehead.

Hunter nodded his head, moving his shoulder as she directed him with a gentle hand.

"I have never doctored anyone before," Shannon informed him as she poured the rest of the antiseptic into the hole in the back of his shoulder. Inspecting the back side of the wound, she realized that he had been right, the bullet had gone straight through his shoulder, and apparently there were no broken bones.

"You have an easy touch, like that of Autumn Woman, the medicine woman in my grandfather's village."

Shannon was startled by his words; she had forgotten that he was an Indian. Without comment she began to bind his shoulder with the bandages.

"If you don't take fever, I would say that you will be all right in a week or two."

Lying back against the pillow, Hunter smiled fully upon her. "I will not take fever, Péta Wicáhpi." He did not add that in a week or two he would be long gone from this cabin. He would rest only for a day, maybe two, if this woman promised to return to tend his wound, then he would be back on his feet and ready to find out exactly who it was that had ambushed him.

There, he had called her that strange name again, Shannon thought as she cleared away her medicines and went back to the sack on the table.

"I brought you something to eat. I hope you are fond of roast beef." She had sliced two large pieces of Cookie's supper roast, and along with half a loaf of bread, and a few of Cookie's famous fruit tarts, she made her way back to her patient's bedside.

With Shannon's help, Hunter sat up against the wall of the cabin, the pillow resting behind his shoulder.

Placing the food down at his side, Shannon stood back and waited for him to eat.

"I will eat if you have something also." Hunter placed the food on his lap, patting the side of the bed, he indicated she should sit next to him.

Uneasily, Shannon sat down on the edge of the bed. She would have refused his offer of sharing the meal, but she decided he was such a stubborn man, he might well refuse to eat altogether, and surely he could not regain his strength without nourishment.

"I'm not very hungry," she stated as she watched him tear the loaf apart and put the slices of beef within.

Hunter's gaze warmed as he reached out and took up one of the tarts and brought it to her lips.

Sheer confusion made Shannon part her lips for the tart to be placed within. As his hand drew away, some of her senses returned and she began to chew the treat slowly.

Watching her intently, Hunter ate the sandwich, the silence in the cabin drawing out uncomfortably.

"What was the meaning of the words you called me earlier?" Shannon softly questioned, disturbing his perusal of her.

Hunter did not immediately answer; his resplendent gaze studied her even closer.

Shannon tried to ignore his intent regard of her. "You called me the same thing this morning when I left the cabin," she reminded him.

"Péta Wicáhpi." Hunter spoke the name as though a gentle caress. "It means Morning Star. I call you this because your beauty rivals that of the star that rises over mother earth each day. You are revealed as a little flame that burns brightly."

Shannon sat speechless. What was she expected to reply to such a statement?

Hunter reached out and pulled the pins from the top of her head that held her braid. The thick copper rope of hair fell freely down her back. "Your hair shimmers with the gold of the morning star. I would see it free, and hanging down your body."

Speechless now as well as breathless, Shannon stared at Hunter, not knowing whether she should comply with his wishes to view her hair unbraided, or jump to her feet and flee before it was too late. She totally took leave of her senses.

Actually, Hunter would have desired nothing more at the moment than to look upon her entire body free of the bindings of clothes that restricted him from appraising all of her perfection. Her hair of fire gold would only heighten his regard of her if he were gifted with the sight of those glorious tresses lying unbound over her creamy flesh.

"I . . . I . . . guess I should be cleaning this up and leaving before Lucas or one of the others begins to worry about me." With a force of will that Shannon did not know she possessed, she pulled her eyes away from his simmering regard and jumped to her feet.

Hunter's smile was tender, his voice huskily entreating as he asked, "Will you return to me tomorrow?"

Some inner sense of caution told Shannon that she should run for her horse and never look back. But looking at him lying there on the bed, she believed him fully dependent upon her care. Drawing in a ragged breath, she forced herself to answer. "Tomorrow. As soon as I can get away, I will return." With that said, she rushed out of the cabin, and for a few trembling minutes she leaned against the wood frame of the door.

Her entire body seemed to tingle with some hidden inner desire of its own. What kind of strange power did this man hold over her? she asked herself. How was it possible that she could feel herself melting from within by the simple sound of his voice? If she hadn't gotten out of there when she had, there was no telling what she would have done. My God, while sitting there upon his bed, she had almost reached out and run her hand over the bronze flesh above his heart!

Shannon arrived at the ranch house shortly before the dinner hour, and fortunately, no one seemed to notice her pensive mood. Dinner, as usual, was shared in the dining room, and much of the conversation centered upon the two guests who had visited the Five Star that afternoon.

Alex mentioned about the murder of the schoolteacher only in passing. For the most part, the talk around the table was pleasant.

Shannon excused herself earlier than usual, leaving the men to their brandy and cigars as she made her way to her bedchamber.

Readying herself for bed, she noticed that her breasts

were more tender than usual as she brushed them with the cloth of her nightgown. The budding reaction instantly brought reminders of Mr. Hunter's gray eyes roaming over her face and lingering upon the swell of her bosom. A groan escaped her lips as she climbed into bed, knowing that sleep that evening would be hard to come by.

Shannon was up before daylight the following morning. Lighting only the small tallow candle on her bedside table, she hurriedly dressed. Distractedly, she ran the brush through her hair. Instead of taking the time to braid the thick strands, she tied the wayward tresses back with a single piece of blue silk ribbon.

Looking into the mirror, she was reminded of Mr. Hunter's heated gaze traveling over her, and his desire to view her hair unbound. If she had any sense at all, she silently cautioned her own reflection, she would climb back into bed and forget all about Mr. Hunter!

But even as she held these thoughts, Shannon knew she couldn't leave the wounded man all alone in the lion shack. He had no food and no horse, and even if he had a horse, he certainly didn't have the strength to ride.

No, she had come this far, she couldn't back out now. Mr. Hunter's very life depended solely upon her.

Going down to the kitchen, Shannon found signs that Cookie had already been up. The heady aroma of strong coffee wafted around the kitchen, and a tin of warm sweet rolls was sitting atop the stove.

Wrapping up a couple of slices of last night's roast, and a loaf of bread in a napkin, she was just starting to take a couple of the sweet rolls and place them in the napkin, when Cookie startled her from behind.

"Here, Honey darlin', let me get you a cup of coffee to wash down all that food."

"Oh, Cookie, I thought I would take along plenty. Last night's roast was delicious."

"Ain't them boys feeding you well enough out there on

the range?" Cookie had noticed the slices missing from his roast the afternoon before, and now, as he silently watched her wrapping up enough food for two large men, he wondered what she was up to.

"Oh, no, Berny is a great cook. It's just that you're much better." Shannon knew that flattery would get her anything she wanted from this kind man. She took the cup of coffee he was holding out in her direction and the napkins full of food, and headed out the back door.

Her words had held the desired effect over the little man. He beamed as he went about the kitchen. From here on out, he would pack Honey a lunch and have it ready before she left each morning. If Berny's cooking didn't suit her, he would make sure she didn't go lacking.

Shannon hated to lie to Cookie, and told herself she would be glad when Mr. Hunter was able to leave Five Star property and no longer need her help. Already she had been forced to lie more times than she wanted to recount because of the wounded man.

Saddling her mare, and stashing the food in her saddlebag, Shannon left the barn alone. That morning she did not take the time to enjoy the beauty of the Five Star. She headed straight to the lion shack, and in the back of her mind she told herself that she would have to explain to Mr. Hunter that she would not be able to come to the lion shack again.

If he felt he needed her assistance, she would have to be able to tell Lucas and the others that he was there on the Five Star. The owners of the ranch had been too good to her for her to have to deceive them any longer!

Hunter had been on his way outside the lion shack to wash the blood from his jeans and shirt, when he heard a horse approaching. Looking out the single window of the cabin, he smiled warmly as he spied the copper-haired beauty on horseback.

Returning to bed, he pulled the blanket over his lower body, and lying back, shut his eyes. The woman appeared

to enjoy taking care of him. By no means did he intend
to disappoint her.

Shannon opened the cabin door quietly, hoping not to
disturb the wounded man. Glancing over at the bed, she
set the food on the table. He appeared to be soundly sleeping. She noticed a small pile of clothes and his boots on
the floor, and wondered if he had had an easy night of it.

She had hardly slept a wink last night; thoughts of this
man had plagued her relentlessly throughout her sleep.
She silently approached the bed. Reaching out, she placed
her hand over his brow.

There was no trace of heat against her hand. His tem-
perature felt normal. As she drew her hand away, his silvery
gaze held her there where she stood.

"I wasn't sure if you would return." The husky tremor
of his tone washed over her, her body reacting with an
inner tingling of the senses.

"I told you I would come back." Her voice was breathless, unusually husky even to her own ears.

"I am glad that you have come." Hunter's gaze silently
traveled over the material of her blue and white plaid shirt,
which stretched tightly over her breasts, and was tucked
into slim-fitting jeans.

Shannon could not halt the blush that traveled up from
her bosom as she felt his eyes upon her. "I . . . I brought
you something to eat," was the only thing she could think
to say.

Hunter's lips pulled back into a generous smile. "Good.
I am very hungry." He watched as she turned and made
her way to the small table across the room in order to
retrieve the food. His argent eyes glistened brilliantly as
he appraised her slim back, the swell of her hips, and
shapely buttocks. The holster belt at her waist and the strap
at her side accented fully her womanly curves.

Bringing the napkins containing the food to his bedside,
Shannon tried to ignore the heat of his gaze as he watched
her moving around the cabin. Setting the food down next

to him on the bed, she thought it safest, if she took herself back over to the table and waited for him to finish.

Hunter somehow sensed her intentions. Before she finished placing the food on the mattress, he had captured her hand within his own. "Do not flee me, Little Flame. I am a wounded man, and can do you no harm. Sit here beside me and share this food. I am lonely for your company."

Shannon knew that she was crazy to comply, but as her blue-green eyes locked with those of brilliant gray, she was powerless. As he gently pulled her hand toward him, her body slipped downward, and she sat upon the blanket next to his large body.

Hunter grimaced a little as he pulled himself into a sitting position, the blanket loosely draped over the lower portion of his body.

Shannon had never been placed in such a position before. In fact, she had never been this close to a man wearing nothing but a blanket. She swallowed nervously as she tried to untie the knot in the napkin containing the bread and meat.

Hunter's hands lightly brushed hers aside as he made short work of the job. "After you left yesterday, I worried that I had frightened you, and that you would not return." With the food now revealed, Hunter appeared more intent on the woman sitting next to him than the hunger he had earlier acknowledged.

Shannon stared down at her hands, not allowing herself to look up into his handsome face. She should tell him now that this would be her last visit to the lion shack, but she simply couldn't get the words out of her mouth.

Easily glimpsing her discomfort, Hunter attempted to put her at ease. Breaking off a piece of the bread, he handed it to her.

"While we eat, you can tell me about your husband, and your life here in Montana." After she left him yesterday, Hunter had had little to do except think about her. He

remembered she had said she had come to Last Chance
to meet her husband, Alex Cordoba.

Like most of the populace of Last Chance, he had heard
the rumor that the owners of the Five Star had sent away
for a woman who would be wife to them all. Such thoughts
had stirred feelings within him that he had not wanted to
explore. He would find out the truth of the matter now.

Shannon glanced up, quickly taking the bread he handed
over. She glimpsed no censorship on his face. In fact, his
features were unreadable as those silver eyes watched her
and he chewed a mouthful of meat and bread. "I'm afraid
that I was mistaken when I told you in the Red Dog Saloon
that I was in Last Chance to meet my husband."

"You are not joined with Alex Cordoba?" Hunter was
confused. He had believed her when she claimed she was
in town to meet her husband. He had been there in the
street when the ranchers had pulled up before the hotel,
and directly had helped her into their wagon and left town
with her.

"It was all a mistake." Shannon felt trapped with him
watching her so intently.

"I thought I was going to be a wife, but . . . but they
only wanted a woman at the ranch. I am more of a . . .
a . . . daughter to them all."

As Hunter ate his meal, he thoughtfully went over her
words. "You care for these men like a daughter cares for
her father?" He didn't care about the ranchers' feelings,
he wanted to be clear about her feelings toward them.

"Every day I am learning to care more for each of them.
They have been very good to me since I arrived in Montana." Shannon saw no reason to lie about her feelings
for the owners of the Five Star.

This was a strange situation. Hunter had believed her
married to Alex Cordoba, and was only mildly curious
about the gossip about the other ranchers. Now he found
that she claimed to be a daughter to all the men; the
wasichu had strange ways.

"Do you like Montana? Do you plan to stay here near

Last Chance?" Unwed as she claimed, there was truly no reason that bound her there, and for some reason he pushed a little harder to hear her plans.

"I will stay for a while." Shannon's answer sounded vague even to her own ears.

Hunter could sense there was more to this woman than what was viewed on the surface. He would have liked to ask more questions, but her features were closed to further inquires. He had to respect her privacy even though he would have had it otherwise, and demanded to know everything there was to know about her.

With caution, he told himself to have patience. He would learn more when she was ready to reveal what she was keeping hidden. "Did you tell anyone that I am here on Five Star property?"

Shannon could sense that it was hard for this man to trust anyone. He had asked her this same question yesterday. She gave the same response today. "I promised I wouldn't tell anyone you're here. You don't have to worry that I will, unless you tell me to do so." Some inner voice told Shannon that now would be as good a time as any to tell him she would not be returning to the lion shack unless she could tell the ranchers she had found him wounded man and had brought him here. But for some reason she still couldn't get the words out.

Hunter had not met a white woman he could fully trust. It was surprising, but he believed this woman's assurances. "Did you wear your hair down this day for me, Little Flame?" Hunter's gaze traveled over the shimmering curls captured by a simple piece of blue ribbon, and hanging down her back in glorious display.

Shannon felt the rush of heat travel up her throat and over her face. "No . . . I . . . I didn't have time to braid it." Somewhere unbiddingly in the back of her thoughts a small voice admonished her as a liar. It would have been a simple thing to braid her hair, taking only a few minutes of her time. Had she not expected the heat from his scalding gaze as he looked upon her hair, had she not even dreamed of this man running his large fingers through her tresses?

Quicker than she could have anticipated, Hunter's hand reached out and caught hold of the silk ribbon. Shannon would have jerked away, but she knew the action would have made her look the part of coward. With indrawn breath she forced herself to remain still beneath his touch.

"Your hair is even more beautiful than I could have dreamed." Hunter's voice was deep, his eyes entranced as they roamed over the freed curls that appeared to shimmer with lights of dancing flame.

Shannon felt a rush of gooseflesh course over her body, her heart hammering wildly in her chest. She could not move, nor could she speak; she was as entranced as he as she stared into the swirling depths of his worshiping regard.

The ribbon fell to the floor, and Hunter's fingers lingered in the lush bounty of her hair. The attraction between them could not be denied. All that had passed had brought them to this moment.

Hunter's hand curved gently around the back of her head, a small amount of pressure applied as he encouraged her to meet him halfway. His head rose from the pillow, their gazes locked. He could smell the womanly scent of her as it swirled in allure over his senses. She trembled slightly in anticipation of what next was to come.

There was no rush in the claiming of what could not be denied. Hunter's sensual lips lightly covered the bow-shaped curve of her mouth, the pressure of the kiss as softly entrancing as a fine wisp of thistledown.

Of their own accord, Shannon's eyes fluttered closed. Lush, feathering lashes fanned against her soft cheeks as she drew in a steadying breath.

The pressure of his mouth against hers slowly intensified, the kiss now a heady, erotic joining. The warmth of his tongue tracing the sculpted contour of her closed mouth slowly slipped through her teeth, invading the sweetness of her essence.

Shannon had never been kissed in such a fashion. Nothing had prepared her for this moment, when she would lose all sense of reality and slip beyond that world where one had complete control of one's actions.

In her heart she knew this was right. It was meant that she and this man share this heat that simmered between them. From the first moment she had seen him standing in the middle of the street in Last Chance Gulch there had been a deep inner attraction of her soul toward him. There was no fear, no regret of what was taking place.

A soft moan escaped the back of her throat, the sound reaching Hunter's ears, further drugging his normal sense of caution. The hand upon her head lowered to her back, gently drawing her closer. Her breasts lightly pressed against the muscular strength of his naked chest.

Their twined tongues did a seductive dance of erotic delight. Shannon's slender hands splayed over Hunter's upper chest in order to hold herself upright, the feel of his smooth bronze flesh igniting fire to her already scalded senses.

The meal lay scattered and forgotten between them. All that mattered was this kiss that they were experiencing.

Shannon desired nothing more than to melt into him, to be filled with him, consumed by the heat of him. Never in her imaginings would she have believed herself capable of such strong emotions where a man was concerned.

She had not truly lived until that moment. Her mind and body had lain dormant until his mouth covered hers, and now she wanted this feeling of incredible pleasure to last forever.

Hunter knew also that what they were sharing was not the usual kiss shared between a man and woman. There was something that stirred within the depths of his being as he held this woman close to his heart. There was a need to protect, a need to comfort and cherish. It was as though she were that missing part of his heart.

He felt as though he were a man who had wandered for years in a vast desert and only then had found his way home. His lips indulged the feelings he was experiencing, searching and seeking. His tongue sought out each hidden crevice of her mouth, wanting to taste, to capture every portion of her essence into his own keeping.

Seared by the flame of their coming together, and unable to withstand the intense heat, Hunter pulled back. For a breathless few seconds he stared at the loveliness of her features as she leaned against him, her breathing ragged, her beautiful eyes closed, her pinkened lips slightly parted. Her copper hair shimmered all around them, falling down her back and over his chest, and as his hand reached out and lightly caressed her delicate cheek, strands of the beckoning fire curls wrapped around his arm, drawing him closer.

Shannon's eyes slowly opened. As though she were only then regaining some of her senses, she smiled with an innocent warmth, "Why did you stop kissing me?"

Hunter had to draw in a deep breath in order to steady the rampage of his wildly beating heart. Looking at her flushed, passion-laced features he knew this woman was his to do with as he would. Something in his soul strongly forewarned to go slowly, to use caution. This woman was not like the girls in the Silver Garter dance hall, to be used and then walked away from without another thought.

The kiss shared impressed upon him that there would be no forgetting her if he did not turn away before it was too late; and even then he wondered if he would be able to chase from his mind the sweet, lingering taste of her upon his lips.

"I have never been kissed like that before." Her words came out breathlessly, her brilliant turquoise eyes transfixed upon his sensual lips.

Husky laughter filled the cabin as Hunter attempted to ignore the need that quickened fiercely within his loins. "Come now, Little Flame, has no man ever held you in his arms and kissed you before?" Hunter was surprised at the instant prick of anger that filled him with thoughts of another man holding her and kissing her until she lay breathlessly against his chest. The question was meant to distract them both away from what they had experienced just moments before, but instead Hunter felt his need flaring dangerously out of control.

"No," came her breathless reply.

Bonny Ingram's bedchamber was one of the largest on the upper floor of the Red Dog Saloon. As she was lighting the rose-scented candles on the bureau, she heard a soft knock on the chamber door.

"Come in," she called, and turning to face her guest, she smiled in welcome. "Oh, it's you. Come in, but you can't stay long. Sammy should be here any minute."

"I have my eye on a new dress in Rose Williams's dress shop window. Sammy promised that if I was extra good tonight, I might just have the money to buy that dress tomorrow." Bonny's pleasant laughter filled the chamber as she turned her back on her company, pulled back the covers on her bed, and adjusted the satin scarf she had draped over the small table near a comfortable chamber chair. Earlier she had brought up a bottle of Sammy's favorite whiskey; this and two glasses were arranged neatly on the table.

"I haven't worn this gown before, what do you think?" Bonny's slender fingers caressed the front of the frilly see-through negligee that adorned her lush form as she turned to face the other occupant of the room.

"What . . . what the hell?" Bonny's eyes enlarged in surprise as she turned and came up short. Her visitor stood close, and within the flashing of a second she felt something soft and unyielding caressing her throat, and slowly tightening.

Bonny struggled against the strong hands that clutched her. She tried to kick out, to push and scratch for her release. As seconds passed and her air was cut off by the tightening of the silk stocking, her resistance slowly waned.

A few minutes later Bonny Ingram lay in a provocative

pose upon the carpeted floor, her eyes wide in disbelief, her heartbeat stilled.

The chamber door softly closed as Bonny's company slipped unnoticed out of her chamber.

NINE

Shannon did not give a moment's thought to lying as those silver eyes studied her intently. There had never been a man in her past whom she had found an attraction toward. There had been the usual childhood infatuations, but none of the young men who had come to her father's house and courted her had dared as much as this man. She knew deep in her heart that no other could have evoked the feelings within her body that this man did.

Hunter could have so easily pulled her back into his arms, but his self-control sustained him in his moment of need. He would have gotten up from the bed and put some distance between them, but he caught himself before he pushed away the covers with the remembrance that he was naked beneath the blanket. "You should not look at a man like that, Little Flame."

"Like what?" she asked innocently.

"Like nothing else on mother earth matters except that I kiss you again."

"Nothing else does matter, Hunter." Her reply came on a ragged breath. Shannon's hands were still pressed against his chest, and beneath her palm she could feel the swiftly drumming beat of his heart.

Hunter needed more time to sort out the feelings that were stampeding him like a herd of mighty *tatanka;* buffalo. He was a loner, a man living between two worlds: a half breed, the white men called him, who was paid to track down and kill other men. In the Sioux world he was Hunter, grandson to a mighty war chief.

There was no room in his life for a woman such as this one, with her wide, innocent eyes looking so trustingly up at him. Drawing both her hands into one of his larger ones, he drew her back away from him. "There can be nothing between us, Little Flame. I am not for you."

"Why?" Shannon had never been denied before, and stung by his rejection, she felt she deserved an answer.

Before he could respond, the thought hit her, that perhaps he already had a woman of his own. Her face began to flame, her eyes filling with betrayal as she accused, "You have someone waiting for you in your grandfather's village?"

Hunter's mind filled with the image of Summer Rose, her doelike eyes and slender form appearing lacking compared to this creature of fire and earth. "No, there is no one waiting for me in my grandfather's village." The last two times he had visited his grandfather, Summer Rose had shared her blankets with him, but neither of them believed their relationship would go any farther.

"Then why do you put me away from you?" Shannon had no shame at the moment. All she realized was that a part of her heart was crying out that she not let this man go.

A lesser man would have easily forgone all thoughts of allowing the woman to escape the lust that burned intensely throughout his body. But looking into her innocent gaze, Hunter drew upon his inner strength, knowing that in the end he would only hurt her, and she deserved so much more than he would ever be able to give her.

He knew she did not understand his reason for desiring they put a halt to the joining of their lips. She was entirely innocent to the ways of a man and woman's reactions to such play; but he was not.

He had to be the strong one, he told himself as he drew in a gulp of air. "I am hungry, Little Flame." He forced his features to close, to appear disinterested in what she was offering him.

It was on the tip of Shannon's tongue to state that she was hungry, too, but not for the food she had brought. Viewing Hunter's cool regard, the words died before leaving her lips. She read in his passionless gaze that what they had shared, however brief, was now over, and would never be rekindled. "I'm sorry. Of course you're hungry." She all but jumped off the side of the bed, and in the process pulled a portion of the blanket away with her.

Staring down at the mess she had caused of the scattered food, her aqua eyes deepened to churning depths of azure blue as they stole over a good portion of Hunter's naked torso.

As her eyes raked over a naked thigh, she realized that his entire body was the color of deep sun-bronze. As her gaze drew upward over a hip and waist, her mouth grew dry as she viewed the washboard of muscles that rippled over his belly, and tapered upward in a V, revealing his powerful chest. His long hair of deepest midnight was held back by a leather tie, but Shannon could see enough of the thick length to imagine the silky feel beneath her fingertips. As an inner trembling beset her, she forced herself to turn away from the sight of her sun-bronzed warrior.

Drawing in great breaths of air as she stepped away from the bed, Shannon's conscience rebuked her for her foolishness. This man did not want her for anything more than someone to bring him food. He was wounded and had only yesterday been on the threshold of death, and now, there she was, wanting him to hold her in his arms and kiss her throughout the morning.

With her back to him, Shannon was able to steady her frayed nerves and strongly admonish herself to force out of her mind the attraction she felt.

He was no more than a wounded man, she the person who had come across him in the woods and saved his life. There would always be that between them, nothing more.

He had made it clear that he wasn't interested in her. He cared only for the food she brought him.

When she turned back toward him ten minutes later, the food was gone, and the blanket had been restored in neat order over his lap.

"I . . . I'll take these out back and wash them for you before I leave." Shannon picked up his jeans and shirt and started to the cabin door.

"I can wash them, Little Flame. I feel much better now, thanks to you." Hunter knew she was hurting because of his words, and wished things could be otherwise. But he lived a life of danger and there was no place in it for a woman such as this lovely white one.

"Don't be silly, your wound will reopen. You still need to rest for a day or so." Shannon exited the door without any more argument on the subject of who would wash out the clothes. Even though she felt like her heart had turned into a great stone, she could still be practical.

When Shannon returned into the cabin, she was in more control of herself. Hanging the clothes over the back of a chair, she turned to face the bed and her patient. "Tomorrow morning I will return with enough food to last you for a few days. I will try to bring you a horse, which you can return to the Five Star whenever you recover your own."

She didn't need to say that tomorrow would be the last time she would return to the lion shack. Hunter already knew that by the determined set to her chin. She was trying to be strong, and Hunter knew that the only way she could do this was by not being in his presence. "Thank you for everything, Little Flame."

Shannon felt tears stinging the backs of her eyes. Turning toward the door, she left without saying anything else. Why did he have to call her that damn name, and why did he have to say it in a way that just melted her heart?

Before going to bed that evening, Shannon gathered enough supplies to last Hunter at least three more days.

In the morning she would avoid running into Cookie and go straight out to the barn. She hoped to borrow a horse for Hunter, and knew if she were caught taking an extra horse she would look very suspect.

After a restless night Shannon left the ranch early, as planned. She told herself this would be the last time she would go out to the lion shack, and thereafter she would forget Mr. Hunter ever existed.

Shannon found Hunter dressed and resting on the bed. He was well enough healed to have left the cabin last night, but Shannon's promise of returning that morning was too tempting for him to resist. Though he knew she could never belong to him, he could not help the need within him to at least look upon her one last time before leaving the Five Star.

That morning she seemed distant, and after laying out the food on the table and indicating that she was not going to draw close to the bed, Hunter sighed heavily as he went to the table and sat down in a chair.

"Are you all right, Little Flame?" Hunter noticed her drawn look and the dark circles around her eyes; his worry apparent in his regard.

"I'll be fine." As soon as she left this cabin and never looked back on these last few days, she would be fine, Shannon told herself.

"I brought you a horse, and enough food for a few days." She wanted to be finished with Mr. Hunter as soon as possible. The kiss they had shared seemed to hang between them like a physical reminder of her wanton needs, and his cold rejection.

"Thank you, Little Flame." Hunter knew she was hurt, but also knew that she would get over the hurt soon enough. One day the right man would come into her life and she would be glad that things had gone as they had between them. With such a thought, a stab of regret filled his heart; regret that the man for her couldn't be he, regret that he would never again taste the honey sweetness of her lips beneath his own.

"I wish you would stop calling me that!" Shannon blurted out, knowing that it wasn't the name so much as the way he said it, in that husky fashion he had, that bothered her so much.

Hunter attempted to break the tension that now filled the cabin. Deep, husky laughter met her ears as he questioned, "Would you like me to call you Honey Belle?"

Shannon knew at that moment that he was aware Honey Belle wasn't her true name. "I guess it doesn't matter what you call me."

She was in no mood to argue with him, and she certainly was not about to confide that her real name was Shannon Stone. This would be the last time they would be alone, the last opportunity for him to call her Little Flame in that melting fashion.

"Everything about you matters, Little Flame." Hunter wished they could part as friends. He did not want her to think about him with ill thoughts. It was fate that would not allow them to experience what could have been if he were a different person. In his heart he wished it otherwise, but his mind knew better than his heart.

"I guess I'd better leave now. The Five Star hands will be waiting for me."

Hunter did not speak the words that he wished he were free to say. He watched her turn and step through the cabin door, knowing that what they had shared for a few minutes the previous day would never be rekindled. There was no turning back what was never meant to be.

Brushing away a tear from her cheek, Shannon cursed herself for being a fool, and Hunter for having to look so attractive sitting there at the table with his clothes on. Maybe it was time for her to leave Montana Territory, she told herself as she reached her horse.

Maybe she ought to strike out for California, or even return to St. Louis. Shannon felt as though she had changed over the past several weeks from an innocent child to a woman with a mind of her own. Perhaps the smartest thing would be for her to turn around and face her past.

Distracted with her thoughts, Shannon was unaware of the two men who watched her from the cover of trees only a few feet away from the horses. Just as she started to mount, one of the men stepped out of concealment and grabbed hold of her arm.

"Hold up there, missy." The tall, gaunt-featured man grinned, the hand clasped around Shannon's forearm tightened its grip as he forced her to stand close to his side.

"What ya got there, Pete?" The man's friend stepped out into the open also, his gap-toothed grin as large as his buddy's as his red-veined brown eyes looked Shannon over from head to boots.

"Get your hands off me!" Shannon glared at the one holding her arm. If it weren't for the fact that the man had a hold of her right arm, she would have pulled her gun free from her holster and warned the pair off with her six-gun. As it was, she couldn't very easily reach over with her left hand for her weapon. The one called Pete would surely be quick enough to waylay her intentions.

"Why, we got us a little sweet treat, Hank. And I aim to eat her up!" The pair had watched Shannon arrive at the lion shack. Not believing their stroke of luck, they had patiently waited for her to appear back outside.

"Do ya think she might have a friend inside?" Hank questioned, his glance going from Shannon to the shack.

Shannon's fear intensified as she imagined these two trespassers barging into the lion shack and taking Hunter unaware. He was still recovering from his bullet wound; he couldn't possibly defend himself in a shootout!

"You're trespassing on Five Star property!" Shannon forced her voice to sound stern as she glared at the pair of unwashed louts.

"If you know what's good for you, you'll get on your horses and ride on before more of the Five Star hands arrive here at the lion shack." Her statement did not appear to have the effect she desired, so she added for good measure, "Lucas and some of the boys were following me and should be here any minute."

The bandit holding her arm laughed gruffly and pulled her up tightly against his chest. "Don't lie to us, little gal. We watched you ride up, and we set up a watch in case someone was following. You're all alone, 'cepting for whoever you got hidden away in the shack. Maybe Hank's right. You got another little ol' gal stowed away in there that's just hankering for a man to be apleasuring?"

Shannon could smell his stale breath, and forced herself not to gag as she squirmed against his tight hold. It was clear these two meant business, and thinking more of saving Hunter than herself, she did the only thing that came to mind. While Pete's attention was held upon her squirming curves, she brought her booted foot down square upon the top of the toe of his boot.

Pete's grip loosened as he cursed her soundly and jumped up and down.

Pulling her gun from her holster, she was about to warn the pair to stand back, when Hank grabbed hold of her from behind.

The gun went off with a resounding bang, and as Shannon struggled for release, Pete cuffed her on the side of the head, the six-gun falling at her feet.

"Get in that shack and see if she's hiding anyone else in there!" Pete shouted at his partner. With his toes aching fiercely, one of his hands plunged within Shannon's thick hair and the other grabbed her by the shirtfront. "You little bitch, you just wait, you're going to pay for that!"

Hank kicked the cabin door open, and looking within, he called, "There ain't no one in here. It's just like I told ya, Pete, the little gal's out here all alone."

"Then what's the extra horse for?" Pete wasn't as convinced as his friend.

"Maybe she stole him," Hank replied.

"Right. She looks like a horse thief, doesn't she?"

Hank stood at the door and looked closer at Shannon struggling against his partner. "Naw, she don't look like a horse thief. Maybe someone was going to meet her, and they didn't show up."

Pete considered this for a few seconds, his grip on his captive tightening with each movement she made. His lust at the moment overpowered his good sense. He didn't press the issue of the second horse any farther. He would force the fight right out of her, he thought as he began to drag her toward the lion shack.

"Well, let's get her in there and have a go at her. We're suppose to be looking for that half breed's body. If'n Billy finds out we've spent the morning messing with a female, he'll have our hides."

Hank and Pete had been partners for going on three years, and Hank had early on learned that Pete was the one with the brains. Whatever he said, Hank did without argument.

Opening the door wide, he waited for Pete to drag the woman inside. This wasn't the first time they had found a young woman alone and forced their attentions on her. There had been another time before they had left Texas when they had come upon a small farmhouse. A woman and a small kid had been there all alone, and kicking the kid out into the yard, Pete and Hank had forced the woman to do all sorts of sexual acts upon them, as they did likewise to her. It had been an afternoon that Hank had not forgotten. It wasn't often that he got a woman without having to pay for a romp on a bed.

"Look around for a piece of rope, or something to tie her down with. I'll get her over there on the bed." Pete had his hands full as Shannon fought in earnest now for her release. She was relieved that Hunter had somehow gotten away before these horrible men could kill him, but now she was left alone to face what she could not even imagine they had in store for her. She tried to kick out once again, but was slapped for her efforts before she could find Pete's shin.

Pete had already dragged her over to the bed when all hell broke loose in the cabin. The sound of shattering glass filled the air, and the next instant Hunter was sailing into the room, his Peacemaker drawn and firing before he hit the floor.

Shannon didn't have time to scream. One minute Pete had his fingers in her hair and was trying to shove her down on the bed, the next, his fingers slipped their grip, and he fell with a dull thud to the floor. Across the room Hank fell backward, a bullet hole between his eyes.

Terror, shock, and disbelief filled Shannon's eyes as Hunter rose from the floor, and without a second thought to the men he had just killed walked straight to her, his arms open wide.

Shannon did not hesitate. With a strangled cry escaping her, she ran to him, and buried her face against the curve of his neck.

"Hush, Little Flame." Hunter's hand rose up, and he caressed her head as he tried to soothe away some of her terror. Her limbs trembled against him as her sobs fell upon his ears, touching his heart with the knowledge of her great fear.

"No harm will come to you, I will take care of you." He was a man used to dealing with death, not with a woman's feelings. But for this woman in his arms he made every effort to comfort her.

"But I thought they would kill you." Shannon wept louder, her fear of minutes earlier overcoming her.

She had worried over his safety, Hunter realized, and his grip upon her tightened. He could not remember anyone truly caring about his safety since he was a child. His grandfather perhaps worried about him, but Two Owls believed that a man's steps were ruled by the Spirit Chief, and what happened to him on his life path was preordained by the hand that led him.

"I am fine, my heart. These two could not have hurt me." He pushed her back from his chest in order to look fully into her face.

But I . . . your wound . . . I thought that they would surprise you . . . and they would kill you." Tears fell down her cheeks. Now that the ordeal was over, Shannon seemed unable to get a grip upon the rush of pent-up fear that filled her.

"My wound is fine, thanks to you, Little Flame." Hunter kissed her forehead, his gaze lingering over the marks made on her cheek from the slap Pete had delivered her. His anger surfaced anew, but he realized it was wasted; the two men would never again hurt a defenseless woman.

Slowly, Shannon's trembling subsided as Hunter held her close and soothed her with tender words.

As Hunter felt her breathing growing even and her heartbeat against his chest slowing, he led Shannon outside, away from the scene within the cabin. Sitting down upon a log, he pulled her down upon his lap. For a few minutes neither spoke as he held her within his embrace.

Finally, Hunter said, his words husky with the emotion he was feeling, "When I heard the gunshot, I cracked open the door and looked out. I saw the man holding you, Little Flame, and I saw you struggling in his arms. In that second my heart stilled in my chest. I knew, no matter the cost, I had to save you from all harm." He lightly brushed back the hair from her face and caressed the bruised cheek. I would kill them again for this," he confessed before his head bent and his lips settled over hers.

Shannon drank in the strength and comfort that Hunter offered. Her arms slipped around his neck as he cradled her against his chest, his mouth plying over hers in a kiss that bespoke more than friendship.

Hunter knew there was no turning back the moment. Though he had little to offer her, he could not halt the feelings that he had tried to push aside where this woman was concerned. If something had happened to her, he knew in his soul that a portion of his heart would have been stolen from him. This woman of fire and earth had kindled some inner need within his body, and he could no longer turn away from the want that filled every portion of his being.

Drawing back and looking into her face, his argent gaze

traced every inch of her features as though he would mark them within his memory for all time.

"I was foolish yesterday when I turned you away. I thought to protect you from myself, but I see now that you and I are meant to be. Medicine Elk, a great shaman of my people, says that each man must recognize from the heart the woman that is placed here on mother earth to share a warrior's life path. I have never thought much upon his words, until I met you, Little Flame."

Shannon listened to his words but was not quite sure of their meaning. All she was aware of at the moment was Hunter's large body surrounding her and the way his silver eyes stared down at her with adoration and warmth. She never wanted him to stop looking at her, or touching her in that gentle way he had. It had been a long time since she had felt this secure.

"You must go back to the ranch, Little Flame," Hunter stated, and, glimpsing one of her buttons undone, he reached down and secured it.

"But . . . but I thought . . . you just said that you and I were meant to be together," Shannon stammered, not understanding how he could make her leave him after what he had just said.

For a second she tried to remember what he had said, but her mind was so confused, she couldn't focus straight. All she knew was that she didn't want to ever leave the warmth and strength of his powerful arms.

"I will come for you." Hunter saw the emotions playing upon her lovely face, and he smiled fully at her. She was as radiant as the sun, and he knew that he would miss her heat, but there were things he had to do. He had to dispose of the bodies in the cabin and make sure the two he had killed did not have more friends who could be approaching the lion shack anytime. Perhaps he would find some clue to their being on the Five Star property in their saddlebags.

"But when will you come?" Shannon questioned as Hunter stood to his feet and she was forced to stand also.

Instead of answering, Hunter held her tightly one last, brief time, and kissed her in a way that stole her breath and forced her to reach out and clutch him for support.

Knowing that the slender grip he had upon his control was slowly slipping, Hunter laughed huskily as he drew back and placed his hands upon Shannon's shoulders. "You are very hard to resist, Little Flame."

"Why should we resist?" Shannon asked innocently. She did not have the worries that were pressing in on Hunter. All Shannon knew was that she had never felt before what she felt while in Hunter's arms. She never wanted those feelings to go away. She wanted to stay at his side and experience all that there was to being a woman; for with a certainty she knew that he was the man who would teach her the great mysteries of her womanhood.

"You must do as I say and return to the ranch. We will have our time." Hunter's words were a pledge.

TEN

Returning to the ranch, Shannon found the house in a great commotion. The ranch hand Sam had reported that over fifty head of prime cattle had been stolen the night before, and one of the Five Star's best men had been wounded trying to stop the cattle rustlers.

As Shannon stood in the great room with the rest of the ranchers, listening to Sam's report, Lucas entered the room with Nancy Inverness's slender hand riding trustingly on his arm.

"I'm sorry to interrupt, but there has been another murder in Last Chance." Lucas looked directly at Shannon, his free hand lightly patting the slender fingers of the woman at his side.

"Who?" Shannon's hand went to her throat, her face paling as she feared the worst.

"I'm afraid, my dear Honey, that your friend Bonny Ingram was killed last night." Lucas saw her sway, and was quick to desert the woman he had entered the room with.

"There, there, my dear, sit down right here." Lucas supported Shannon as he helped her to sit down in a comfortable chair.

Shannon had known from Lucas's first look that he would reveal the murdered victim as Bonny Ingram. Silvery tears spiked her thick lashes as she attempted to keep some control over her emotions.

The rest of the ranchers hovered around Shannon, wishing to help her get through this terrible ordeal.

Cookie handed her his handkerchief, and after wiping away the path of tears on her cheeks she forced herself to question Lucas. "What happened to her?"

"I'm sorry to be the one to tell you this, my dear, but Bonny was strangled."

"Strangled? Oh, no, not Bonny. She was so full of life, I can't imagine . . ." Shannon couldn't go on. It was unbelievable that Bonny could have been the victim of such a horrible death!

"Did they find the culprit who did the deed?" Logan asked.

"Not yet. Marshal Taylor is investigating, but so far he hasn't found her killer." Lucas returned to Nancy's side.

"She was killed just like Abigail Primer," Shannon whispered, fighting the image in her mind of Bonny attempting to fight off a vicious attacker.

"Yes, that's exactly right. When the body was found, there was a silk stocking wrapped around her throat just like the schoolteacher's.

"That's the reason why I have brought Miss Inverness out to the ranch. She will be staying out here at the Five Star for a few days," Lucas announced.

Shannon nodded her head, too upset in her grief over the loss of her friend to say anything more.

"Oh, you poor dear." Nancy Inverness whisked past Lucas and the ranchers in a cloud of perfume and made her way to Shannon's side.

"Come along now, Honey, and I will see you to your room. I know that you and Bonny were close. She told me all about the friendship that had developed between the two of you on the stagecoach. You need a few minutes alone. Time to pull yourself together."

Shannon allowed Nancy to help her from her chair and lead her upstairs to her room. Lucas and the rest of the men stood silently by, glad that Nancy Inverness had come to the Five Star and apparently was capable of handling a woman's grief; which none of the men had confronted before.

"There now, let me help you out of these clothes." Nancy's throaty voice held no censorship over Shannon's unwomanly apparel. She appeared totally concerned with her well-being as she went to the wardrobe and pulled out a satin robe.

"You need to try and rest for a little while, Honey. Once you are wearing something comfortable, things will look a little brighter."

Shannon was suffering from shock at hearing about Bonny's murder, and with Nancy's help she undressed and slipped on the robe.

At the moment she doubted anything she did could ease the hurt she was feeling, but as Nancy puttered around her bedchamber, she was glad she had come out to the ranch. She loved the ranchers well, but it was easier to share her grief with another woman. "I just can't believe Bonny's truly gone."

"I know, dear. That is exactly the same reaction I experienced this morning when I received the news. The whole episode is so horrible. A woman is no longer safe in Last Chance Gulch, and I don't know what I would have done if not for dear Mr. Atwater."

Nancy busied herself by bringing a perfume-dampened cloth to Shannon's bedside. "Here, dear, just rest back on the pillows and press this over your forehead. My mother always said that a woman's pain is always lessened by a scented cloth."

Shannon did as Nancy bid her, but dared not close her eyes. She feared that with the closing of her eyes she would see her dear friend's face and be sent into even worse despair. "Who would have done such a thing to Bonny?" she questioned, knowing that she would receive no answer.

"Why, I guess whoever killed Abigail Primer." Nancy pulled up a chair close to the bedside, appearing with her actions to care only about Shannon's welfare.

"I saw the dear girl for a short time last evening, and

she appeared to be the picture of good health. You know she was seeing the owner of the Red Dog Saloon, Samuel Sterling, exclusively. She told me once that he had threatened to beat her if he caught her with another man, but I'm sure he would never . . . he certainly is the not the type who could strangle two women!"

And what kind of person was the type to take the life of a young woman like Bonny Ingram? Shannon wondered as she listened to what Nancy had to say on the subject.

"I hope you don't think I am imposing here at the Five Star, but ever since Abigail Primer's murder, I have felt uncomfortable in Last Chance. Now, after what happened to Bonny, I don't mind telling you, just like I told Mr. Atwater, I am scared to death that I might be the killer's next victim."

Shannon's look was one of question as she wondered why this woman would believe herself a candidate for such a horrible crime. "What makes you believe so?"

"Why, I am a woman, and newly arrived in Last Chance, my dear. It would appear that Bonny and Abigail Primer had these things in common." Nancy's dark, searching regard for another minute or two continued to study Shannon before she once again spoke. "You know, Honey, you might want to use a bit of precaution from here on out yourself."

"What do you mean?"

"You did arrive in Last Chance Gulch on the same day as both these young women who have been murdered. I wouldn't wish to imply that the killer will come after you next, dear, but I don't think it unwise if you are a little more careful for the time being."

Shannon's hand automatically went to the bruise on her cheek as she remembered the two men who had attacked her at the lion shack. Could they have possibly been Bonny's killers? Was Nancy right about her being the killer's, or *killers'* next victim? If she were right, and it was the two men, they had run into more trouble than they had bargained for when they had come across Hunter!

"I noticed that mark on your cheek earlier." Nancy watched Shannon hurriedly draw her hand away.

"I took a fall from my horse this morning," Shannon lied, for some reason not feeling comfortable confiding in this woman. Nancy had been Bonny's friend. Shannon would have to get to know her a little better before she would be able to completely open up to her. It would be nice, though, if she had another woman to share her thoughts with. Hunter's image played within her mind, and as she remembered his promise to come for her, a slight trembling took hold of her body.

Nancy's sharp eyes missed nothing. She knew the young woman had not fallen from a horse, but for now she would not concern herself with such a trivial matter as a bruise on Shannon's face. "I had better leave you for now to your rest, my dear. I'm sure that darling little man, Cookie, will be more than willing to show me to a chamber that is not in use."

Shannon would have asked the woman to share her room, but something stilled the invitation before she could get it out. Nancy appeared friendly enough on the surface, but there was something about her that bothered Shannon; she just couldn't put her finger on what it was about her that was disturbing. She was sure that the feeling would go away, or she would recognize the woman for what she was soon enough with her staying as a guest at the Five Star.

When Nancy left the chamber, Shannon remained in bed for a while longer. Her mind wanted to mourn the loss of her friend, but her heart wanted to reflect on that morning, and how wonderful it had felt being held in Hunter's arms.

The house seemed unusually quiet for the rest of the day. Dinner was served in the dining room as every evening, but Nancy Inverness appeared the only one with a hearty appetite and a lively spirit. The ranchers' mood reflected Shannon's; they could all sense her grief and understood the loss of a friend.

After dinner Nancy retired to the great room with the men, promising all that if asked just right, she would be more than willing to sing for them. The ranchers seemed pleased with the prospect, but Shannon excused herself and retired for bed earlier than usual.

It was not until shortly after the house quieted that Shannon's restless mind was able to ease and sleep began to overcome her.

She had just closed her eyes, when a noise at her window had her sitting straight up in bed. Remembering what Nancy had said about herself possibly being the killer's next victim, she clutched the covers up to her chin, her eyes wide as she tried to make out the reason for the intrusion of her sleep.

Nervously, her fingers lit the candle at her bedside, her gaze fastened on the window. Her six-gun was on the bureau, and anxiously she wondered if she should retrieve the weapon in case she had to defend herself.

Seconds passed as Shannon stared at the window. Her breath expelled in a whoosh as Hunter climbed through the open portal. "What are you doing here?" she gasped aloud in whispered tones as she scrambled off the bed and hurried across the room.

Hunter looked surprised at her reaction to his entrance into her chamber. "Did I not tell you that I would come for you?"

"Well, yes, but I'm surprised that you would come to me in this fashion."

Hunter's grin was genuinely warm as his regard traveled over Shannon. Her glorious fire curls were in wild disarray about her shoulders and down her back, the thin gown covering her body leaving little to the imagination as the flickering light from the candle illuminated the shadows of lush feminine curves. Even her tiny feet peeking out from the hem of the sheer gown captured Hunter's imagination as his desire for this woman magnified.

"Come with me, Little Flame." Hunter's hand reached out to place hers within.

"Now?" Shannon had not thought things would go this fast.

Hunter's smile never wavered. "You had no doubts this morning about us. Do you hesitate now?"

It was not hesitation that held Shannon on the spot, staring at him as though he had taken total leave of his senses, it was practicality. Having always been practical regarding major decisions in her life, she was a little reluctant to jump into this man's arms and let him sweep her away.

But then, on the other hand, she had not been too practical the morning she had left Honey Belle's room with the intention of claiming her identity and coming to Montana. Perhaps practicality was something Shannon found she could no longer be afforded.

Looking at Hunter's handsome face, she wondered what he was offering, but in the same reflection realized that she did not have the power to turn down the promise that she read in the depths of his silver eyes.

Slipping her hand within his, she made her decision. "It will take me only a minute to dress and leave a note telling Lucas and the others who I am with."

"Do not leave a note, I will send word of your whereabouts in a day or two." Hunter didn't want their trail to be hounded by the owners of the Five Star. He could well imagine what their reaction would be when they discovered that their houseguest, whom the men considered a daughter, had run away with him.

They would have every lawman and bounty hunter within five hundred miles searching for him. That is not what Hunter wanted for the beginning of his relationship with Little Flame. He wanted her to have time in which to decide if she was willing to become a part of his life; they would not have this time if they were being chased like common outlaws.

Shannon did not argue. It was easier to place her trust

in this man who was offering her what every woman alive would jump at the chance to reach out for.

Going to her bureau, she pulled out a pair of jeans and a shirt. Slipping the jeans up under her gown, she turned and found Hunter's steady gaze watching her. A flush stained her face and throat and, turning away from his heated perusal, she slipped the gown over her head and pulled on the shirt.

Hunter's eyes traveled over the flesh of her back with all the hunger of a starving man. In the candlelight her skin looked creamy smooth, beckoning for the touch of a lover's caress. The full curve of her bosom was revealed as she lifted her arms to slip into the sleeve of the shirt, and with the revelation, Hunter felt the stirring of his manhood. With a will he forced control over the impulse that filled him to separate the distance between them, and have finish with his raging desire and lose himself within the heat of her passion.

When Shannon turned around and faced Hunter once again, she glimpsed none of the raw emotions that he was fighting to control. She saw him as she always saw him, strong, and in control. "I guess I'm ready." Her voice was low, tentative.

The smile returned to Hunter's sensual lips. He held his hand out once again. "All I have to offer is my heart, Little Flame." The husky promise of his words washed over Shannon in a wave of undiluted desire.

Was the promise of this man's heart enough to make Shannon turn her back on the Five Star and the ranchers, and even life as she knew it? She did not know where he intended to take her, nor what tomorrow would have in store. Was she truly prepared to leave with him?

That more wayward side of her mind forcefully challenged the more practical. *And just what are you leaving behind? A life that is a lie? Lucas and the others don't even know your real name, nor do they know what made you run away to Montana Territory. Are you willing to remain here, living this sham of a life, when this man is offering you all that he has?*

Feeling somewhat light-headed, Shannon walked the few steps across the room. Slipping her hand within his, she spoke softly, her words barely reaching his ears. "What you offer is dearer to me than you can know. In return, I have only my own heart to offer you."

What she offered was all that Hunter would ever desire. He was a man who had always made his own way in this life. He would share with her all that he was, and would pray to the Great Spirit that his offering would be enough to keep this woman happy in the days ahead. Bending his head toward her, his lips covered hers in a kiss that was not meant to tempt, but instead to seal the promises made.

A short time after the couple had climbed out of Shannon's bedchamber window to the roof of the porch below, and, aided by the trellis on the side of the porch, made their way to the ground, the bedchamber door silently opened. The candle burned low at the bedside, revealing the room to be empty. The door eased shut once again.

ELEVEN

Hunter had secured two horses beneath a tree a few hundred yards from the house. Shannon noticed that neither was the Five Star horse she had taken to the lion shack that morning.

"Where are we going?" Shannon asked after Hunter lifted her up into the saddle of the horse he had brought for her use.

"We will go up into the mountains to my grandfather's people." Hunter watched her features as closely as he was able beneath the moonlight for any sign of a negative reaction.

Viewing the slight nodding of her head, his relief was great. He wanted her to share that portion of his life that was different from the white man's. He did not want her to look back with regret that she had given her heart to a man whose culture and past were worlds apart from her own. He wanted her to have time to meet his people and for his people to fall in love with her, as he already was doing.

"Do you think your grandfather will approve of your bringing a white woman into his village?" Shannon was not frightened at the prospect of going with Hunter into an Indian village. In fact, the thought was rather exciting, but she did remember what she had heard about his grandfather, and how he and his band of warriors, long ago, had attacked white settlers.

"My grandfather and my people will not be able to help falling in love with you, Little Flame. They will see, as I have seen, the goodness that lies in your heart. All will know that it was meant that you and I should share our life paths as one."

This was all the assurance Shannon needed. Hunter seemed so sure of himself and his belief that the two of them were supposed to be together. How could she think otherwise?

They left the ranch house quietly and rode throughout the night, Hunter insisting they put as much distance between themselves and the Five Star as possible before daylight broke.

Sometime after dawn Hunter reined in his mount in a wooded glade. Having watched Shannon's slumped form for the last few hours, he knew that if he didn't stop to rest soon, she would be falling out of her saddle. "We will rest here, Little Flame."

Shannon had thought this moment would never come. Never had she felt so weary. Pulling her horse up next to his, she all but fell into his arms as he came to her side and reached up to help her dismount.

With a soft sigh she leaned her body full against his support. "Hmmm, I could grow to like this." Her soft smile was quickly followed by a large yawn.

Hunter laughed low in his throat. "I did not mean to push you so hard, my little star. I wanted to make sure we are not being followed."

"And are we?" Shannon was content to remain in his arms forever.

"Our trail will not be followed. We cross-trailed a couple of times. That is why we have traveled all night. We will rest for a few hours here. I know a better place, were we will camp tonight, and tomorrow we will arrive in my grandfather's village."

Shannon was too tired to worry about anything. It was wonderful to have someone else take charge. It seemed like she had been making decisions most of her life, and at the moment she saw nothing wrong with letting this man take control.

Enjoying the feeling of her pressed up tightly against his body, Hunter was reluctant to let her go. For a few more minutes they stood close before he untwined the hands wrapped around his neck and untied the blanket secured behind the saddle of his horse.

"Come, Little Flame. There is a spot here beneath the trees that will make a soft bed for you to rest in." He covered a hill of pine needles and leaves with the blanket.

Shannon was more than willing to lie upon his blanket if this handsome man was going to lie down beside her. Forgetting her exhaustion for a moment, all she could think about was the kisses they had shared before she had left the lion shack. He had not kissed her since he had come for her at the Five Star, and in expectation her body trembled slightly as she stepped over to the blanket and stretched out.

Hunter stood over her, his brilliant regard full of hunger as he let his eyes roam over her shimmering copper curls spread out over his blanket. At that moment he desired no more than to bend to her and capture her body against his own.

Forcing a reviving breath of air into his lungs, he fought off the inviting temptation. In his heart he knew it was not the right time for him to take her. He was unsure if she fully understood the magnitude of what giving herself to him would mean. He did not want to join with her now and tomorrow she realize that she desired more than his life could give.

He knew deep in his soul that once he joined with this woman, there would be no letting her go. What they would share would bind them through this life and all those that eternity would guide them to. With a soft sigh, Hunter turned away from the sight that gave him so much pleasure to look upon.

"Where are you going? Are you not going to rest here next to me?" Shannon's features plainly revealed her surprise. One minute she had viewed the want upon his features, the next his face had closed to his true feelings and he had turned away from her.

"You tempt me greatly, Little Flame, but I will keep watch here near the horses."

"But you said yourself no one was following us." Shannon was loath to let go her desire to share his kisses.

Hunter laughed deep in his throat, knowing her needs, and promising himself that soon he would shower her golden body with kisses that would leave her breathless for more. Soon, but not this day, not here in this forest, where someone could come upon them, and not until she fully knew her heart. "Rest, my heart, for soon enough we will be back on the trail."

It was on the tip of Shannon's tongue to ask him why he had taken her away from the ranch if he didn't want to be with her, but as she rolled over on her side and watched him tend to the horses, she calmed herself with the thought that he only worried over her safety. When they made camp tonight, he would once again take her in his arms and kiss her like he had at the lion shack. A soft smile settled over her lips as her eyelids drooped, and she silently appraised his large body.

It seemed that Shannon had only just fallen asleep, but in truth a few hours had passed, when Hunter was leaning over her and shaking her awake.

"No, I'm tired, I don't want to go out on the range today." Shannon tried to push the insistent hands away from her shoulders.

"It is time that we get back on the trail, Little Flame. If we stay here much longer, we will be late making camp this evening."

Hearing Hunter's voice, she immediately remembered where she was. Pulling herself upright, a small groan escaped her lips. Every muscle in her body was sore from their hard night-long ride.

Hunter's smile was one of sympathy. He knew she was being pushed, but there was nothing else to do. "I have some biscuits and meat that you left with me yesterday. We will share this food before we ride." He sat down next to her on the blanket and pulled out the food from a leather parfleche.

God, Shannon wondered, *what have I gotten myself into?* She was tired, and aching, and all she really wanted was a warm bath and to sleep in a soft bed for a day or two. Instead, here she was, sitting on a blanket of leaves and about to share a meal with a man, admittedly, she knew little about.

But as Hunter's hand touched hers as he gave her a biscuit, and those gray eyes swept over her so warmly, some inner sense told her that the feelings this man stirred within her had to be searched out. she could not turn away now without fully discovering what more there was between them. Taking a bite of the biscuit, she smiled, and watching her, Hunter grinned back.

The ride during the day was easier going. Hunter led Shannon over unseen forested paths, and through flower-covered valleys. Always he took an upward route higher into the mountains. Several times they stopped and drank from his canteen, and allowed their horses a few minutes rest. But for the most part they traveled at an easy pace.

The couple rode mostly without speaking, Shannon believing Hunter's silence due to his caution and concern that they not be taken unaware, and she followed his lead. Once Hunter halted the horses when they were deep in the woods and quietly pointed out a doe elk and her calf drinking from a swiftly flowing stream. Shannon delighted in the beauty of the place and would have lingered there in the coolness and watched the animals, but Hunter pushed on, wanting to reach camp before dark.

It was shortly before dusk when Hunter called their traveling to a halt within the shelter of a densely wooded glen. The stream they had been following for the most part of the day appeared to be deeper in this part of the forest.

Dismounting, they unsaddled the horses and allowed them to graze and drink their full.

"We will stay here tonight. My grandfather's village is not far away."

"Why don't we just go on into the village now?" Shannon was surprised to learn that his grandfather's village was not far from where they were. One would think Hunter would want to be with his people, and sleep within whatever type shelter they had, instead of spending the night in the woods.

She certainly had no intention of arguing with his decision though. She would be happy to have the opportunity to have him all to herself for another night. She didn't know what would await them in his grandfather's village. But she supposed they wouldn't have such privacy as in the woods.

"We will refresh ourselves here. Tomorrow will be soon enough for me to share you with others." Hunter smiled warmly, bringing a slight blush over her flawless features. "I will start a fire. The stream is deep here, why do you not wash away the dust from the trail?"

The invitation of a bath was too tempting to refuse. "You're sure you don't need my help here in camp?" A minute's guilt washed over Shannon as she watched Hunter picking up twigs for his intended fire.

Hunter's eyes sparkled brilliantly as he smiled at her. This woman who had stolen into his heart was as easy to read as the white man's books. He had not missed the initial response of joy that crossed her face with his offer of a bath, as well he had seen her thoughtful expression due to her leaving him to set up camp alone. "There is nothing for you to do here, Little Flame. I will build a fire and see what I can find for us to eat."

"Well, if you're sure you don't need me, a bath sounds wonderful." Shannon's hesitation fled. After all, she had no means to start a fire, and she certainly didn't have any idea where to find food in the woods.

Kicking off her boots and stripping off her clothes,

Shannon waded out into the cool, swirling water. A sigh escaped her lips as she submerged entirely, letting the refreshing liquid revive her body and her senses.

Breaking the surface, her copper curls twined around her body, then floated upon the top of the water in a shimmering display as the last remnants of afternoon sunlight broke through the canopy of trees overhead.

For a while she floated on her back, kicking her feet against the current that gently pulled at her with an insistent will to carry her downstream. With her eyes tightly closed she delighted in the feel of the liquid caressing her flesh.

It was erotically indecent of her to be lying in the water totally naked. Never had she dared take a bath out in the open before. Her father's housekeeper, Mrs. McGuire, who had scolded her father constantly that he was allowing her to grow up with unladylike attitudes, would be shocked if she could see her now! A smile filtered lazily over Shannon's lips as she imagined Mrs. McGuire fainting dead away as she chanced upon her in her unladylike state of undress.

Hunter's intention had been to go downstream only the few yards to where Shannon was bathing and give her the soap he had purchased in Last Chance the previous day and tucked away in his saddlebags. But as he stood along the bank and his regard feasted upon her incredible beauty, all of his pent-up passion stormed through his body in a flood of heated desire.

Glad that she did not see him, Hunter stepped away from the streambank, turning away from the sight that tempted him beyond all the temptations that had come before his life path.

Drawing in great breaths of air, he forced himself to call upon his inner strength. As a child, he had been taught to fight off the will of the flesh and make it one with the mind. Several times he had gone on vision quests, and in the tradition of his people, he had pushed aside all temptations of the body. He had three times endured the trails of the Sun Dance ceremony, and had been blessed greatly by the Great Spirit for his endurance and strength of will, and his ability for fighting off all temptations that had come upon him.

But this woman, with her golden body, and curls of fire, was a temptation, Hunter realized, that was stronger than any he had thus far known.

Closing his eyes, he saw her as he had moments before, her beautiful body lying inches below the surface of the water, her fire curls fanning out around her curves in a swirling web of glistening beauty.

His body began to tremble as he inwardly reflected on how her full breasts had trust upward, their swollen rose tips beckoning his resolve.

If the woman in the water were any other, Hunter would not have hesitated to strip his clothes away and join her, but this woman was not one of those from his past. He could not rob her of the choice that was hers alone to make.

He wanted her to meet his people, to go among them and see the true man that was inside of him. With all his heart Hunter wanted this woman, but he would not deprive her of knowing her full heart.

He would not take her only to one day witness the regret on her face. Nor would he be able to turn away from his own people and live the life of a white man no matter how much he believed this woman was the one that the Great Spirit had placed upon his life circle.

Slowly, his body stilled its trembling, and his heart resumed & normal beat. Looking down at the soap still clutched in his hand, Hunter smiled in anticipation. Turning back toward the stream, he called out be fore stepping out into the open along the bank. "I have brought you some soap for your bath, Little Flame."

Shannon immediately shrank down into the cover of water, her neck and head all that could be seen, and at the moment, these features were blushing brightly. Hunter's sudden presence there along the edge of the water pushed all thoughts of Mrs. McGuire out of Shannon's head. Her daydreaming about the overbearing housekeeper stumbling upon her in all her naked splendor had been comical to think upon. But the reality of Hunter standing only a few feet away, and she, totally naked except for the rushing water covering her body, was no dream. "Soap . . ." she gasped out as though not understanding the word.

Holding his hand out, Hunter displayed the bar of soap in his palm. "Would you like me to bring it to you?" The question was voiced in a teasing manner.

Shannon swallowed hard, her eyes widening at the question. It was true that she believed this man the only one for her, but was she prepared for what would happen if he did as he questioned? There was little doubt that if he came to her in the water, she would not be able to resist whatever would follow.

Glimpsing the hesitation on her features, Hunter gently laughed as he threw the soap into the water next to her. As the creamy bar of soap splashed and immediately sank out of sight, his breath stilled in his throat as she dove down into the swirling depths to retrieve it. The curve of her shapely buttocks and long, beautiful legs filled his vision, and in so doing tempted all his firm resolution of moments earlier.

Pushing back up through the surface water, Shannon laughed delightedly in triumph as she clutched the bar of soap in her fist. "It smells wonderful, Hunter." The flowery scent swirled around her Senses reminding her of the soap she had purchased for herself at the dry goods store in Last Chance Gulch.

A groan of pleasure-pain escaped Hunter's throat as he viewed her delighted features. As well, the swell of her breasts was barely covered by the water, the rosy tips appearing to play a game of hide-and-seek as the water gently lapped against her body. Fearing that to remain another minute would strip him of the slender thread of will that he still claimed, he turned away from the water and the woman that was creating havoc in his usual calm world.

Shannon watched him leave with a frown gracing her brow. She had enjoyed this interchange with Hunter. There was always that slight challenge of tempered passion just below the surface of their conversation, and she was inquisitive enough to wonder what would be the outcome of their exchange. For just a minute she had caught a look upon his handsome face that made her believe he was going to join her in the stream, but as quickly the look had vanished, and he had turned away.

She lathered her hair and body with the fragrant soap, she rinsed and left the stream. Hunter had left a piece of fur for her to dry with her clothes.

After drying, she dressed and returned to camp to find Hunter sitting a few feet away from the small fire he had made in the center of camp.

Looking up at her approach, he patted the blanket at his side. "Come, Little Flame, sit near the fire. The warmth will dry your hair."

Shannon immediately did as bid, finding the sensations that stormed her body every time she was close to Hunter pleasurable, and something she wished to explore fully. As she sat down next to him, she wondered if he would kiss her again.

The fresh, flowery scent of her ensnared Hunter's senses and held him stiffly there upon the blanket. It was all he could do not to turn and take her in his arms and have finish with the aching need deep within his body that seemed to be growing by the minute.

"The water was wonderful." Shannon's words came out on a single breath. Her side lightly pressed against his, and the contact held the effect of stirring to wake little shivers of anticipation coursing down her spine.

Any minute now she expected him to turn to her, wrap his arm around her shoulders, and draw her close. After all, this is why he had come for her and taken her away from the ranch. They had wanted time alone to fully explore these daring feelings that overcame them both when they were near each other. Now was as good a time as any, to Shannon's way of thinking, to start the exploration.

Hunter's arm did reach out, but not to wrap around Shannon's shoulders and draw her close as she had dared hope. Instead, both of his strong hands wrapped around her shoulders and set her somewhat at a different angle on the blanket. "I will brush your hair. It will dry sooner, and there will be fewer tangles if it is combed while still damp."

Shannon was not about to argue. Her thick lashes fluttered against her cheeks as she closed out all sensation except that of Hunter's hands upon her body.

Having earlier retrieved a comb from his saddlebags, Hunter gently drew it through the copper strands. As his fingers followed the comb, and tangled within the thick, glorious mass, he knew that he had been waiting for this moment since the first time he had set eyes on this woman. She was a goddess of fire and sun, and sitting close to her, Hunter could feel the heat that lured him ever nearer.

Her hair came alive, the ruddy sheen darkening to shimmering highlights due to the warmth of the fire and Hunter's attentive ministrations. Relaxing back against Hunter's chest, Shannon indulged the impulse to forget everything except that moment.

Hunter's powerful thighs circled her, his strength surrounding her as his hands stroked and freed the tangles from her hair. Any minute she expected him to turn her around to face him, and put a finish to the craving that gnawed at her insides with a fierce desire to feel his mouth upon her own.

It did not take Hunter long to realize the folly of his desire to brush her hair. Her closeness blinded his good intentions with a throbbing sensation that started deep in his abdomen and settled in his loins.

Her copper curls came to life beneath his hands, the thick tresses twining around his wrists and clutching his forearms as they fell in a glorious display over his lap; the fiery tips brushing against the blanket. A small groan of inward pain blended with piercing pleasure as Hunter forced his hands away from her hair, and at the same time he drew away from her as though she held the ability to scorch him with flame.

Without a word spoken, he stood to his full height. Staring down into her questioning turquoise regard, Hunter was at a loss. A part of him fought against the imposing restrictions he had set for himself and desired only to return to the blanket and pull the woman up close against his heart. But once again his good sense won out as he defeated his weaker needs where Shannon was concerned.

The full bounty of her favors would be that much sweeter to savor when he knew in his heart that she desired him for the man he truly was. Just a little more time and he would be sure of her responses, he told himself. Just a little more time in her presence and he would go insane with the want of her! his weaker self lamented.

Turning away from the confused look he read upon her face, he headed for the stream. What he needed at the moment was to submerge himself entirely in cold, head-clearing water!

Shannon was left at a total loss to understand what had just taken place. One minute she had been leaning against Hunter's strength, his heartbeat dashing strongly against her cheek; the next minute, he was standing over her and glaring at her as though she were the cause of all his problems.

Brushing a tear away from her cheek, Shannon asked herself what had ever possessed her to leave the Five Star with this man in the first place. It was obvious now to her that Hunter's feelings were not those of a same nature as her own. Her passion for the man had ruled her decisions. She was not sure what had ruled Hunter's.

A short time later Hunter stood silently on the outskirts of camp. His silver regard instantly sought out the woman

sitting before the fire. His breathing caught on a inward
sigh as her beauty caught and held his rapt attention. Her
mood appeared silently reflective as she stared into the
flames, and he wondered at her thoughts. Was it regret he
viewed upon her features? Regret that she had left the
security of the ranch to come with him into a world of the
unknown?

His heart trembled with such thoughts. Was she already
plagued with feelings of dissatisfaction that she was with
him? What would tomorrow hold if already she regretted
that she had left the Five Star? Would she look upon his
people with the contempt that he had viewed upon the
features of other white people? Was this woman of his
heart like all the rest?

Something drew Shannon's gaze away from the fire pit;
some inner knowledge of Hunter's presence caused her
gaze to travel around the outer boundaries of the camp-
site.

A shiver of highly charged anticipation filled her as her
regard caught and held with his gaze of purest silver. The
trampling of her heart charged unwillingly in her chest as
her wide eyes slowly lowered from his face and traveled
over his broad, naked chest, down his muscle-rippled midriff, to the breechcloth tied over his hips. Her ragged
breath exhaled as her glance filled with the sight of his
powerful thighs.

At that moment Hunter saw no regret upon her brow.
His thoughts of moments earlier vanished with the heat
of her gaze as her eyes swept over his body. *This woman is
different; she is not like all the rest.* His heart leaped with the
announcement, and happiness filled him with the realization.

As he advanced toward her, all Shannon's earlier
thoughts of worry and regret vanished before his tender
regard. Here before her was the powerful warrior she had
always dreamed would one day come into her life and
make her world worth living.

TO A. D. ARMSTRONG
  HAVE EXPERIENCED A SLIGHT SETBACK STOP WILL SOON HAVE SITUATION UNDER CONTROL STOP
  N. IVEY

TWELVE

All reason fled Shannon as Hunter came to her. Bending down to the blanket, he stretched out next to her, his arms gathering her close against his wildly beating heart.

"For a moment, while I watched you, I thought I viewed regret upon your features." His husky tone raced over her flesh as his heated breath caressed her ear.

Regret? What woman could hold regret while being in the arms of such a man? Shannon's fingers traced the hardness of his bronze chest, trailing over his shoulders to twine around his neck. Her body shuddered at the close contact of him.

Tenderly, Hunter kissed her brow. "I am a man who has been taught early in life to use restraint, Little Flame. I fear, though, that where you are concerned, my will has been sorely tested."

"Why would you wish to use restraint?" Shannon placed a trail of small kisses over his heart. "Why do you not kiss me, Hunter, and let what happens happen?" She had thought he was rejecting her, but now she was beginning to understand that for some strange reason, he was fighting off this attraction that they held for each other.

His heart raced madly beneath the ardent flame of her kisses. Hunter's husky laughter escaped his throat as he gently pushed her somewhat away from him. "Do not tempt me, little one, you know not what you ask. I would

4 BESTSELLING HISTORICAL ROMANCES BY YOUR FAVORITE AUTHORS CAN BE YOURS, FREE!

Kensington Choice brings you historical romances by your favorite bestselling authors including Janelle Taylor, Shannon Drake, Bertrice Small, Jo Goodman, and Georgina Gentry, just to name a few! Each book is filled with passion, adventure and the excitement of bygone times!

To introduce you to this great club which is part of Zebra Home Subscription Service, we'd like to send you your first 4 bestselling historical romances, absolutely free! And once you get these 4 free books to savor at home, we'll rush you the next 4 brand-new books at the lowest prices available, as soon as they are published.

The way the club works is that after your initial FREE shipment, you will get our 4 newest bestselling historical romances delivered to your

doorstep each month at the preferred subscriber's rate of only $4.20 per book, a savings of up to $8.16 per month (since these titles sell in bookstores for $4.99-$6.99)! All books are sent on a 10-day free examination basis and there is no minimum number of books to buy. (And no charge for shipping.) Plus as a regular

subscriber, you'll receive our FREE monthly newsletter, *Zebra/Pinnacle Romance News*, which features author profiles, subscriber benefits, book previews and more!

So start today by returning the FREE BOOK CERTIFICATE provided. We'll send you 4 FREE BOOKS with no further obligation: A FREE gift offering you hours of reading pleasure with no obligation...how can you lose?

We have 4 FREE BOOKS for you
as your introduction to
KENSINGTON CHOICE!
To get your FREE BOOKS, worth
up to $24.96, mail the card below.

FREE BOOK CERTIFICATE

Yes! Please send me 4 Kensington Choice (the best of Zebra and Pinnacle Books) Historical Romances without cost or obligation (worth up to $24.96). As a Kensington Choice subscriber, I will then receive 4 brand-new romances to preview each month for 10 days FREE. I can return any books I decide not to keep and owe nothing. The publisher's prices for Kensington Choice romances range from $4.99-$6.99, but as a preferred subscriber I will get these books for only $4.20 per book or $16.80 for all four titles. There is no minimum number of books to buy and I may cancel my subscription at any time, plus there is no additional charge for postage and handling. No matter what I decide to do, my first 4 books are mine to keep, absolutely FREE!

KC0199

Name _____

Address _____ Apt. _____

City _____ State _____ Zip _____

Telephone (___) _____

Signature _____

(If under 18, parent or guardian must sign)

Subscription subject to acceptance. Terms and prices subject to change.

AFFIX
STAMP
HERE

KENSINGTON CHOICE
Zebra Home Subscription Service, Inc.
120 Brighton Road
P.O.Box 5214
Clifton, NJ 07015-5214

ll..l..lll.....lll.l.l.l.l.l.l.l.ll.l.l..lll..l

give you the chance to know your heart before you are taken beyond that point where there is no turning back."

"But I don't want to turn back." Shannon could no longer kiss his flesh, but her fingers trailed over the hard contour of his shoulders, and her body yearned for something elusive that was just out of reach.

"You are innocent to the ways of a man and woman, and do not understand of that which I speak." Hunter's resolve to remain in control was reinforced by her innocent words. She was too trustful for her own good, and he would not take advantage even though he desired nothing more at the moment than to pull her back up against his body and have finish with the aching want that filled him.

"We will reach my people tomorrow, and then you will know if you can accept me as a woman takes a man without regrets of what tomorrow will bring."

"I am sure now, Hunter," Shannon whispered, but much of what he was trying to impart to her was beginning to become clear. He feared that once she arrived in his grandfather's village she might realize she had made a mistake.

A tender ache began to slowly build and grow within her heart for this man. He was honorable enough to put his own desires aside in order that she have time to be sure of her feelings for him. She was not very wise about the heart of a man, but she doubted there were many who were this thoughtful.

She would have told Hunter then that she held no doubts about the feelings she harbored for him, but wisely, she knew her words would make little difference. He would not risk his heart so deeply by sharing all and then later feel the downfall of rejection. She knew that he was a man who had suffered hurt greatly in his past. The risk was too great for him to take without assurance that she would not one day turn away from him.

The tension within her body eased as she turned these thoughts over in her mind. A small sigh of contentment escaped the back of her throat as she laid her head against his shoulder.

"Perhaps you are right, Hunter. I know so little about you except for the stories I have heard. Why don't you tell me about yourself?" Shannon didn't care at the moment what he told her, she desired only to have the husky tremor of his voice circle her with the security that it always did.

Hunter was a little taken off guard by her easy manner of turning softly against him, and for a moment he could not speak. She fit easily against his side, her shapely body curving in just the right places against his partially naked one. When he could speak again, he questioned her about the stories she had heard about him.

"Oh, I'm sure they are just the usual stories that circulate about a man people call a bounty hunter and a gunslinger." Shannon smiled against his neck as she felt him move somewhat to try to get a better view of her face.

"Oh, those stories?" Hunter's humor was not lost to Shannon as he also seemed to ease against the curve of her body. "I guess the stories started when I began working for Robert Pinkerton a few years back."

Shannon sleepily listened as Hunter explained that he had met Robert Pinkerton in Texas, and had scouted for a couple of his men who were tracking down two men who had killed a rancher and his family.

"At first I took the job for the money, but then I began to pick those jobs that affect my people. Such as, when I shot Mike Snyder that first day I saw you in Last Chance. He and his brother, and a fellow called Rufus Murdock, have been running stolen army guns to a band of Crow who are enemies of my people."

"I met the man they call Murdock, and Billy Snyder." Shannon paid more attention when Hunter mentioned the men she had met in Last Chance the day she had gone into town with Cookie and Logan.

"They are very dangerous men. Some call Murdock a preacher, but he's no friend of the white man's God." Hunter's grip tightened a little around Shannon when he thought of her amid men as potentially dangerous as Rufus Murdock and Billy Snyder.

Remembering the day she had stood outside the Red Dog Saloon and was stopped by the men who worked at the Bar-K, Shannon was reminded of Bonny Ingram. So much had happened to her since yesterday, when she had heard the news of the young woman's death, she felt somehow that she had betrayed her memory by allowing herself to forget.

"Did you hear about the murders of the new schoolteacher and Bonny Ingram, one of the girls who worked at the Red Dog Saloon?" Shannon didn't know why she asked Hunter about the murders. She knew only that she needed to talk about the women.

"I heard some talk about it yesterday in Last Chance." Hunter enjoyed talking to this woman. He could not remember ever talking so companionably with a woman in his past.

"You know both women came to Last Chance Gulch on the same stage as I did. I didn't know Abigail Primer that well, but Bonny and I were slowly becoming friends. She came out to the ranch for a visit the same day I found you wounded. Nancy Inverness implied in a roundabout fashion that I might be the next intended victim of the killer. Do you think the two men at the lion shack could have been the ones that killed Bonny and the schoolteacher, and their attack on me was planned?"

Hunter could hear the unshed tears in her voice, and he gathered her closer, hoping to offer her comfort. "I do not believe the men at the lion shack were the killers of the women. I knew both women arrived in Last Chance the same day you did, but I did not know you and the one who worked at the Red Dog Saloon were friends."

"I am sorry that you must feel this pain of losing a friend, Little Flame. I too have lost friends, it is not an easy thing. My grandfather says that those who go on to climb the star path are never forgotten, but lie within our memories to enrich our knowledge and our days." Hunter wondered who this woman Little Flame called Nancy Inverness was, but he did not question her.

"Everyone I have cared about in my past leaves me sooner or later." Shannon could not halt the self-pity she was feeling at the moment. It was true, she believed that everyone she cared about eventually left her.

"I will never leave you, Little Flame." Hunter reached down and turned her chin so that she looked fully into his face. "Trust me, my heart. I promise you I will always be there when you need me."

"How can you make such a promise?" Shannon gazed into his face, the overhead moon highlighting the silver streaks in his eyes. Not even her father could make her such a promise. He had left her just like her mother had when she had been no more than a child. Why now should she believe this man's words?

"You have brought something into my life that I feared I would never know again. It is not an easy thing to allow love to fill one's heart, because to do so leaves one open to pain. As a child I was innocent to such pain, until one day my life as I knew it was forever changed. My brother, my mother, and myself were taken away from all that we loved." For a moment Hunter was quiet, the night sounds of the forest all that stirred around them as Shannon lay in his arms and waited for him to continue.

"We were taken far away from my people to a place the white man call Texas. My mother's people lived in this place far away from the sacred lands of the people. We were not happy in this place, and wanted only to return to those we loved. One day my mother, Trapper, and I took my uncle's horses and left my grandfather's ranch. We wanted only to return to our people."

"What happened?" Shannon whispered as he again quieted.

Hunter did not hear her question, he was reliving that hurried flight from the Texas border, as he had so many times in the nightmares that now and then stalked his dreams.

"My mother was happier away from her own people. They could not understand why she would want to return to my father. I remember how often she smiled on the trail, and how she sang the songs of my people to me and my brother before we fell asleep each night beneath the stars.

"We were several days away from my grandfather's village, when buffalo hunters came into our camp one night. I tried to help my mother and brother fight off the attackers, but I was beaten in the head with the stock of a buffalo rifle.

"When I awoke the next morning, I found my mother and brother both dead." Hunter did not tell Shannon the grizzly details of his kin's death, he alone would keep those memories until the day the Great Spirit called him to climb the star path.

"I found the same buffalo hunters two days later." There was no need for him to reveal what had taken place upon this meeting.

"I tell you this part of myself as I have told no other, to let you know, Little Flame, that I am worthy of your trust. I will not leave you as others have. The Great Spirit led you to me to walk this life path at my side. I swear this night that I will fight all the enemies of this life in order to stay at your side. Nothing will ever come between us." Nothing except her own feelings, Hunter inwardly thought. He still tried to shield his heart against the chance that she would not find his life one that she wished to share.

Hot tears escaped Shannon's eyes as she heard his heartfelt pledge. How could she not believe in such a declaration? Be had bared his soul to her and asked nothing in return but her trust. Could she dare place her trust in his keeping? "I want to believe you, Hunter." No one could imagine how desperately Shannon wanted to turn her heart and trust over to someone strong and capable, who would ensure she not be hurt again. But could anyone truly give her such assurance?

Looking down into her tear-filled gaze, Hunter lowered his head, his mouth covering hers in a kiss of promise. The contact was brief, a pledge that was sealed in a promise that would not be broken.

The next morning, shortly before daylight, Hunter awoke to find Shannon's slight limbs entangled with his own. Her head was cushioned upon his collarbone, her even breathing caressing his throat.

A gentle smile touched his lips as he inhaled her sweet scent. This woman he called Little Flame was like a branding flame to his senses, blinding him to everything but her radiance. She was like the first breath of sunshine on a cloudy day. She awoke in him all his inner desires to protect and cherish. He knew in his heart that if she rejected his lifestyle among his people, he would find it hard to turn away from her. She drew him as no other ever had.

The early morning peacefulness of the forest enveloped the couple as they lay next to the now-cooled fire. Hunter enjoyed the feeling of the woman pressed up tightly against him; she felt right lying there in his arms. For a few minutes his mind turned over their conversation of last night, and he wondered about those things she had not revealed. He had sensed there was much she had not been willing to share. With time, he hoped she would learn to trust, and realize that he would do all in his power to see she remain safe and happy.

Trust was gained with time, and Hunter was afraid that time was not something he had on his side just then. He still had a job to do for the Pinkerton Agency, and by all rights, at that moment he should be back in Last Chance gathering more information about Rufus Murdock and Billy Snyder, not in the mountains on his way to his grandfather's village.

He had thought he had his life under control, until this flamed-haired beauty stormed into his life and set his world upside down. And even then he had thought he could put off his attraction for her until he finished his job.

Getting himself shot and her finding and tending him had messed everything up. That first kiss there in the lion shack had sealed his fate.

He had been unable to think of anything except the sweet taste of her, even though he fought an inner battle to try to forget. Those two Bar-K hands who attacked her at the cabin had brought all his feelings to a head. But still, he wasn't willing to risk his heart entirely until he was sure that she could accept him for the man he truly was, and the only way to find that out was by taking her to his people's village.

If everything worked out as Hunter hoped, he would leave Little Flame with his grandfather for the time it would take for him to finish the job he had begun. This would be the last job he intended to do for the Pinkerton Agency. He would stay in the mountains with his people, and he hoped Little Flame would remain at his side.

As the first traces of daylight filtered through the trees overhead, Shannon stirred against Hunter's warmth.

Hunter placed a kiss upon the crown of her head as he spoke softly. "The morning star beckons us from our blankets, Little Flame. We should rise and ready ourselves to go to my grandfather's village."

"I would much rather stay right here." Shannon snuggled closer against his large body. She rather enjoyed waking to find herself pressed up tightly to Hunter.

Low, husky laughter filled her ears. "It would be pleasant to spend more time here, but I fear my grandfather will be sending out scouts if we do not arrive in the village this morning."

Shannon became alert at this announcement. "Your grandfather knows we are coming?" She drew back out of Hunter's arms and sat up on the blanket.

"I sent him word that we would arrive this morning." Hunter grinned warmly as he took in her tousled appearance. If possible, she was even lovelier than he remembered.

"But how could you send word? Why didn't you tell me your grandfather knew I was coming with you? I thought we were going to take him by surprise. Does the entire village know we're coming then?"

Hunter's laughter washed over her. It was apparent that Little Flame had been caught off guard. "I sent word to my grandfather through Little-Horse-Man. He will also take a message back to the Five Star for you, so you can let everyone know that you are well. And, yes, I am sure my grandfather has told everyone about our coming arrival."

Hunter was sure the old man would be pleased with the message that at last his grandson had found himself a woman. He would be expecting Hunter's arrival in the village to mean that he was ready to settle down among his people.

"Are you sure your people are going to like me, Hunter?" Shannon had not allowed herself to worry overmuch about what would happen once they arrived in Hunter's village, but now that the moment was almost upon them, her worry increased, especially with the news that everyone would be expecting them.

"You wouldn't just tell me that they will like me because you do, would you?" Shannon knew that she was babbling on, but she couldn't help herself. She had never even seen an Indian village before. In fact, Hunter was the only Indian she had ever met, and he was only half Indian. Would the villagers be fierce and angry over her presence in their village? Would they shun her . . . or, even worse, would they try to hurt her?

Hunter glimpsed her worry, and sitting on the blanket next to her, he pulled her into his arms. "My people will love you, not because I do, but because of the person you are."

Shannon's eyes widened over his statement. He had said he loved her. None of the rest of his words mattered; all she heard was his confession of love. What did it matter that she would be traveling into the unknown? This man would be at her side, and in her heart she knew he would let no harm come to her.

"I will do my best not to disappoint you." She placed a kiss upon his chin. It was easier knowing his feelings. Shannon was learning that Hunter was a man who did not easily reveal those things he felt within. This confession of his love was hard won, but something she could hold onto in her time of need.

"I will go to the stream and wash, and then ready the horses. There is still some food in my packs if you are hungry." Hunter was pleased that he had been able to calm her worry. Whatever he had said appeared to have eased her fear of going to his grandfather's village.

Shannon watched him leave camp, her turquoise eyes following his powerful build until he disappeared through the trees. In her heart Shannon was sure that Hunter was the only man in the world for her. He was her destiny, the reason she had come to Montana.

Witnessing her uncle murder a man had been her reason for fleeing St. Louis and finding herself in Honey Belle's room, and taking over her identity had been her means. But Hunter had been what had drawn her. All her life she had been seeking someone to share her heart with, and this warrior was the one.

She had understood him last night when he had tried to explain that he desired her to know him for who and what he was before she made a final commitment. Shannon believed she knew all she needed to know about him.

Heated gooseflesh traveled over her body as she could only imagine what that final commitment would detail. She yearned for him to take her as a man takes a woman. Her body ached deep in the nether reaches of her womanhood for something that only he could give.

Rising from the blanket, she began to unbutton her blouse as she began the short walk that would lead her to the stream. Why should they wait? She was sure she wanted him. Nothing would ever change her mind. Hunter was the man she longed to belong to, and she aimed to have him that very morning.

As Shannon stepped out of the cover of the trees and underbrush, she felt flushed, her limbs trembling even as she kicked off her boots and began to pull off her clothes.

A noise from downstream caught her attention. Shannon's gaze enlarged as she spied Hunter standing next to the stream, his arms upraised, a pipe clutched in his hands and raised upward to the heavens.

He stood facing downstream, the breechcloth no longer tied around his hips, the morning sun bathing his body in a golden radiance that left Shannon standing breathless with desire to run her hands over the muscular planes of his torso.

The chanting of his prayers calmed the wild desire that drummed within her with a covetous appetite to take the steps that would bring her to his side. Instead, she finished undressing and dove into the deepest portion of the stream.

Hunter heard the splash several feet away from where he stood along the streambank. Turning, he caught sight of a tangle of copper hair, and abundance of satin beauty.

Drawing a breath deep into his lungs, he forced reason to overtake the initial desire that swept over his body. Setting his pipe and tobacco pouch down in the thick grass, he picked up the bar of soap and dove into the water, hoping that the cold water would help him to cool his ardor.

"I see that you are not hungry, Little Flame." He had not wanted this to be the turn of events for the morning. He had thought she would remain in camp until he finished with his prayers and swim.

"I am not hungry for food, Hunter." Shannon called across the few feet of water that separated them. Food was, in fact, the furthest thing from her mind at the moment.

Hunter was not lost to the shades of passion that stirred in the depths of her blue-green eyes. He would have called out at that moment to the Great Spirit to grant him strength, but feeling her gaze holding upon him, he dared not show his weakness.

"My prayers were long this morning. I have much to be thankful for. I will wash and return to camp so you may bathe in privacy." Hunter brought the soap out of the water and began to lather his chest and neck.

"I had hoped that you would want to help me wash my hair." Shannon congratulated herself with her quick thinking. She took a couple of steps toward him, and noticed that he took a couple of steps back.

Hunter inwardly groaned. "I thought you washed your hair last night," he ventured to say. Splashing water over his chest and neck, he was more than ready to get out of the water and put some distance between them. After all, he was only human, and a man who possessed a raging desire to claim this woman as his own. He knew now that it had been a mistake for him to dive into the stream with her in the water.

"I did wash it last night. But I want to look my best when I meet your grandfather and your people." He certainly couldn't refuse such a sweet request, Shannon told herself.

She was right. Hunter couldn't refuse her, nor could he flee from the temptation of having her naked body close to his own. Though the sweet agony of her was painful, he could not resist. "Come closer, then, and I will wash your hair." He could barely get the words out of his throat.

"Don't you think you could do a better job nearer the bank?" Shannon had never attempted to seduce a man before, but she was finding herself quite able at the moment. She ignored the heat that rose in her cheeks as she began to swim toward him.

Hunter swallowed hard as he glimpsed the curve of her buttocks and the smooth angles of her back as she approached him. "It is better that I wash your hair here, where the water is running swiftly." He murmured the first thing that came to mind, knowing that if they went toward the bank, and he was confronted with the full bounty of her charms, he would not be able to resist her any longer.

Shannon sighed softly when she stood but a foot away from him. Her wide eyes gazed boldly up into his heated regard, and glimpsed the battle that was raging in his body. "Should I turn around?" she asked softly, and before he could speak, she spun in the water, her bottom softly grazing his thighs.

The air within Hunter's lungs stilled with the contact of her soft buttocks brushing against him. She was so innocent, she didn't know what she did to him, he told himself. For a full minute he stood staring down at the back of her head, his heart dashing wildly in his chest, his manhood lurching to life, as hot, coursing blood flowed through his veins and centered in his loins.

A small smile played over Shannon's lips as she waited in anticipation for him to make the next move. The contact of her body touching his only reinforced her determination to have finish with waiting to become truly his. He might have some sense of doing the honorable thing by not taking her until she was sure that he was the right man for her, but she had no such crazy hesitation. She knew he wanted her, and she wanted him, that's all that mattered.

Hunter's hands trembled as he began to lather the soap in her hair, and silently he rebuked himself for being so weak by allowing his lust sway in the ruling of his life. It would not be fair of him to take her before giving her the chance to fully know the man he was. But at the same time these thoughts filled his head, his body was being drawn closer to her tempting shape.

The fragrant scent of woman and soap swirled around his senses, his fingers massaging her scalp as the glistening strands of soapy copper hair twined around his arms.

Shannon leaned back against his strength, her eyes dreamily closing as she felt the consuming heat of his nearness.

Hunter's hands slipped to her shoulders, his fingers

stroking in circular motion as they trailed over the fine collarbone, and downward to the full bounty of her breasts.

"You alone hold the power to destroy my will." The words were released from deep within his throat as he pulled her full against him, her back pressing against his chest, her buttocks curving into the blazing heat of his loins.

Shannon felt the thick length of his manhood as it rose up and pressed fully against the junction of her legs. Her breathing grew ragged, her heartbeat hammering against her ribs as scorching blood raced through her veins.

Hunter's hands cupped her breasts, his thumbs rubbing back and forth against the rushing tips. Never had he wanted a woman as badly as he wanted Little Flame. His body craved joining with hers.

Shannon turned within his arms, her arms rising up and wrapping around Hunter's neck. "I want you, Hunter. Take me now," she whispered as she pressed herself back against his heat.

"You know not what you ask, Little Flame." Hunter fought for some slender hold upon his control. It he took her now, she would have no choice. There would be no turning back for him. He would never allow her to leave him.

"I know that I burn from within with the wanting of you." Shannon felt tears welling in her eyes. She ached deep in her womanhood to feel him move within her.

As he stared down into her face, her innocence was clearly revealed. Her trust in him to lead her into the unknown touched him deeply in his heart. A fierce, possessive groan escaped his throat as he gathered her to him, his mouth covering hers in a scalding kiss of unleashed passion.

For timeless moments they stood in the middle of the swiftly rushing water and clung to each other. Shannon felt the full temper of his desire as the fiery blade of his lance pressed fully against the soft curve of her femininity, and she clung to his large body with a need that burned out of control.

Hunter forced his mouth to pull away from the offering she willingly presented, a ragged sigh escaping from deep in his throat. "You blind me to what should be, Little Flame. You are innocent, but I know the power that would be let go by our joining."

His fingers brushed away the strands of hair that fell over her face. "I would offer you all, because you are the woman of my heart. If I take you here and now, I would be cheating not only you, but the strength of character that I have forced upon myself since my childhood. I would give to you the offering of my honor."

"But I don't want your honor, Hunter, I want you!" Shannon cried aloud in frustration.

"As I want you."

"Then take me. Let us have end to this thing that rages out of control between us."

"There would be no end if I were to take you now. This would be the beginning, and there would be no turning back."

"I am willing to risk whatever will happen." Shannon was more than willing to face whatever tomorrow would hold. She wanted this man, and didn't care about anything else. She tried to press herself back against him.

Hunter had regained a portion of his control and dared not tempt his will again. Gently, he held her a few inches away from his body, knowing that if they came together again, there would be no halting their passions. "It is not you who will pay the price of what this day could bring. I am the one who would be bound by our joining to keep you at my side. No matter that you find you cannot adjust to my life, or my people, I would not allow you to leave me. Do you not see that it is my heart that would be placed upon this offering? I would be the one to live with your unhappiness."

Shannon would have argued that she never wanted to leave him. She would live anywhere that he wished, she cared only that she remain at his side. But the burden of his feelings was plainly revealed in his brilliant regard, and before it she could not say the words that would challenge his strong belief. She would have to show him that he could trust her. He would learn that he could trust in her love, for she knew now that she loved this man with all her heart.

"You should rinse the soap from your hair. I will go and ready our things for travel." Hunter felt the disappointment of the moment as keenly as she, but in his heart he told himself there was no choice. The risk was too great to chance, even though their young bodies hungered for fulfillment.

Shannon did not attempt to restrain him; she knew there would be another time for them. Soon she would know the full meaning of being a woman, of being Hunter's woman.

THIRTEEN

When Shannon returned to camp, her gaze widened in astonishment as her eyes fell upon Hunter. No longer did she see any sign of the white man she had known. The man standing across from her looked every inch the part of a tribal warrior.

He still wore the leather breechcloth, but now his legs were encased in fringed leggings, and beaded moccasins covered his feet. An intricately beaded vest adorned his broad chest, and around his neck he wore a choker of dentalium shells and brass studs. His midnight hair hung freely down his back, thick braids hanging over each shoulder, and entwined in each braid was a strip of red trade-cloth. Above his right ear hung an ornament, a blue circle with white spokes, and eagle breath feathers clasped within the center piece of gold which had been hammered into the image of a wolf.

Shannon had never seen anyone as magnificent, nor as frightening-appearing. She had been so blinded by her feelings for Hunter, the man she had met the day she arrived in Last Chance Gulch, she had not imagined him as a Sioux warrior. There was nothing left for her imagination now. He boldly stood before her, and as he did he portrayed in her mind all the fierce some stories that the penny magazines had conjured up of the enemy red man.

"Come to me, Little Flame." Hunter's gaze clutched her own as he held his hand out toward her.

Shannon swallowed hard, not daring to take the necessary steps that would bring her to his side. This was the same man she had told herself only a short time ago she was in love with. He spoke with the same tender concern in his tone, his hand reaching out to her for acceptance. But could she accept him as he was now?

Her indecision was clearly revealed on her features. Hunter waited patiently for her to either accept him as he was, or turn her back on what the future would hold for her if she reached out and took his hand.

Time spun upon the axis of a barely discernible passage as Shannon stared at the hand she could either accept or reject. To accept the man Hunter was now would be the first step in accepting his people, and the life of an Indian.

Did she have such courage? Tentatively, her hand reached out toward his, for she lacked the strength that it would take to turn away from all she viewed within his searching regard.

Hunter met her more than halfway. Quickly banishing the few steps that separated them, his powerful arms wrapped her within the strength of his love.

She had taken this first step, and as she felt the security of his body enfolding her, Shannon knew she had made the right decision.

Hunter's finger lay beneath her chin and eased her face up in order for him to look into her eyes. "You see before you the man I truly am, Little Flame."

His primitive trappings did not make him the man Shannon had fallen in love with. There was an attraction of spirit and soul that came to life each time she was near him. Even now in his arms there was no thought of Indian or white man, there was only Hunter.

The Sioux village was encamped high in the mountains in their summer valley. The couple kept a steady pace, traveling upward for the better part of the morning. They

had been on the trail over two hours, when Shannon
thought she saw a horse and rider up ahead.

Hunter seemed unconcerned with her announcement
that they were being watched, and as they drew close to
the spot there was no sign of the horse and rider she had
fleetingly glimpsed.

Shortly before midday, Hunter pulled his horse to a halt
atop a small summit. Shannon halted her mount at his
side, and peering down into the valley below, she was astonished as she gazed upon the primitive beauty of the
Lakota village. Spread out on the valley floor in a pattern
of graceful respite there were over one hundred conical-
shaped lodges set up along the banks of a sparkling river.

Never having viewed anything as breathtakingly beautiful, Shannon said the first words that came to mind. "I
thought your grandfather lived in a small village." Her
vision filled with the sight of hundreds of horses dotting
the valley floor, and wisps of smoke curling out of the tops
of many of the hide shelters.

Hunter laughed in relief as he glimpsed the pleasure
on her features. She appeared to be drinking in the beauty
of the valley just as he did every time he crossed this same
peak. "The survival of my tribe depends upon the number
of warriors that lends it protection. In the past several years
two smaller bands have joined their number with my people."

"I have never seen such a sight before. I admit, I am
nervous about going down there and meeting your people." Shannon remembered how taken off guard she had
been when she saw Hunter in his Indian garments. She
could not even begin to imagine how she would feel when
she rode into his village and was surrounded by men and
women in like garments. Their customs and manners were
obviously very different from her own, or anything she had
been exposed to in the past.

"All that matters is that you remember I will be at your
side. No harm will come to you. You are my woman."

Well, that seemed simple enough, Shannon told herself

as she began to follow Hunter's lead down into the valley. But still, she trembled inwardly as they made their way into the heart of the village and she glimpsed people leaving their homes and following in their direction.

What if these people did not want a white woman among them, she asked herself, and knew that it was a little late for such thoughts. She had made her choice that morning by the stream when she had reached out to Hunter in acceptance of who he was. It was far too late for her to turn tail now and run back to the Five Star. She would see this thing to the end, because she had no other choice. Hunter had summed it up when he stated that she was his woman.

Hunter halted his horse before one of the largest lodges in the center of the village. The outside hide was buff in color, and much of the structure had been painted in artful designs of animals in vermilion and blue. On both sides of the entrance flap a large owl had been painted, and a visitor would have the impression that the birds' brilliant dark eyes were fixed upon him as he pushed past the hide flap and entered.

Shannon remained upon the back of her mount as she and Hunter were slowly encircled by seemingly the entire village. The men appeared dressed similarly to Hunter; the women wore beaded and fringed hide dresses, and moccasins. Their thick, long, midnight hair braided or hanging free down their backs, with hair ornaments of brilliant color and design, caught Shannon's eye. She paled as she felt questioning stares directed fully upon her.

Hunter appeared at ease as he called out greetings and responses in the Sioux dialect to many of the men. Shannon wished she could understand the Indian dialect in order to better gauge their reception here in the village.

Shannon's attention was fully captured as the entrance flap of the lodge before them was thrown back, and a large, bronze-skinned elder man with gray-streaked hair stepped out into the sunlight.

"It is good that you have come, grandson." Two Owls

greeted Hunter, his shifting gaze going from Hunter to the woman on horseback.

Hunter instantly jumped to the ground, and within seconds was clasping the older man's hand and forearm. "I see you have not changed in these moons I have been gone from my village." He spoke in the Sioux tongue as his grandfather had spoken to him.

Two Owls's grin widened with his grandson's words. He knew in his heart that his grandson loved his people, but upon occasion he needed the assurance that this son of his son did not wish to live always among the people of his mother. He had been happy when he received the message that Hunter was coming to his village, but he was not as sure that he approved that his grandson was bringing a white woman among them.

"This is Little Flame, *Tunkasila;* Grandfather." Hunter was eager for his grandfather and people to meet this woman of his heart. He spoke loudly, and by so doing, all the people who stood nearby were able to hear his words. "Little Flame is the woman that I would take within my life circle. She is the one that I will join with."

Two Owls, like most of the villagers, turned to look fully upon Shannon. His features were closed to his thoughts as his intelligent eyes went over her from head to foot. He would have wished his grandson to take a woman from his village, to strengthen the Lakota blood of his children.

Admittedly, the woman was beautiful with her hair of curling fire and her eyes of grass and sky. She appeared nervous under his regard, but not frightened as he knew most white women would be. "You are welcome here in our village, Star-Of-Fire." Two Owls greeted Shannon in English. Perhaps there was still time to talk sense to his grandson. He would not wish the same pain upon Hunter that he had known his own son had endured because of the white woman he had loved.

Hunter knew his grandfather was reluctant to accept fully a white woman as his grandson's mate. He told himself that the old man would soon see the goodness of Little

Flame's heart, and within no time he would come to love her as he had his mother.

Shannon was caught by surprise that the man she assumed was Hunter's grandfather could speak English. Some of the tension in her features eased with his welcome.

"When we received word that you were coming, Summer Rose prepared a fire and food in your lodge." Two Owls's words were reaffirmation that he would prefer his grandson forming an alliance with the family of his old friend, Spotted Elk, Summer Rose's father.

"That was good of Summer Rose. I will thank her for her thoughtfulness." Hunter knew the old man's mind well. "Little Flame is tired from the long days on the trail and will have this day to regain her strength. She also will thank Summer Rose." He wanted no doubt in anyone's mind that Little Flame was the woman of his choice.

Standing toward the back of the crowd circling Hunter and the pale-faced woman, Summer Rose heard the conversation, and her own name mentioned. She knew that Two Owls wished his grandson and she to join their life paths together. For the past three summers she had desired the same thing. Each time Hunter came to the village she was always more than willing to see to his needs. She had denied him nothing, asking little in return, but hoping that the day would come when he would ask her to join with him.

The sting of his rejection pierced her heart, but even as she felt the intense pain, her dark gaze held upon the white woman. She had stolen the man that Summer Rose desired, but she could find no anger in her heart for the other woman. Hunter was a man that many women desired. She had heard the maidens of the village talk about him with longing in their hearts. She could not fault another woman for desiring him.

"Why do you not take Star-Of-Fire to your lodge and return to my fire, where we can speak of the things you have done since you last visited your village?"

Two Owls hoped that given the time alone with his grandson, he would be able to speak to him about the problems he would face in the future if he kept this white woman in his lodge. He was unable to forget the pain his own son had suffered up until the hour of his death because of his own claim upon one that was not of his own kind. The white men did not want the Indian to live in peace, nor would they allow one of their own to find happiness with the people they held hatred for.

Hunter knew that his grandfather had not lightly given up his hope that his grandson take the white woman back to her own people. There would be talk later about Little Flame, and it would be up to him to say the words that would make Two Owls understand there would be no giving back that portion of his heart that claimed this woman of fire and light.

His grandfather would bend to his decision in the end because of the love he held for Hunter, but Hunter did not welcome the confrontation. He released a sigh as he nodded his head. "I will see that Little Flame is made comfortable, and then return to you, Grandfather."

The elder man watched as his grandson turned back to the woman. Before taking up the reins to his horse, he reached up and helped Star-Of-Fire dismount. The villagers parted as Hunter left the center of the village to make his way to his lodge along the bank of the river.

Shannon glimpsed many of the villagers smiling in welcome toward her, and she in return did likewise. Though she had sensed something in Two Owls's manner that told her he was not too pleased about his grandson's choice of a woman, his welcoming words in front of the villagers had prepared the way for Hunter's people to accept her. She had not expected things to go so easily. Her relief was evident in the way she kept smiling up at Hunter, as she studied everything around her.

Hand in hand the couple made their way toward Hunter's lodge. The villagers returned to their own tepees or outside fires, having welcomed this intrusion to their normal daily activities. That evening there would be reason to celebrate. One of their own had returned among the people, and many of the villagers having heard his words to his grandfather wondered how soon a joining ceremony would take place.

"Where are we going?" Shannon questioned Hunter, having understood nothing of what had passed between him and his grandfather.

"To my lodge."

"Is that proper?" Shannon grinned. "I mean, you seem a little reluctant." She stopped there, but would have liked to have reminded that he had left her at the stream that morning. Was he not afraid she would attempt to take advantage of him again when they were alone in his lodge?

Reluctance was the furthest thing from Hunter's mind. Keeping his sanity and his will while in this woman's presence was his greatest concern.

His fingers squeezed hers before he spoke. "It is not that which is proper, or reluctance that keeps me from claiming your body with my own, Little Flame. It is my wish for you to know your heart fully that makes me suffer the torment of having you close and not being able to satisfy my desires."

Shivers of inner wanting traveled over Shannon's body with his words. She had been only teasing when she taunted him about being reluctant. But her teasing had become a doubled-edged sword, taunting her with her own body's awakening need for a fulfillment she had never experienced, but knew when she was in Hunter's presence, that it existed.

"And when will you deem that I know my heart?"

Hunter was surprised by her bold question, realizing the import that it held. She was as ready as he to experience the full depth of the feelings they held for each other. "You will be the one who will tell me."

"And if I say to you that I know my heart now?" What more did this man want from her? She had come to this village with him, and faced his people, and still she was at his side and holding his hand. Was this not enough to tell him that her heart was his?

Obviously not, Shannon thought when he laughed heartily at her suggestion.

"Tonight there will be feasting and dancing in the village." He turned the subject away from what stayed in both their minds.

"Because the prodigal son has returned home. I bet your grandfather would have liked you to have returned to your village alone." Shannon was still a bit put out because of the restrictions he was imposing on their relationship, and though she didn't mean for her words to sound sharp, she couldn't help that they came out that way.

"My grandfather will learn to love you as he loved my mother. He only fears that I will be hurt."

Shannon was instantly contrite. "You can tell him that I would never intentionally hurt you, Hunter. I didn't mean to sound so ungrateful. It was kind of him to welcome me to his village in English."

"My mother taught him to speak the words of the *wasichu*. He thought it good, in those days, that he learn the tongue of those that were coming upon our land."

"He doesn't believe this any longer, does he?" Shannon knew the answer to her question before asking.

"My people have suffered from the coming of the white man into our sacred mountains. My grandfather blames the *wasichu* for my father giving up the will to live this life here on mother earth, and going on to join the sky people. For a while after my father's death, my grandfather warred against the whites."

There was no blame or censorship in Hunter's voice, there was only an acceptance. "I do not hold these thoughts as my grandfather does. I have seen for myself the influx of the white man. I have lived among them, and some I call friends. I know that the One Above rules a man's fate, and if we are to survive, we must adapt. My father's heart became cold and his will to live left him because of his great love and loss, not because of the color of the skin of the woman he loved."

Once again Shannon realized how very wise Hunter was. He was surely a man of his times, a man who could walk in between two worlds and understand them both.

They arrived before Hunter's lodge, and the somber mood that had settled around them silently disappeared. "This was my mother and father's lodge. The custom of the people is to give away the belongings of those who climb the star path, but my grandfather would not allow my father's things to be shared. He gave the poor his own horses, and instructed his wife to give away many of the things from his own lodge.

"When I returned to my people, he told me he had never given up the hope that my brother and I would one day return. He makes sure that my lodge is set up after each move the people make."

The hide lodge was almost as large as Two Owls's own, the tall lodgepoles reaching up from the center smoke hole and framing the tight buffalo hides in a conical form. Many of the depictions that had been painstakingly drawn on the bleached hides were now faded, but still the viewer could clarify the many scenes of battle and warfare. The newer paintings were of animals—a large wolf with pale eyes was near the entrance flap, a warrior atop a prancing stallion, and the same warrior fighting a grizzly bear with only a knife were positioned also at this front portion of the tepee.

As Hunter pulled aside the leather flap that allowed entry, Shannon bent and stepped within. Her surprise was evident in the small gasp that escaped her as her eyes adjusted to the dim lighting, and she looked around the interior.

A small center fire had been readied, and a fragrant pot of bubbling stew was placed against the glowing coals. A colorfully beaded and fringed backrest was at one end of the fire, and on both sides inviting furs had been positioned.

Off to the far side of the center fire, a great portion of the lodge floor was covered with hides, and a mound of silver furs covered a sleeping couch.

On the opposite aide of the lodge a warrior's weapons were tied to the structure by leather thongs. Shannon glimpsed a beautifully crafted bow in a bobcat-hide case, a beaded quiver of arrows, and a war shield with a painted wolf with pale eyes in the center. A war ax and lance with eagle feathers dangling from the top were also arranged upon the wall. Here also she glimpsed parfleches, small leather bags, and baskets arranged on the floor against this side of the lodge. Shannon assumed these contained Hunter's clothes and personal belongings.

There were paintings of stars, the sun, and moon, and many small animals on the inside walls. The effect upon the senses was pleasantly soothing, and Shannon admitted to herself that she had not expected to be presented with such quaint but lavish surroundings.

She truly had not known what to expect when she agreed to come with Hunter. Perhaps she had thought they would stay with his grandfather, or another relation. She was more than pleased to find such privacy here within the cool interior of an Indian lodging.

"You are pleased with my home?" Hunter had remained quiet as she had slowly appraised the interior of the lodge. Viewing her pleased expression, he could no longer wait to hear her thoughts put into words.

"It is beautiful, Hunter. I never expected anything like this."

"What did you expect?" His smile turned to a wide grin.

"I'm not sure what I expected. Truthfully, I have seen only a few pictures of Indian villages, and the white man's interpretation was nothing like I have seen this day."

"I also have seen some of these pictures. The white men who discredit the Indian do so out of fear and ignorance."

Shannon agreed, for there was no other answer for the sketches that had made their way back east depicting dirty savages who lived in filthy environments, and whom the government was attempting to civilize.

"Summer Rose prepared us some food. Are you hungry?" Hunter was pleased that everything was going so well. Little Flame looked upon his people and lifestyle as one who looked with an open heart.

Shannon was hungry and eagerly nodded her head. "I'll help you with the horses and then we can eat," she said even though she knew Hunter would tend to the horses himself while she filled her belly on the savory-smelling food next to the fire. But she had no desire to be pampered by this man. She wanted him to realize that she was willing to do her part.

It was not long before their packs and saddlebags were brought into the lodge, and the two horses they had brought to the village were loosed with Hunter's grandfather's herd.

"Who is this Summer Rose that made the stew? It is delicious, I will have to thank her," Shannon said as she finished the last in her bowl.

Hunter held no guilt where the Indian maiden Summer Rose was concerned. There had never been any promises made between them. He did, however, know that he would sooner or later have to answer this question. Many of the people of his village, including his grandfather, had expected an alliance between Hunter and Summer Rose's family. If he did not tell Little Flame about the young woman, he could be sure someone else would.

"She is a maiden from this village. When I return to my people, she often cooks and tends my fire."

Shannon's gaze rose from the bowl in her hands, and for a few seconds she studied Hunter's features. She could sense there was more that he wasn't telling her. "Is this usual for a maiden to keep house for a man?"

Hunter's regard did not waver under her close perusal. "Not if the maiden is interested in the brave as a mate."

"And is this Summer Rose interested in becoming your wife?" Shannon's breathing stilled as she awaited his answer. All manner of horrible thoughts were swirling through her head. She had heard of Indian men who had more than one wife. Was Summer Rose and Hunter already married? Was she to be his second wife? Were there even more women in this man's life that she didn't know about?

Hunter would not lie to her. Slowly his head nodded. "Summer Rose hoped we would be joined one day."

"And what about you, Hunter?"

"I am a man with a man's needs, Little Flame. There were no promises made between Summer Rose and myself. She took from me as I took from her."

Shannon let out a long, trembling breath. No wife, only an angry Indian maiden who had been jilted by a lover who desired a white woman!

FOURTEEN

His words rang in Shannon's mind long after Hunter left the lodge to go and visit his grandfather. *I am a man with a man's needs, Little Flame.* It would appear that he held no reservations about sharing his needs with any maiden—except her!

Hunter had instructed her to rest until his return, but how was she to rest when she couldn't chase from her mind the images of him lying in another woman's arms?

In her mind this Summer Rose was every bit as exotically beautiful as her name implied. Her lush, overly abundant curves, and dusty charms had lured Hunter to her robes on past occasions. What would keep him out of her bed now that he had returned to his village?

The coolness she had noticed in his grandfather's manner was more than likely over the fact that he wished his grandson and this other woman to wed.

Shannon fought back the tears that threatened to spill. How could she fight this attraction that Summer Rose held for Hunter, when she couldn't even seduce him into claiming her body with his own?

He claimed that he would not take her until she knew her inner heart. But what if he were putting her off only because he wanted someone else?

Though she knew such thoughts were unreasonable, Shannon couldn't help their springing to life within that most insecure portion of her heart.

As she lay upon his soft bed of furs, deep in her own misery, a call from outside the lodge came to her ears. Before she could reply, the flap was thrust aside, and a young Indian woman stepped inside.

Shannon quickly sat up on the side of the sleeping couch, her azure eyes wearily taking in this visitor. Who was she, another one of Hunter's women?

The woman's dark gaze was warm as she appraised Shannon. Slowly, she took the steps across the space of the lodge. Standing before the sleeping couch, she held out her arms. She carried a doehide dress and a pair of moccasins.

"I bring for you."

"You can speak English?" Shannon instantly warmed to her guest.

"Hunter teach *wasichu* words to Summer Rose."

"You're Summer Rose?"

Summer Rose's smile was answer enough as she set the clothing on the sleeping couch. "Summer Rose wish to be Star-Of-Fire's friend."

"But I thought you . . . you and Hunter?" Shannon couldn't say the words aloud.

Summer Rose nodded her head in understanding. "Summer Rose loves Hunter also."

"But . . . you can't love him, too!" Instant anger sprang to life in Shannon's breasts.

Summer Rose understood that the white woman understood little of the people's ways. She smiled softly in the face of Shannon's heated emotions. "Summer Rose realizes Star-Of-Fire knows little of Lakota traditions. I will be Star-Of-Fire's sister. I will also be Hunter's second wife."

Shannon jumped away from the sleeping couch, staring at the young woman, unable to speak. *Second wife!* Was the woman insane? She must be crazed if she believed for one second that she would share her husband with another woman!

"I'm afraid you're mistaken, Summer Rose. Hunter told me himself that there were no promises made between

the two of you." Shannon attempted to pull her wits together as she realized that she would either have to face
this conflict head-on, or tell Hunter that he was right all
along; she wasn't cut out for this kind of life.

The smile on the other woman's face never wavered.
"You will see in time that it is easier for everyone with
two women in a lodge. There is much work to be done
when one's husband is a mighty warrior like Hunter. Meat
must be cut and cured. Skins will have to be staked and
scraped."

Shannon didn't know how to respond to all of this. The
only thing she knew was she would not share Hunter with
anyone!

"I will leave you to ready yourself for the dancing and
feasting that will take place tonight. The people are happy
Hunter has returned. They will celebrate long through the
night."

Summer Rose was not threatened by the white woman's
reaction to her words. Soon enough she would realize that
it was better for a strong warrior to have two wives. Two
women could provide Hunter with many children. He
would be a warrior envied by many braves.

Shannon stared at the other woman's retreating back as
she exited the lodge. She was tempted to fling her offer
of clothes right out the entrance flap with her, but some
semblance of control held her standing there next to the
sleeping couch.

Of all the nerve! Shannon fumed inwardly. As she had
imagined earlier, the other woman was shapely and beautiful, and altogether too sweet to believe!

Summer Rose had acted as though it was the most natural thing in the world for the two of them to share Hunter.
Well, it wasn't so natural for Shannon! Why, just the
thought of the other woman touching Hunter's beautiful
bronze body made her want to scream!

In a fit of tempter Shannon knocked the hide dress and
shoes off the sleeping couch. She would have stomped her

booted foot on the apparel, but she stilled the impulse before she could act it out.

She should just march right up to Two Owls's lodge that minute and tell Hunter she wanted to leave this dreadful place! She paced back in forth within the lodge, every now and then her gaze settling back on the clothes on the floor.

The thought of giving up didn't appeal to Shannon. Not only would she be running from the beautiful Indian maiden, but she knew in her heart that she would lose Hunter forever.

This thought alone is what stayed her emotions from erupting into a full-fledged rage. The thought of losing Hunter left a cold, empty spot in the depths of her heart.

As the minutes passed, she waged an inner battle with her emotions. An hour later she slowly began to calm as a plan surfaced. The only way that Summer Rose could become a part of her life was if Hunter invited her. She would just have to see to it that he had no desire to bring another woman into his lodge.

Shannon's turquoise eyes sparkled with inner lights of warmth as she told herself that the only way to ensure he desire only her was by making his wanting of her flame out of control. Once they came together, there was no doubt in her heart that there would be no room for anyone else in their lives.

As her eyes fell on the dress and moccasins this time, she kicked off her boots and began to pull off her clothes. She would put forth a valiant fight, one in which she would meet the other woman on common ground.

Entering the lodge a short time later, Hunter stood immobile for a full minute there near the entrance flap. He had been about to call Little Flame's name, but the words died within his throat. He was struck as though dumb as he stared at the ravishing beauty sitting upon his sleeping couch.

A blue and white glass-beaded headband encircled her

brow. Her bright gold hair shimmered in fallen rivulets around her body and over the pale silver furs. A bleached doehide dress adorned her body. The dress boasted a beaded yoke of blue and white, a wolf with pale eyes had been designed in beadwork in the center of the yoke, and tufts of eagle breath feathers were secured around the wolf's throat. Bleached fringe fell from the bottom of the yoke to the waist of the dress, and pale fringe adorned the length of the sleeves.

Hunter's eyes fell from the bottom of the fringed dress to slowly roam over Little Flame's shapely calves, and downward still to the pair of artfully beaded moccasins that covered her feet.

Shannon smiled warmly in greeting. No words were needed. She grasped the adoration in the depths of his silver eyes. And as his gaze held upon her, she stood and took a step toward him, as though she would welcome him.

In reality, she desired him to note the way her shapely curves filled out the dress to perfection. Her breasts were much fuller than Summer Rose's, the hide material stretching across her bosom and tapering to her tiny waist, and the flare of her shapely hips.

Hunter was overwhelmed by her beauty. Never had he looked upon a maiden so lovely of form and face. She alone held the power to steal his breath, and set his heart to drumming wildly in his chest.

All his thoughts were revealed upon his handsome face, which usually remained closed to his thoughts.

Shannon's slender hand reached out for him to take. "I have been waiting long for you, Hunter," she said in a tone that was abed to seduce, and keep his full attention upon her.

Taking both her hands within his own, Hunter pressed them against his heart. "My grandfather and I had much to speak to each other about." He would have rushed on to reassure that he had thought of nothing except her waiting for him there in his lodge while he sat before his grandfather's fire and smoked the pipe of peace with him.

But he knew his words would give this woman too much power over his heart. He had to be sure of her before he entrusted all his feelings into her keeping.

"How do you think I look in the clothes of your people?" She turned this way and that before him to better allow him to view all her shapely curves.

Never had Hunter imagined in his wildest dreams that this woman would so utterly fulfill the image in his mind of the perfect maiden. "Your beauty astounds me, Little Flame. Never have my eyes been so blessed."

His husky tone washed over Shannon and left her inwardly trembling. She would have easily thrown off the gown and moccasins and fell back upon the bed of furs with him if he but said the words.

"Your friend Summer Rose paid me a visit and brought me these clothes." Her aqua eyes sparkled brightly, and her lips revealed a generous smile that did not allow her thoughts to be shared. "I will have to thank her later at the celebrating." She closed the step that separated them, her full breasts brushing against his broad chest.

Hunter drew in a ragged breath. He could barely understand her words. Her scent and nearness combined to overwhelm all his reason. His hands spanned her waist as he pulled her closer, his body molding against her feminine bounty. His head bent, his lips covered hers in a kiss that pushed aside all resistance. Lust . . . want . . . need—these were the only thoughts that filled Hunter's mind, and were imparted in the heat of his mouth as his tongue swirled within her honeyed depths, and he burned for release.

"Hunter . . ." The call from outside the lodge entrance broke through upon Shannon's senses first.

Hunter's name was called again, and as Shannon pulled back and out of his arms, the entrance flap was thrown aside and a brave entered the lodge.

"I hope I am not disturbing you." Spotted Eagle instantly knew that he had made a bold mistake in entering the lodge without leave. In past days when his friend was there in the village, a call from without was enough of an announcement before he entered. He could see now from the flushed features of the woman standing close to Hunter, and his friend's dazed look, that he had took much upon himself. "I could come back at another time." He turned around as though to leave back through the lodge flap.

"No . . . no," Hunter called out. "You are welcome, my friend." Both men spoke in the Sioux tongue. With Little Flame standing a few feet distant, already Hunter's senses were clearing. He cursed himself for being weak, and wisely knew that another minute with her in his arms and there would have been no stopping what would have taken place on his sleeping couch.

Looking at Spotted Eagle standing across the lodge, he drew in a deep, steadying breath before he turned his back on Little Flame and approached his lodge fire.

"Come and sit by my fire, Spotted Eagle. It has been a long time since we have shared a pipe." He sat down upon the beaded mat of his backrest and pulled forth his pipe from the mountain-lion-fur pipe-case his father had made years before.

"I did not mean to intrude. I thought I might walk with you to the celebrating this evening." Spotted Eagle looked from his friend to the woman across the lodge, standing with her back toward the men.

He silently admired his friend's choice in the woman he had chosen to join his life circle. He had not seen the couple when they arrived in the village, but he had heard much of what had taken place outside of Two Owls's lodge. There was no denying that the woman the people were calling Star-Of-Fire was very beautiful, and by Hunter's manner it was obvious his friend was very much taken with her.

Feeling that he had regained most of his normal senses, Hunter called Little Flame to join them. "Come over here, Little Flame, and meet spotted Eagle. He and I have been friends for many years."

Shannon knew that her face was still flushed from Hunter's kisses, and would have lingered there near the sleeping couch until the other man left the lodge. Hunter's invitation dispelled such hopes.

Turning toward the men sitting near the lodge fire, her gaze never lowered away from his as she took the necessary steps to gain Hunter's side.

Hunter reached up and clasped Shannon's hand within his own, his voice low as he spoke to Spotted Eagle. "This is the woman of my heart. I call her Little Flame. She is the reason I shall soon remain here in the mountains with my people."

Spotted Eagle was entranced as the woman drew close, and as she stood next to Hunter, he found his own heart beginning to beat erratically in his chest. "You are indeed a lucky man, my friend."

The warrior had never looked upon such beauty as this woman held. Her hair rivaled the moon and stars combined, her beautiful eyes comparing only to the trappings of mother earth herself. "I envy you your wondrous find, Hunter."

Shannon understood none of what the other man said, and then and there she swore to herself that as soon as possible she would begin learning this Indian language in order not to be left out of the conversations going on around her.

She felt his dark, searching gaze upon her, and knew that his words were in compliment to her appearance; she assumed he admired her in her Indian apparel. She could only hope that whatever he was saying, Hunter was paying close attention. She could use all the help she could get from any direction in order to claim Hunter as her own.

Hunter also noticed his friend's heated appraisal of Little Flame, and his own reaction surprised himself. Swift, and sharp as a blade twisting in his gut, he was overcome with jealousy. "She is mine alone, friend."

His hand tightened for a few seconds upon Shannon's before he let it drop and roughly spoke to her in English.

"Go back over to the sleeping couch. I will be ready soon, and we will go and join the others in the celebrating."

"I did not mean any offense." Spotted Eagle heard the hard edge in Hunter's voice, and was quick to assure his friend that he had no designs on his woman. Hunter was not a warrior whom Spotted Eagle would wish to make angry.

Shannon stood where she was, her anger beginning to clearly show on her features as twin spots of heat settled in her cheeks. "I am not like your other women, Hunter. I don't meekly take orders from you or any other man." Instead of going back to the sleeping couch as he demanded, she turned away from the men and silently stepped through the lodge flap.

Hunter was instantly sorry for the manner in which he had taken out his jealousy on Little Flame. He would have jumped to his feet and followed her, and tried to explain his reasons for being such a fool in front of his friend, but Spotted Eagle was staring across the fire at him as though he had just sprouted two horns atop his head.

Knowing that he had already made a fool of himself, he attempted to ease the tension in the lodge. Filling the bowl of his pipe with kinnikinnick; Indian tobacco made from willow bark, he offered the only excuse he had. "A warrior who is in love for the first time in his life can make a big fool of himself." Hunter laughingly admitted as he exhaled the smoke, and it curled around his head before traveling upward through the smoke hole.

Spotted Eagle laughed loudly, relieved that his friend had not lost his good nature with his heart. "You need not explain, my friend. A woman such as your Star-Of-Fire has the looks that could make any warrior weak in the knees, and in the brain."

Hunter handed his friend his pipe, their camaraderie restored. "I must go and apologize to her, my friend. I fear her anger as much as I fear my loss of will in her presence."

"What did you say to her that made her so angry?" Spotted Eagle could speak some English, but when it was spoken quickly, it was a challenge for him to understand all the strange words. He drew deeply on the stem of the pipe.

"I told her to go over to the sleeping couch and await me."

Spotted Eagle laughed once again. His friend had much to learn about women. Even he, Spotted Eagle, who was still unattached, knew that it was a dangerous undertaking for a warrior to boss a strong-willed woman around. "Well, we had best go and find her. I am sure that the women have set out the food that that they have been preparing all day for the feasting this evening."

The two men left Hunter's lodge arm in arm. Shannon looked up from where she was standing gazing at the river when she heard their laughter.

Her anger sparked anew as she glimpsed Hunter and Spotted Eagle coming toward her. Hunter wore a cocksure smirk upon his features that added to Shannon's temper. If he thought he could order her around, and then laugh at her upset, she would set him straight right from the start. She might be the outsider in his Indian world, but she would not be treated as anything but his equal.

Right away both men noticed that her temper had calmed little since she had left the lodge. Hunter's steps outdistanced Spotted Eagle's as he quickly made his way to her side.

"I am sorry for how I treated you, Little Flame. I admit that I behaved very badly. The next time a man looks upon you, I will try to keep you from witnessing my jealousy." Perhaps the next time, he would just take his anger out on the one who provoked his emotions. Inwardly he admitted that a good fight might be just the thing he needed to help him keep his mind clear.

"You were jealous?" Shannon's anger instantly was replaced by the feeling of joy that leapt within her breast.

"It was because I recognized the hunger that filled my friend's eyes when he looked upon you. He understands me well, and is not angry.

Hunter was the most remarkable man in the world! Shannon wanted to throw her arms around his neck and kiss every inch of his handsome face.

"You are no longer mad?" Glimpsing the wide grin that came over her lips, his own heart filled with joy. "I promise I will remember you are the woman of my heart, and will not take orders from me or any other man." His own lips drew back into a wide smile. It was so easy to love this woman.

By the time Spotted Eagle reached the couple, he, too, was grinning. The pair were contagious as they stood and smiled at each other. "You are wise in the way of women, my brother. Tell me what you said to make her look upon you with such devotion and happiness?"

Hunter wasn't about to admit to his friend that he had simply told her the truth. It was better for his ego if Spotted Eagle thought he had some great gift with women. Puffing out his chest, he stated boldly in the Lakota language, "There are things that a man learns over the years. Special things that one can say to please a woman."

Shannon elbowed him in the ribs. "What are you two talking about, Hunter? I have already told myself that I have to start learning these words, or I won't know what is going on around me."

Hunter laughed loudly and pulled her tightly against his side. With Spotted Eagle's questioning look, he informed, "She wishes to learn our language."

"Good. I will then be able to ask her about these special things a woman wishes to hear."

The dancing had already begun around the large central ceremonial fire when the threesome arrived in the center of the village.

Shannon's mood was lighter than it had been all day, due to Hunter's admission of jealousy. It was crazy for her to be so happy over his confession, but the fact that he was jealous over another man looking at her spoke volumes about his feelings for her.

Food was pressed upon them by the women of the village, who attempted to communicate with Shannon by signing with their hands while speaking in their native tongue.

Trying to remember the names that Hunter related after the many introductions was too hard. Shannon smiled warmly at all, more determined than ever that she would learn the Sioux dialect.

It was while a group of young women were dancing in a shuffling manner around the blazing fire that Shannon caught sight of Summer Rose. The maiden smiled in a friendly fashion, her glance straying from Shannon to Hunter.

Glancing up at Hunter and catching sight of the smile he directed at the Indian maiden, Shannon's mood suddenly took a plunge. *Oh, you green-eyed serpent of ancient lore, your bite can be as sharp as the prick of a pointed blade.* Jealousy, raw and cutting, pierced her heart at that moment.

As the young woman's dancing took her to the other side of the fire and out of sight, Shannon attempted to restrain the impulse to step forward and snatch her out of the line of dancers and let her know that Hunter was already taken.

Such actions would do little more than let everyone see her for a fool. It was common practice for the men in this village to have more than one woman. They would probably believe her insane by causing such a scene. And what would Hunter think? That she was as crazy jealous of him as he was of her?

"Let's go for a walk, Hunter." She pressed her bosom against his arm, her features revealing none of her heated thoughts as she smiled up at him.

"Do you not wish to watch the dancers?" Hunter was aware how dangerouS it was for him to be alone with Little Flame. Sweat began to bead upon his forehead, and he felt his palms beginning to dampen. How the hell was he supposed to handle this situation for much longer?

Cold dread inched up his spine as he thought about the evening to come. He should have made arrangements for her to stay in his grandfather's lodge until they had worked out all their problems, he told himself belatedly.

"It is a beautiful night. Why don't we go for a swim in the river while everyone is here celebrating your return?" Shannon was desperate to get him away from the other woman's proximity.

Vivid images of the last time they were in the water together came swiftly into the forefront of Hunter's mind, and he was loath to say the words that would refuse her. As though a man without a will of his own, he allowed her to draw him to the outskirts of the celebrating, and then through the village, and toward the river where his lodge had been set up.

The night air revived his spirits somewhat as Hunter counseled himself silently that he was a man in charge of his own destiny. His will was strong enough to fight off the attraction this woman held for his senses and body.

A few minutes later he was not so sure. Reaching the river, Shannon immediately pulled off her moccasins, and clutching the sides of the hide dress, she started to pull it up and over her head.

Hunter's reaction was quick and decisive. "We must talk, Little Flame." He caught both her hands into his own.

"What is it, Hunter?" Shannon asked innocently, her flashing, wide eyes appearing indigo beneath the moonlight.

"Come and sit with me beneath this tree. There is much that must be said between us" He pulled her toward the tree a small distance from where they stood, but as she drew back, he realized she was barefoot, and with a sigh of impotent need he lifted her into his arms.

Shannon sighed, too, but her response was of a different nature than his own. Wrapping her arms over his shoulders, her fingers toyed with the silken length of his hair that reached well down his back. "I feel so safe in your arms, Hunter," she whispered against the side of his neck.

The feel of her in his arms and her soft breath caressing his neck was almost Hunter's undoing. Gratefully, he reached the tree and set her down to her feet.

She leaned against his full-length, her arms still entwined around his neck, and at the same time placed a trail of small kisses in the hollow of his throat. She would have him tonight, she silently vowed.

Her kisses shattered much of Hunter's will. With a groan escaping the back of his throat, he pulled her to the ground with him. "Sit here beside me, Little Flame." He could barely speak, his body was so aching already for the release only she could give him.

Shannon knew that he was weakening to her charms just as he had earlier in the lodge before Spotted Eagle arrived. She did not sit next to him on the ground as he instructed, but instead climbed into his lap, her bottom pressed tightly against the heat of his loins.

This is not how Hunter had imagined their talk to take place. He had hoped to speak reason with her, and to gain her agreement that they would wait for a short time longer before joining together.

She had arrived in his village only this day. There had not been enough time for her to make a clear decision about spending the rest of her life with him there in the mountains.

As Shannon drew her hands back up around his neck and pressed her breasts against his chest, Hunter attempted to take some control. Capturing her hands in one of his larger ones, he lightly brushed the long strands of golden hair away from one of her cheeks.

"I cannot bear this any longer, Little Flame. We must talk."

"I don't want to talk, Hunter. I want you to kiss me." She wiggled somewhat on his lap, letting him know the full impact of her wanting.

Looking down into her upturned face, for a few seconds

he felt himself drowning in the liquid of her trusting gaze. He was tempted; the only Great Spirit knew the temptation she presented. But gathering together the last dredges of his discipline, Hunter traced his finger over her lips before responding. "You charm me as the hawk does a squirrel before swooping down for the kill."

"But what I offer is not so deadly."

"What you of fer can be paradise on one hand, and later turn into the white man's hell for the other."

"Never! Our love will grow and remain beautiful," Shannon declared in all of her girlhood fancy of finding her one true knight, and everything thereafter turning out to be happily-ever-after.

This was the first time she had used the word *love* in regard to her feelings for him. Hunter felt his spirit soar. But caution held him within tight talons of control. "You are happy here among my people?" He knew the question was foolish. She had not had enough time to fully digest the custom and lifestyle of his people. He wanted only to hear the words on her lips, and to feel his inner hope ascend.

"I couldn't be happier. I will always be happy wherever you are, Hunter." He had freed her hands, and she lightly caressed his firm jaw. Her eyes were entranced with the way the moonlight created the illusion of smoky fire within the depths of his eyes.

"Then you would live with me forever here in these mountains?"

"Hmmmmm," she dreamily responded as she pressed her cheek against the firm flesh above his heart.

"Would you be able to learn my people's ways, and adapt to their lifestyle?"

His questions broke through the pleasant sensation that touching him was evoking in her body. Summer Rose's words that afternoon in Hunter's lodge, about cutting and curing meat, and staking and scraping hides, stilled her hands as they caressed the bulging breath of his forearms. "There may he a few things that I would wish to change."

Such as the custom of a warrior being allowed to have more than wife, she thought to herself, sobering even more at this thought.

"Why are you so concerned about me adjusting to your people's ways?" She sat up straighter so she was eye level with him once again. "You were able to adjust to the life-style of the white man easily enough. I think I will be able to fit into both worlds, just like you have been able to do." She avoided talking to him about the one matter that truly lingered in her mind.

Hunter knew at that moment that she did not fully understand his desires for their future together. "I do not wish to walk the path that leads me into the direction of two very different worlds, *mita wicanti;* my heart. I wish to live here with my people, with you as my woman."

"But of course we would still go down into civilization. We could even purchase a ranch near Last Chance Gulch. I have an inheritance that my father left me. I will soon be of an age where it will have to be handed over to me. We will be rich. We will he able to do anything we want." Thoughts of her uncle Graylin, and that the only way to gain her inheritance would be by facing him, were pushed aside as she noticed the frown appearing on Hunter's brow.

"I wish only to know peace, Little Flame."

She would have argued that they would find this peace together. They could have everything . . . both worlds . . . each other. Her words stilled upon her lips as she glimpsed the slight shaking of his head.

"The only peace I have ever known has been here in these mountains which he long to my people. When I finish with this last job for the Pinkerton Agency, I will return here to my people, and not go back down among the *wasichu.*"

There would be no arguing Hunter out of his decision. Shannon saw within the set of his features that his mind was determined, and nothing she could say or do would sway the plans he had made for the future. This is the reason he had kept himself from taking her with his body. He had cared enough about her to allow her to make her own decision. But how could she turn her back on the life she had known? Was she strong enough to live with him in his mountains and not resent the fact that she could have had anything a woman could have ever dreamed of?

FIFTEEN

His fear of losing her completely was at last being realized. The pain that filled his heart was crushing, but he knew it could have been much worse.

"And what of you, Hunter? Am I the only one in this relationship who is required to give things up?"

"What is it that you ask of me? I have told you I cannot give up these sacred lands, nor will I turn away from my people any longer. I have kept myself from joining with you, though the task has been almost more than I can bear, because I would offer you this choice."

"What about the horrible custom that your people abide, of a man being able to have more than one wife?" Shannon knew in her heart that she could not give this man up. If he wanted to live out in the open, beneath the elements, she would face anything to stay at his side. But she would get something out of this interchange, and the paramount subject in her mind was Summer Rose and her promise that she would become Hunter's second wife.

Hunter was astonished that she would even think of a tradition like this at the moment. "The tradition of a man taking more than one woman into his lodge is not all that horrible, Little Flame."

"At times it is the kindest thing that can happen to a woman without a man to give her protection and bring her meat. During wartimes, if a warrior is killed, his wife may go to the lodge of her sister or cousin and become second wife to her husband. This is a custom that has been practiced to secure the survival of the people. But I do not understand what this custom has to do with you and me?"

Shannon wasn't interested in the semantics of the custom. All that concerned her at the moment was the question of that, if she decided to stay in the mountains with him, would he see the need to take another wife besides her? "And what of you, Hunter? Would you desire two wives in your lodge, and would you take them both to your bed?"

Hunter didn't know what she was getting at, but he spoke from his heart when he answered. "You are my heart, Little Flame. You alone are the reason that I have walked this path upon mother earth. All that has been before matters little beside the feelings that fill my heart when I look upon you. I lived, but did not know the full meaning of life until I met you. I would need no other woman in my lodge. With you I would have no desire to look upon another. I would cheat a second wife of love, because my heart would be fully given to the first."

Shannon's heart leapt with the sheer joy of hearing this man's most inner feelings.

Still, she did not tell him that she would stand at his side no matter what came against them. Having remembered Summer Rose's words once again, she dared to ask him one more question. "And if I agreed to stay here in your village, would you think badly of me if I were not like the other women of your tribe? I'm really not sure if I know how to cure meat and stake and scrape hides."

Her face revealed the concerns she held, and Hunter trembled with the desire that overcame him to gather her close into his arms. "You are the one of my heart because you are not like any other, Little Flame. I do not want you to come to me because of the needs of my lodge. I wish you to join your life with mine so that I can spend each day trying to make you happy. I would see your smile when I awake upon my sleeping couch, and each night before I fall asleep. I would ask nothing more of you."

Shannon needed to hear nothing more. Flinging her arms around his neck, her lips settled fully over his. "That is all I need to hear, Hunter. I will stay here with you in your mountains, or, in fact, any place you wish," she murmured against his mouth.

"You are sure of these words that you speak?" Hunter looked closely into her features, wanting to impart to her that now was the minute of reclaiming her declaration; tomorrow would be too late.

Tears of happiness spiked Shannon's thick lashes as she nodded her head. "I have wanted you since the first day I looked upon you. I am sure there will never be anyone else for me but you, Hunter."

Hunter clasped her tightly against his chest. For a few minutes he did no more than allow the thought to seep into his mind and heart, that this woman was truly his.

The self-imposed restraints that had stayed him from fully claiming her as his own vanished as though they had never existed. Hunter's mouth hungrily covered hers, his tongue pillaging her sweetness as though a man lacking sustenance.

As their tongues sucked and dueled, drawing and filling, their hands traveled over each other's bodies. They searched in hungry unison.

Shannon's hands trembled over the muscular strength of his upper torso; seeming not to be able to get enough of his closeness. The very heart of her womanhood ached with a fierce need of searing want. She burned deep within, the heat spinning out of control as she moved against his lap, and came against the thickness that pressed against his breechcloth.

Hunter's ravishment of her mouth only made his wanting of her that more potent. He rained kisses over her face and down her throat, his tongue tantalizing the pulse beat near her collarbone with the brand of his tongue. His hands sought out the outline of her full breasts, finding his freedom obstructed by the material of the hide dress.

As she clung to him, his hands roamed over the satin-smooth texture of her thighs, trailing upward to caress the womanly shape of her buttocks. His fingers wandered over her flesh, twining within the copper curls that guarded her sweet fountain of need.

Searching fully all that lay in wait for his taking, Hunter's strong fingers parted the lips of her paradise, and seductively he stroked the moist cleft of her desire.

A moan touched his ears as Shannon's head fell back to receive the full pleasure given by his mouth and tongue. Her lower body pushed closer to his searching touch, wanting to feel him there between her thighs, to experience the ultimate bounty of his caresses.

"I am a man gone mad by the simple touch of you." Hunter's warm breath bathed her face and throat. With a deep groan of pent-up desire, he clasped her tightly to his chest as he stood up from the ground.

His long, powerfully built legs carried them swiftly to his lodge. The sound of drums carried upon the night breeze from the villagers celebrating, but neither Shannon nor Hunter noticed; the drumbeat of passion that raced fiercely through their veins left little room for anything else in its wake.

The minute Hunter entered the lodge and dropped the hide flap back into place, he set Shannon to her feet.

Her silken arms clutched tightly around his neck as her body molded against his larger form. Shivers of unleashed passion danced over her length, aroused by his nearness.

Hunter greedily kissed her lips. Now within the shelter of his lodge, he took time to savor every second of their passion. Her fingers laced within his hair, her body pressed to his, her eyes closing out all but the sense that feeling could evoke.

Looking upon her, Hunter knew her to be the most glorious woman on the face of mother earth. Without a thought to her reception of modesty, he reached down and lifted the hide dress up and over her head.

The sight of her perfection held the power to take his breath away. The dim glow of firelight cast about the lodge from the shallow pit fire bathed her in a golden sphere of rapturous beauty. Her skin appeared satin, her breasts were full, her nipples rosy, and her soft, womanly curves were exquisitely proportioned. As his silver eyes sought out and fully savored each feminine inch of her beauteous form, his ravenous desire flared threateningly out of control.

Shannon's eyes slowly opened as though awakening from a rapturous dream. Gazing up into Hunter's eyes, she saw revealed in their pale depths all the praise a woman could ever need. Words were unnecessary. He drank of her beauty, and she gave all that she was into his keeping without reservation.

Without leave or instruction, Shannon's hands reached out and slowly began to unlace the tie that bound the vest together across Hunter's chest. It took only a few seconds before the intricately beaded garment dropped to the floor in a pile with the hide dress.

Shannon's gaze churned with lights of deepest indigo as she devoured the length and breath of his upper torso. He was a man above all other men, a warrior without equal.

Her fingers trembled as they took hold of the ties that held the leather breechcloth about his loins. With the slightest tug upon the bindings, the breechcloth fell at his feet.

The perfect creation of a bronze, invincible, goldlike warrior stood before her. Shannon's breath stilled in her throat as she took within her gaze the full magnitude of his manliness.

The thick, turgid length of his manroot surged upward with raw vitality as Hunter felt her searching gaze traveling

over his body. The power of his sex held her gaze transfixed. In the following passage of seconds he viewed the
fleeting expression of fear cross her countenance.

The fear of the unknown stole within Shannon's heart
the first sight of his powerful manhood. He appeared
so large, she trembled at the thought of his filling her
body.

He silently drew her back into his arms, her wide eyes
staring up at him. He read in their depths her innocence.
Bending to her, he kissed her long and hard. He was deliberate in his seduction, wishing to bring her back to the
ease in which they had dealt with each other in the past.
With the touch of their lips, the lure of tasting her overrode all thoughts of caution.

Without thought of resisting, she opened her mouth
for him. His tongue moved against hers to take complete possession. Her body melted against him then.
His mouth trapped her escaping sigh. And only then
did he begin to deepen the kiss. He was hard and hot
against her, his senses hungry to give her the taste of
him inside her.

For breathless minutes they mated with their mouths.
Desire swept over Shannon, the likes of which she had
never known. Caught up within the overwhelming tide
of passion, each time his tongue slid in and out of her
mouth she silently yearned for more. Her grip upon his
shoulders tightened, and her body rubbed against his,
expressing to him without words spoken how much she
wanted him.

As his lips plied hers, he lifted her off her feet and carried her over to the sleeping couch. With tenderest con-
sideration he laid her upon the pallet of silver furs, her
curls of shimmering flame spread out in wild disarray over
the hides and around her body.

For a few seconds he stared down at the intoxicating
beauty she presented. His heart hammered wildly in his
chest. His body clamored for release, but he forced a measure of self-control over his desires, reminding himself that

this was her first time with a man. He would stir her arousal to its keenest point, and once the flame flared out of control, he would carry her with him to experience the full bounty of ultimate fulfillment.

As her eyes locked with his, he gave no time for the fear to return that he had viewed seconds before. He lowered himself to the bed and pulled her into his arms and held her close.

As her body moved to accommodate his larger form, he buried his face in the crook of her neck and inhaled her scent. The pleasure of her curves consumed him, her breasts pressing against his chest branding him with scalding intensity.

The pleasure that his body created as she pressed against him was incredible. Each time Shannon rubbed against him, the feelings of induced pleasure abounded in her body, the friction creating a tingling of heat throughout her limbs. It was deliciously wanton.

For a time they kissed. The sweet pleasure of their mouths joining slowly and became a ravenous search as their tongues plundered and sought out the taste of each other.

As Hunter's mouth left hers, he feathered kisses along her cheek and down her jawline to the tempting swell of her breasts. Licking and nibbling the tender flesh, he lavished his attention over first one breast and then the other. His straight white teeth caressing the underflesh of her bosom drove Shannon mad with desire as a moan escaped from deep within the back of her throat. Then his dark head lowered to the line of her ribcage and the tempting space of her waist and hips.

Long, tanned fingers slowly wound their way down over her belly, causing a shudder to course over her body. They lowered to the nest of her womanhood, and with his touch she gasped as his fingers sought out her sheath of warmth, the very fountain of her pleasure.

Moaning aloud, Shannon was totally consumed by the feelings that Hunter caused to erupt within her. His mouth rained sensations of igniting heat over her body, his fingers gently probed and tantalized until she felt the heat of her body's passions flooding her entire being. Her slender form rose up from the couch to meet the movement of his hand.

Not wishing to rush these first moments of passion's awakening in her body, Hunter did not heed her cries of fulfillment. He desired her to be on fire for him, totally and completely consumed with her need for her body's joining with his.

With gentle movements he pressed her back down upon the sleeping couch. The taste of her sweet young flesh and the feel of her satin-smooth body combined and seduced Hunter into a physical wanting that knew no bounds. His hands splayed over the firmness of her belly, then gathered her lightly beneath the hips as he drew her closer. With his fingers he parted the tangled nest of curls, and she felt his warm breath on her. She trembled violently as she watched and waited for what next he would do.

His fiery tongue sent scalding sparks throughout the lower portion of her body as he laved the insides of her thighs. As the searing touch of his mouth followed the path made by his hands and touched upon her woman's treasure, Shannon's body bucked in reaction.

Sweet, forbidden pleasure snaked its way within her womb and throughout her limbs. Soaring high upon this newfound tide of incredible pleasure, Shannon clutched Hunter's hair, her fingers twining in the thick strands as his mouth opened her luscious pink woman's petal to reveal the coveted treasure within.

His tongue plunged inside, tasting the bounty of her sweet essence. The caress of his mouth spiraled Shannon headlong into boundless pits of storming rapture. The pleasure she was experiencing was keen beyond bearing, akin to pain in its intensity, but woven together in a million glittering particles of ecstasy. Her body arched forward with the first assault of his branding tongue, his strong hands upon her hips keeping her positioned as again and again he filled her with his stroking heat.

Her mind whirled out of control as Shannon began to rock against his tugging lips, his tongue, which held the power to tame and send her spinning upon the outer edges of a swirling vortex of unbelievable feeling.

Shannon was subject to an igniting deep within the lower depths of her belly, which slowly began to gush hot, molten sparks of insatiable desire coursing over her body and pulsing throughout her womanhood. She was consumed by a blazing inferno. The burning flamed higher and erupted. Her hands clutched his hair, raked his back; her head and shoulders rose off the furs as a cry of trembling pleasure burst from her lips, and her entire form shook with a convulsion of satisfaction that she had never known existed.

Hunter continued his love play for a time longer, his tongue plunging into her moist, sweet depths, lingering over the nub at the center of her woman's peak as she quaked with shudder after passionate shudder. The sound of her cries filled his ears, furthering his desire to pleasure her to the very fullest.

With the relaxing of her fingers in his hair and the calming of her trembling, Hunter rose from his position between her thighs. He held her with one arm drawn around her waist and leaned down to kiss her. His mouth was ravenous now, for the pressure building inside him was making him wild with need. His tongue moved inside her mouth, then withdrew, only to thrust back inside again and again in a carnal mating ritual.

Instinctively Shannon knew there was more. His kisses drew her closer. His body pressing fully against her as the hot, thickened length of his throbbing rod sprang between them and sought out that place where only short moments previously his mouth had left her breathless.

There was no recourse but to open to him; nor were there thoughts to do otherwise. As his tongue kept up its heady skill of moving in and out of her mouth, the sculpted marble head of his manhood made contact with the opening of her moist, shivering cleft.

Hunter's buttocks drew upward, and as an inch of his shaft entered her, he felt the tightness of her warm, pulsing sheath of love. Another inch, and the velvet trembling of her inner sanctum drew forth a rumbling from deep in his chest, the noise filling the space of the lodge with an animallike groan.

With the breaching of her virgin's body, Hunter's own body stilled atop her, his manhood buried deep within the heat of her passion. His dark eyes glimpsed the small pain that crossed her delicate features, and he allowed her time to adjust to his presence within her. "I am sorry there must be pain at first, my love. If I could change this, I would take the pain unto myself. I can only promise that it will soon leave."

Shannon heard little of what he was saying, she was too surprised by the sharp pain that had ripped through her lower body and continued to throb within her womanhood.

Once again Hunter's mouth covered hers as he kept a steady assault upon her senses, gently lulling her toward that passionate burning of moments earlier.

As his tongue plunged into her mouth, she felt the first stirrings of her body's response. Slowly at first, she moved, the feeling of pleasure replacing the pain. She moved again, more fully against him, as though seeking out that elusive delight that she knew was within reach.

Hunter felt her movement, but forced his will over his body, remaining still atop her. He desired her to fully accept him, holding no desire to cause her further pain.

Softly whispering her name against the side of her cheek, at that moment he wished to share all with her. Even her pain he took to his heart. His lips drew over her face, seeking her lips in a kiss that caught her within the blooming of a tender budding, and slowly grew to a tempting hunger.

He did not hold back for long. His body began to move

in a slow rhythm, not allowing the full thrust of his massive size to claim her, but remembering always to be considerate of her virgin's body. Slowly, he probed deeper into her velvet depths, then withdrew to the lips of her moist opening. Over and over he plied her with his skillful seduction, until at last she gave over completely to his masterful touch.

Shannon clutched at him, her head thrown back in mindless ecstasy as the fullness in her loins drove her toward a frenzy of swirling desire. Each time the brand of his lance drove into her hidden regions and stirred her, her body of its own will moved toward total fullness. Her legs slowly rose as she sought to capture the entire length of him deep within the heat of her desire.

Even as he felt the first stirrings of a shudder convulsing in her depths and traveling the length of his manhood, even as her sheath suddenly trembled and tightened, Hunter forced himself to draw in deep gulps of air, willing himself not to let go of the true fury of his raging passions!

Shannon's entire body centered upon the branding flame of his probing shaft. Ecstasy coursed over her as her movements stroked and tightened around the swollen length of him. She slipped beyond control as her body thrashed wildly about, her hips jerking convulsively as she was swept into the realm of true and utter satisfaction.

Hunter realized the power of her climax, and for a moment fought the heated need that raced through his loins. His hungry gaze looked down into her features, and he witnessed the passion that filled her, heard the climatic moans escaping her lips. Each thrust was now torture-laced as he fought off the aching need for his own fulfillment. It was only when he knew she was descending from the dazzling heights of satisfaction that he allowed himself to give vent to his own steaming desires. His mouth covered her lips, and as he plunged just a fraction deeper into her soft, velvety depths, scalding pleasure burst from the center of his being and showered upward, racing through his powerful shaft and erupting in a shimmering burst of pearl-essence

It was the most incredible release Hunter had ever experienced. His arms tightened around Shannon. He had known that their joining would be glorious, but never would he have believed that anything could be so wonderful.

"Are you all right?" Shannon softly questioned in great concern as Hunter's shudders began to calm. She was not sure if she had done some great hurt to him and should go and seek help. She had never seen him so vulnerable, his breathing heavy against the side of her neck, his body having appeared collapsed atop her.

Hunter chuckled over her regard for his condition. "I have never felt so well, Little Flame."

"Then I did not disappoint you?"

Hunter lifted himself to his elbows and peered down into her face. "You could never disappoint me, my love. You are my heart, my breath, the stirring of my blood. I have been a man lost, without purpose, until this very night when my body joined with yours. You are my reason, never a disappointment."

Shannon heard his heartfelt declaration and tenderly reached out and caressed his jaw. "I feared that my lack of experience might be a disappointment. I am glad that you are so blinded by your love for me."

Hunter glimpsed the small smile on her lips, and relaxing his body upon the sleeping couch next to her, he drew her against his larger curves. "Indeed, I have been blinded by love from the moment I first set eyes upon you."

"It took you long enough to realize it."

With his questioning look, Shannon added, "We could have been sharing these wonderful feelings a long time ago if you had not been so stubborn." She sighed softly as she reviewed the past hour; a small shudder swept over her body.

Hunter hugged her tightly against his side, a grin pulling back his lips. "It was your feelings that were in question, Little Flame, never mine."

"My love for you is obvious, Hunter." Her body squirmed against his, the feel of his hard, bronze flesh inducing shivers of excitement chasing down her back.

"Keep still, my heart." He tightened his grip on her body. With the movement of her silken limbs brushing against him, he felt the surging of his manhood.

"But I would claim what we shared once again." Shannon couldn't believe that he would hold back now after what they had experienced.

"I would not wish to bring you more pain, Little Flame. Your body will need time to rest. Tomorrow will be soon enough for us to join together once again."

"Tomorrow?"

Hunter could hear the disappointment in her tone, and his smile settled over his lips as he tucked her head beneath his chin and wrapped his arms loosely around her.

A few minutes passed before Shannon spoke once again. "Hunter?"

"Yes, sweet?"

"Will it always be so good between us?"

"Always, my love. The Great Spirit brought us together. He makes no mistakes. You and I are meant to walk this life path together. No matter what comes against us, we will share it together, and our bodies will sing out praise with our joining."

"You have the most wonderful way of saying things." Shannon stated sleepily. "I can almost believe that everything will turn out all right."

Hunter would have turned her in his arms and questioned her now about her past, but already he heard her even breathing. He made a mental note that tomorrow he would begin questioning her about her life, and what had brought her to Montana. Now that she was truly his, he believed he had the right to share her past as well as the present. At times he sensed an inner fear she was hiding. He wanted her to know that she could trust him to keep her safe.

TO: N. IVEY

GRAYLIN STONE WILL ARRIVE IN LAST CHANCE GULCH BY END OF MONTH STOP WILL SEE MATTER PUT TO AN END, IMMEDIATELY STOP
A. D. ARMSTRONG

SIXTEEN

Shannon awoke to the smells of meat roasting over the open coals of the lodge fire. A small smile filtered over her lips as she stretched contentedly, her eyes remaining closed. The movement brought to life a tender ache in the depths of her womanhood, and also brought to mind full remembrance of what she and Hunter had shared the night before upon this soft bed of furs.

The smile did not waver. She held no regrets. In fact, she had welcomed their coupling. The initial pain had been a surprise, but the rest, before and after, had been wonderful, beyond words. Hunter was a man among men, and he was all hers! This thought pleased her very much.

Watching for any sign of life from the sleeping couch, Hunter silently approached when he spied Shannon's movement. Looking down upon her, he silently thanked the One Above for allowing him to be the owner of her beautiful smile.

His heartbeat drummed with joy as his eyes traveled over her lush figure. She was perfection in his mind. All that a warrior could desire, she was his heart.

Bending to the sleeping pallet, Hunter reached out and lightly traced his finger over her kiss-swollen lips.

Shannon kissed the finger before opening her eyes. "Good morning, Hunter." She smiled with all the happiness she was feeling.

"It is a good morning, my heart. You are here in my

lodge, and in my bed. What more could a man ask for of a morning than this?"

"I guess he could ask for a wife who would get up before him and prepare his breakfast." She grinned.

Hunter grinned back. "To me, it is enough that you are here to share this day."

Shannon sat up on the bed, dragging a piece of fur up to cover her breasts. She did not wish him to believe she was one to lay abed throughout the morning. Why, on the ranch she was usually up before the ranchers, except for Cookie, of course.

For the first time, Shannon noticed that Hunter held a piece of tradecloth and a leather bag in his hand.

Seeing her eyes upon the cloth and parfleche, Hunter clarified, "I bring water to wash your body, Little Flame."

"Thank you, Hunter. If you just set it down, I will wash in a minute or two." She would do the job as soon as he left the lodge, she told herself. Some of her modesty had returned now with the light of morning.

Hunter smiled patiently. "I would do this chore for you, Little Flame."

"You . . . you want to . . . wash my . . . ?" Shannon couldn't finish the question. She admitted that she had been a little brazen where this man was concerned. But for the most part, it had been when she had been overwhelmed with the intense lust that filled her when she was near him. This deliberate desire of his to have free access to her body in order to wash her was something else entirely.

"This day I would see to all your needs, Little Flame."

What exactly did he mean by all her needs? A flush of heat traveled up Shannon's throat and covered her face.

Setting the parfleche of warm water down next to the sleeping couch, Hunter sat down at her side and gently eased the fur from her hands.

"My love for you is humbled when I look upon your beauty." His pale gaze roamed over her naked body, and then slowly rose back to her flushed face. "You and I are one, Little Flame."

He drew the dampened piece of tradecloth over her breasts and down each arm. "When I was a young man I often wondered how I would feel when I found the one that was meant to join my life path. I imagined that I would love her with all my heart, but the power of my love for you compares little to the thoughts that a young brave reflects upon as he sits alone by his campfire." He spoke to her in that low, husky tone that held the power to melt her from within.

As he drew the cloth over her belly and gently pushed her back upon the sleeping couch, his voice captured her within a web of total submission. "I remember the day when my friend Lone Step tried to explain the feelings he felt for his woman. I had inwardly laughed that a man could allow himself to fully lose all that was his inward self into the keeping of another's heart. Now I know that I had been foolish in my thoughts. To share one's heart so fully is to know life with all the energy and power that the Great Spirit wishes us to experience."

Shannon shivered as Hunter's hands traveled over the flair of her hips, the dampened cloth roaming lower over the curve of her buttocks and her upper thighs.

"Life is the gift that only a woman can present. Never have I felt more keenly aware of the beauty and strength that is woman's than I do when I look upon you." Dampening the cloth once again with the warm water, he drew it slowly over each shapely leg and delicate foot.

"I wish for our love to take seed and grow. He tenderly spread her thighs, and drew the cloth between her legs, washing away the flecks of virgin blood that stained her body. "I wish for my child to live within the shelter of your body, and to experience the nourishing love that our joining brings."

Shannon shuddered as much from his words as his touch. In this man she had at last found shelter from the turbulence that life usually offered her. She could stay here at his side forever and be content.

As he set aside the cloth, he drew her upright once again. "Come and dry your body near the fire I will comb your hair."

Stepping to the side of the sleeping couch, Shannon reached for the hide dress Summer Rose had given her.

Hunter stilled her hand as he clasped it within his own. "There is no need to cover yourself here in my lodge. Only my eyes will look upon your beauty."

Shannon would have argued that for her own modesty's sake she would feel more comfortable with something covering her, but Hunter drew her toward the warmth of the center fire, and as they reached his backrest, he pulled her down upon the beaded mat.

His hands lightly trailed over her forearms, his senses filling with her nearness as the soft curves of her body adjusted to fit before his larger frame.

Shannon sighed softly as she leaned her back against him. The warmth of the fire before her, the strength of Hunter behind her held the power to totally ensnare her senses in the erotic spell he had cast within the lodge.

Pulling forth a tortoiseshell comb, Hunter gently ran it through the fiery strands of her thick, lush hair. As he brushed the tresses, they wrapped around his wrist and twined over his lap, caressing him in a rich display of shimmering curls. "Every time I look upon you, I desire to run my fingers through your hair, Little Flame. You are the little flame of my desire that burns out of control."

Shannon wanted nothing more at the moment than to have Hunter carry her back to the sleeping couch and join his body with hers.

Hunter held other plans. Taking his time, he controlled the wayward strands of fire curls and braided the tresses into a thick, plump length that fell down the middle of her slender back.

Turning her slightly upon the beaded mat in order to

view her features, Hunter smiled warmly as he questioned. "Are you hungry, Little Flame?"

Shannon's eyes widened with the question, and she was tempted to respond truthfully by telling him that her hunger for his body was raging out of control.

"Of course you must be hungry. You ate very little yesterday." Hunter answered the question himself and pulled a bowl of sliced meat sitting next to the warm coals, closer to the backrest.

Taking up a piece of the succulent meat with his fingers, he brought it up to Shannon's lips. Obediently, she opened to him, allowing him access to place the choice morsel upon the center of her tongue.

Hunter smiled before placing a piece of meat within his own mouth, his left hand idly tracing a path over her forearm, his fingers lightly brushing the fullness of her breast, and at the same time hearing her hiss of released breath.

For a few minutes Hunter continued to feed Shannon in this same manner. With the finish of the meat in the bowl, his mouth settled over hers and fully sampled the sweet bounty that was hers to offer.

Shannon pressed herself closer to his lap, her breasts pushing against his chest, the rosy tips tingling at the contact with his hard flesh.

As his mouth drew back, Hunter's thumb lightly caressed one hardened bud. "It is time for you to dress, Little Flame. I thought we would go for a ride this morning."

"A ride?" Shannon asked dumbly, her mind whirling from the things he was doing to her body.

"Come, I will help you dress." Hunter rose, and pulled her along with him to her feet, not giving her time to voice a protest.

Shannon's body and mind were keenly attuned to Hunter's every touch, every word. As he helped her to pull the hide dress over her head and settle it about her hips, his hands roamed freely over her flesh, his touch seducing her senses.

Before she awoke, Hunter must have readied his horse, because when they stepped outside the lodge, the stallion was hobbled outside the tepee. Looking around, Shannon did not see her own mount. As her gaze went to Hunter, he pulled her along with him, and reaching his horse, he set her on his back.

"I thought this day we would ride together, Little Flame."

Shannon released a small moan. She was not sure how much more of his tender handling she could bear up to.

Hunter seemed unconcerned with her reaction. He mounted behind her, and with strong hands turned her so that she sat almost in his lap. His arms went around her as he reached for the reins, and as he inhaled her flowery scent, he smiled. "You are exactly where I want you."

"Where are we going?" Shannon attempted to control the feelings of want that filled her by being so near Hunter. He appeared unaffected by their closeness; she would have to learn to keep a tight leash upon her passions.

"We will have this day to ourselves with no intrusion. That is why we leave the village. I wish to have you all to myself. We go to a place where I will hold you naked in my arms throughout the afternoon."

Shannon should have known better than to ask questions. The flame within her woman's depths began to burn wantonly out of control. The promises he made were enough to make any woman hot for him. Although she only had had a taste of what joining with him held, her anticipation of what the afternoon would bring sent her senses spinning out of control.

For a time they rode in silence. Shannon attempted to understand these feelings she was experiencing, and Hunter put his attention on their surroundings. He was a wise warrior, knowing the value in keeping a keen eye on the trail up ahead as they followed the path of the winding river.

An hour after leaving the village, Hunter pulled his mount to a halt near the edge of the river. "There is a place over there"—he pointed a short distance from where they sat—"where there is a pool of heated water. The people believe this water has healing powers. One's body is relaxed and invigorated when they rest within the waters."

The idea sounded wonderful to Shannon. "Are we going to spend the rest of the day here?" The river appeared sparkling blue beneath the midmorning sun. It was a most inviting place to spend an idyllic afternoon.

Hunter heard the pleasure in her voice. Dismounting, he reached up and helped her from the horse's back. "I cannot imagine more pleasure to be found here on mother earth than having you at my side here, alone."

He pulled her up close into his arms, and bent his head to sample the sweet taste of her. "Your taste is pure and sweet, Little Flame." He breathed the words softly against the side of her mouth with the finish of the kiss.

"And yours is the touch of an untamed blending of man and beast. If possible, I would draw the essence of you into my own keeping." Shannon held no thought to speak anything but the truth; her words coming from her heart.

Her ragged breathing stilled as his lips took hers once again. This time the kiss was languorously overlong, holding the power to fully explore the draft of erotic pleasure that passed between them. Hunter's heated tongue probed and plundered, swirling around her moist tongue, leaving her clutching his shoulders for support.

Honey-sweet nectar filled Hunter's mouth as the kiss was prolonged. Her lush curves pressed against his hard body, goading the sensual pull of the moment. As his tongue drew back, he caught hold of her bottom lip and sensuously sucked.

This new assault touched off a searing flame deep in the heart of Shannon's womanhood. An ache of unbearable want came to life, and without conscious thought she began to press against the hard line of his maleness.

Shannon would have spoken aloud about the pleasure she received from him as his hand began to lightly caress the fullness of her breasts. But lost within the spell of his closeness, she could not speak; it was hard enough to even draw breath.

"Why do you not show me all of your body?" His husky tone circled her and sent shivers of anticipation coursing over her length.

As her trembling hands lowered from his shoulders and began to pull the hide dress up over her hips, Hunter reached out and helped her, pulling the dress over her head.

Without saying a word, she stood before him in all of her woman's glory; proud at the moment that she was able to view the pleasure within his silver regard as his eyes slowly swept over her naked length.

"Your beauty is as a flame that burns out of control. I am unable to quench my heated hunger for you with just a look. I wish to bury myself deep within you, and feel the searing warmth as your body's liquid flows over my manhood."

Shannon felt instant heat flare between her legs, then begin to throb. She would have willingly lay down upon the grass with him, but Hunter's husky voice held her where she stood.

"Does your body ache with need, Little Flame?" His silver eyes locked with hers, not allowing her to turn from him, demanding an answer to his question.

"Yes, I ache," she got out on a ragged breath.

"What is it that you ache for, my love?"

Shannon felt the heat of a flush traveling up her throat and over her face, but still those eyes would not give her release. "I . . . I want you, Hunter." She spoke her words in a low whisper.

"Do you feel this ache deep inside your woman's heat?" His words were a husky caress. The very air around them was electrically charged by this passionate interchange. His questioning of her was a potent seduction of Shannon's senses. Her legs felt weak where she stood before him, her gaze at last breaking away from his as her eyes roamed over his muscular torso.

Before she could move or speak, Hunter's voice washed over her once again. "Reach out and help me to undress, Little Flame."

Standing still before her regard, Hunter watched her silently as she took the step that separated them. Silently, her hands reached out, and with a movement the leather tie was unlaced.

The breechcloth fell to his feet, his hard, blood-filled manhood jutting upward with a need that only this woman standing before him could satisfy. His hungry gaze watched her lowered look, witnessed the parting of her lips as her glance slid over him, and she inhaled a ragged breath.

Shannon felt the ache in her lower depths widen, then spread upward as her gaze filled with the sight of his magnificent body. Her tongue lightly dampened dry lips as she greedily devoured the bold display of his turgid lance; the vein-ridged protrusion swollen to engorged proportions. Her gaze rose and locked with his, and lost to the spell, she welcomed his embrace as he pulled her upward against his chest, her arms twining around his shoulders, her legs wrapping around his hips.

He filled her then. The pulsing length of his lance surged with power as he felt her tightness surround him, holding him close, the trembling of her inner sanctum vibrating around him.

For a moment, forgetting everything except the woman in his arms, Hunter walked toward the grassy patch of knee-deep sweet grass at the river's edge. Each step he took pushed his manhood that much farther into Shannon's passion, her womanhood tightening and then releasing with the movement.

As Hunter stood beside the river's edge, he softly questioned, "Do you still feel the soreness that you experienced last night?" Her kisses feathered over his throat and chest, and her breasts pressed against his chest overwhelmed him with intense need, but some small warning of caution to have a care for her body overrode his own desires.

"I feel no pain, Hunter. I feel you . . . only you," Shannon whispered in response.

Hunter's senses took flight as he laid her down upon the grassy bed, their bodies still entwined. They stirred against each other in a wild, tempestuous joining that knew no bounds or restraints.

The smell and feel of the grass, and soft, moist earth beneath their bodies, as well as the sun's warmth kissing their flesh served as a heady inducement to the surging rapture that stormed through their young limbs.

Shannon gasped softly as Hunter's lips and tongue stole a flaming path from her mouth to her full, straining breasts. As he filled her, his mouth caught the rosy tip, and he greedily sucked.

Her lips parted as she cried out; a contended keening sound of pleasure circling the area as, again and again, he filled her and drew back out.

Hunter sank hilt-deep inside her warmth, his breathing ragged as pleasurable sensations stormed through his body, blood, and brain. He had almost believed that last night had been a dream, but she was far better than he remembered, far better than any dream could possibly be. Her body fit his to perfection . . . the fit of her tight and smooth around his shaft, the feeling driving him mad when she lifted her hips to draw him in more completely. Swirling enchantment streaked up his spine and expanded throughout every portion of his body.

As his ram-hard lance took up a rhythm of languid withdrawal and penetration, Shannon's hand stole down his muscular back and pressed against the base of his spine, driving him onward as he braced his feet against mother earth and glided in and out in a primal dance of tantalizing passion.

She wanted this moment to go on forever. She wanted

to feel him over her, and in her. Her hands roaming over his flesh, their bodies entwined, as he filled her depths with a fullness that stoked the farthest reaches of her body. In his arms was pleasure beyond compare . . . sweet, rapturous bliss!

As his heart pulsed harshly against her breasts, and his mouth plundered her with heated kisses, Hunter held nothing back as he thought only of pleasing this woman who laid claim to his heart. Her yielding body was like a temple of love, quenching his thirst with its heady liquid, setting his soul afire with her passion. Never had he felt such intense pleasure.

Her breathing instantly changed, intensifying in the flashing of a heartbeat as he pressed farther into her trembling depths. Exquisite sensation peaked, Hunter matching her new rhythm, following as Shannon's sheath convulsed and trembled around his manhood, drawing him fully into her satisfaction, as climatic keening sounds escaped her parted lips.

Hunter drove in, holding himself hard against her womb as Shannon arched into the hard length of him and clung to his shoulders, knowing that he was all that truly mattered in her spinning world.

As her shuddering intensified, he poured into her with a surging intensity that exploded in his depths and carried them higher . . . toward a tumultuous, soul-shattering experience.

Gasping for air, Shannon's heart raced with rapture as Hunter clutched her tightly against his body. She kissed his mouth, his eyes, his cheeks, her lips covering his face as she breathlessly attempted to express her feelings without speaking them in words.

Hunter's fingers brushed aside the stray wisps of copper curls, his eyes tracing the beauty of her face and marveling that he had been so blessed.

"I should truly be angry with you, Hunter." Shannon sighed as she melted against him and reviewed the tenderness in his eyes.

"And why is that, my heart?"

"Because of the times I tried to coerce you into making love to me, and you refused. When I think of the other times I could have experienced these wonderful feelings . . ." She did not complete her sentence.

Hunter knew full well her feelings. "I promise I will make up to you all the deprivation you have suffered, Little Flame." Hunter grinned, enjoying the aspect of the job he had set for himself.

"I don't know if I have told you yet, but I love you." Shannon spoke the words as a heartfelt declaration of all the feelings she harbored inside for this man.

Hunter felt the skipping of his heartbeat with her confession. He had been waiting all his life to hear these words from this woman's lips.

"I don't mean to sound greedy, but do you think we could do this again soon?" Hunter was still within her, and she squirmed her bottom just a little to emphasize her meaning.

"I rather like this greedy side to your nature, Little Flame." Hunter chuckled, and felt his manhood responding to her movement. "I think we should rest in the hot pond for a while before we join again. I fear that my size may leave you sore, and I wish you to know only pleasure with our joining."

How could Shannon voice any kind of argument when he placed all his concern upon her well-being, but as he pulled out of her, her first thought was to draw him back and once again be filled by him.

Hunter carried her against his chest to the hot pond, and still holding her, he stepped within the water, submerging them both in the steaming depths.

They lingered there within the warm water beside the edge of the pond, now and then their lips joining, or their hands reaching out to caress or tantalize.

The water made Shannon's limbs feel like liquid, and perspiration beaded her brow as steam rose up from the surface. "Hmmmmm, this is wonderful," she sighed against Hunter's chest.

"I think it time that we left this heat and swim in the river." Hunter had come to this place many times, and enjoyed diving into the cool depths of the river after idling in the hot pond. He always felt refreshed, as though he had come out of a sweat lodge.

Shannon sleepily nodded. If he wanted to go to the river, she offered no resistance; in fact, she was too tired to make an effort at argument. She would have been content to lie there within the hot pond throughout the rest of the afternoon, or in fact do anything he wanted.

Hunter's husky laughter washed over her as he pulled her up the pond's edge, and, clutching her hand, led her to the river. "Follow me, Little Flame," he called as he dove headfirst into the water.

Though contentedly tired, Shannon followed. She came up sputtering, her body tingling from the chill of the water.

Hunter came up behind her and pressed his body against hers. "Grandmother river has the power to make you feel the blood flowing fiercely through your veins." He laughed as he witnessed her teeth rattling together.

"I think I prefer the heated water in the little pond." Shannon made a pout.

The pursing of her lips was hard for Hunter to resist. Grabbing her around the waist, he covered her mouth with his own and pulled her body with his below the surface.

Their limbs twined, his midnight hair cascading out around their bodies and joining hers of shimmering titian. Their senses were fully attuned to every nerve ending in their bodies. The touch of each other stoked their passions to full wakefulness.

His shaft instantly hardened, and without resistance slipped within the warm haven of Shannon's passion. As the feeling of cool water rushed before his manhood and caressed her womb, Shannon's mouth opened beneath his and filled with water.

Hunter carried them closer to the river's edge, his big body surrounding her as he cushioned their joining. The cool, circling water encased them and parted with velvet smoothness as she pressed her belly against his, her slender arms feeling weightless as they automatically wrapped around his neck. At the same time, Hunter's large hands cupped the fullness of her rounded buttocks.

A timeless moment passed as Hunter stared into her gleaming turquoise eyes, the raging passion flickering like quicksilver in his own regard as his head slowly lowered and his mouth slanted over hers.

Shannon clung to him as though he were her only lifeline. As she brought her legs up and wrapped them around his hips, his legs braced apart to carry the full burden of their steaming desires, he moved sensuously in and out of her. Her body shuddered, the sound of a small gasp filling his ears.

The water intensified Shannon's sensitivity. She felt each curve and muscle of Hunter's large body, her breasts pressing against the muscular contours of his chest, and with the contact, the dusty-rose buds turned to hard nubs.

The contact of Hunter's hands caressing her buttocks, her breasts pressing against his chest, her legs settled around his hips, held the power to draw her breath away. As she felt the velvet smoothness of his lance touch the heart of her passion, her breath clutched in her chest. She could feel the cool water circling her and filling her, a small amount of the coolness traveling before the heated brand of Hunter's powerful shaft, and showering within the depths of her womb. The feeling was so erotic, it set off a trembling that left Shannon rocking back and forth upon the hardness of his manhood.

Hunter was lost upon the raging tide of their passion. He felt every caress she gave, every pulse of her body as she moved against him. The flaming cauldron of white-hot passion stirring within the depths of his loins raced up-

ward, and the moment he heard Little Flame cry aloud
his name, her body coursing with trembling shudders,
head thrown back and eyes tightly closed, Hunter met her
release with own storming climax.

SEVENTEEN

Lingering there in their forested paradise, twice more the couple explored this newfound passion that flared up with the slightest provocation. The sun was high in the cerulean sky, the late afternoon shadows encircling the area, when Hunter deemed it time for them to start back toward the village.

Shannon contentedly relaxed in his arms as he directed his horse back over the trail through the forest they had traveled that same morning. "This has been a wonderful day, Hunter. I hope we can come back her often."

Hunter lovingly kissed the crown of her head, which was tucked beneath his chin. "Never have I had such pleasure here at the hot pond."

"I would hope not!" Shannon lifted her head and smiled up at him.

"You have told me little of your past, Little Flame." Hunter hoped that she felt comfortable enough to confide in him. Thinking to pass the time on the trail, he entreated her to trust him. "What brought you to Montana Territory?"

Shannon would have liked to forget all about her past and think only about tomorrow in this man's. arms. Knowing that she had to tell Hunter something, because to keep quiet would only make him curious, she stated softly, "My father died two years ago, and I had to live with my uncle.

He was not a very kind man, so I decided to leave his house."

Hunter waited for her to continue, but when she didn't he pressed. "Why did you come to Last Chance Gulch?" He knew that she was leaving much unsaid.

"I . . . I didn't exactly choose Last Chance Gulch as my destination. It just happened that I wound up there." After spending such a wonderful day with Hunter, Shannon didn't feel like thinking about the circumstances that had brought her to Last Chance Gulch.

Hunter would have reminded her that she had come to Last Chance Gulch as a supposed bride for Alex Cordoba. But he understood even less about those arrangements. She claimed to be a bride one day, and then she swore she wasn't, and the ranchers went along with whatever she declared. He could tell that she wasn't sure yet if she was able to trust him, and he would not press her for the time being.

"In a few days I will have to leave the mountains to go and finish the job that I started for the Pinkerton Agency."

Hunter had received word before leaving Last Chance about a meeting that was to take place in a few days at Moccasin Wallow Canyon, between Rufus Murdock and his boys and a band of Crow Indians. If everything went as he hoped, he might be able to wrap up this assignment right then and there, just a few miles outside Last Chance Gulch.

Shannon had known that sooner or later Hunter would have to go back down to Last Chance. She was surprised only by the suddenness of his announcement. She had hoped that they would have more time together before the outside world would press back in on them. "I will be ready to go whenever you say," she responded softly.

Hunter's arms tightened around her with her response. "I want you to stay here in the mountains with my people, Little Flame."

"Stay here in the mountains without you?" Shannon

drew back away from his chest and stared at him incredulously.

"I will not be able to do my job if I have to worry about you." Hunter tried to make her listen to reason.

"I can go to the ranch while you finish up your work." She knew even as she made this statement that she was not stating the truth. She wasn't about to let Hunter out of her sight. He had been shot already by the men he was after; she would be at his side in case he needed her help the next time he came against those same outlaws.

"I have already sent word to the Five Star Ranch that you are safe; and have chosen to stay with me and my people. I have invited the ranchers to come here to the mountains if they wish to visit you."

"Well, I won't stay here without you!" Shannon pouted. "Your people don't even know me, and I noticed how cold your grandfather received me yesterday when we arrived. If you leave the village, so do I!"

Hunter was just as determined to have his own way. "You are being unreasonable, Little Flame. My people know that you are the woman of my heart. My grandfather will realize that I will have no other. I will be gone only a few days."

"Your grandfather probably hopes that you will send me away so you can join with Summer Rose!" Shannon's temper was beginning to simmer, and she said the first thing that came to mind.

Hunter certainly did not want their pleasant day to end like this. For a while he remained quiet as they traveled through the forest. He did not speak again until he heard her ease in her breathing, and was assured her temper had calmed.

"Why do you speak of Summer Rose when you are angry? Have I given you reason to believe I want anyone but you?"

"She told me yesterday that I would become her sister and she would become your second wife." Shannon felt tears stinging her eyes over the fact that she and Hunter were having their first argument.

Hunter's husky laughter filled her ears as he pulled her tightly against his chest. "So that is why you questioned me about taking a second wife."

"I had to be sure that you didn't agree with what she said."

"And are you not sure about my feelings for you, Little Flame?"

Shannon slowly nodded her head. How could she not know what Hunter's feelings were. He had expressed them so wondrously throughout the day.

"And you also know that I wish only to keep you safe from harm's way?"

Once again she nodded, but silently she was determined that she would not be left behind when he left the Sioux village.

Hunter was pleased that she was being sensible. "Perhaps it is time that I help Summer Rose find a warrior of her own."

Shannon looked up sharply, unsure that she wanted Hunter anywhere near the other woman.

"I have seen Spotted Eagle looking upon her in the past," he was quick to explain. "I believe he did not pursue her because he believed I was interested."

"You can certainly set him straight on that account, and the sooner the better!"

Again Hunter laughed. This woman of his heart did not hold back her words, and he was delighted that she belonged to him.

For the next two days the couple spent as much time in each other's company as possible. They seemed unable to get enough of the taste and feel of one another. They awoke with their bodies tightly pressed together, and fell asleep with their limbs entwined.

Life here in the mountains was idyllic. There was no further mention of Hunter's leaving the village to go back down to Last Chance Gulch, nor did Shannon bring up the subject of Summer Rose.

The second day of Shannon's arrival in the village, she found herself with time alone, after several warriors arrived at Hunter's lodge and coaxed him into joining them as they went to inspect a small herd of ponies that had been stolen from a band of Crow.

Finding herself alone, Shannon decided to wander through the village. She knew that the villagers were tolerating her presence because of Hunter, and decided that the only way they would get to know her was if she went among them and visited.

The first evening when the villagers had celebrated Hunter's arrival, she had met several of the women, and as she walked through the center of the village now, she hoped she would see someone she recognized.

As she passed a small group of women sitting before a lodge, sewing and laughing companionably, she was motioned closer by one of them.

Shannon didn't hesitate. Drawing in a deep breath, she made her way to the group and eagerly attempted to communicate. The most she was able to do was smile and nod as they hand-signed and spoke in their tongue, which to date she understood very little of.

The women didn't seem to mind that she could not communicate well. They were friendly enough, and entreated her to sit among them.

Shannon sat down and watched on as their busy fingers stitched and beaded tradecloth and hides. A few of the small children appeared to find her a great curiosity, but within a matter of minutes she had had them sitting around her as she entertained them by making images of small animals out of the shadows in the dust with her hands.

The mothers were grateful for the reprieve from having to watch over and chase the younger children, and Shannon found more and more of the women laughing along with the children as she made sounds in her throat to accommodate the beasts.

An hour had quickly passed, when Shannon looked up to find Hunter's grandfather standing a few feet away, watching her. Never having been one to shy away from a confrontation, she excused herself from the group and silently approached the elder man.

"My people welcome you as Hunter's woman," Two Owls stated in gruff English. There was no pleasure in his voice.

"Perhaps," Shannon conceded. "But the children accept me for myself."

Two Owls grunted in agreement. He had watched the children around her and had viewed the animation on their features. He could not take from her the small headway she had made.

"I hoped that once you realized that I care a great deal for your grandson you also would accept me for myself." Shannon was unsure where she had drawn up the courage to speak directly to this large, imposing man. But she knew that if she were to be happy here among Hunter's people, the first step was in gaining Two Owls's approval.

For a full minute Two Owls's dark, unreadable eyes stared at the woman standing before him. "Come to my lodge, Star-Of-Fire, and we will speak on this subject of my grandson." Two Owls turned before she gave her agreement, and began to make his way to his lodge.

For a few seconds Shannon stood in hesitation, unsure if she should follow him to his lodge or turn back to the safety of Hunter's tepee. Good sense won out. Surely Hunter's grandfather would not harm her. He would not dare. Hunter would be furious if harm befell her, and the old man was wise enough to know that by doing her harm, he would lose his grandson forever.

Two Owls's lodge was larger than Hunter's, and after quickly adjusting her eyes to the darkness of the interior, Shannon spied the old man sitting before his lodge fire.

His hand rose upward and motioned for her to come

closer. "Sit here, nearby, Star-Of-Fire." Two Owls directed her to sit at his right, but Shannon decided to sit down across from him.

"I love Hunter, Two Owls, and he loves me. We will be together." Shannon wanted to let the old man see exactly where she stood on the matter of his grandson, and for him to realize that they were going to stay together.

His eyes suddenly filled with tiredness as Two Owls studied the white woman. "I feared long ago that I had lost my grandson forever. The Great Spirit returned him to me, and I would not see him depart the people and their ways again."

His inner vision relived the day when Hunter had rode into his village carrying the heart of his brother and mother, and once again he felt the sharp sting of pain he experienced whenever he thought of that day. Hunter had tried to appear strong that day in his grandfather's lodge, but Two Owls had seen and shared the pain of his loss.

Two Owls understood Hunter's desire to go among the white eyes, but he never feared that his grandson would not return to the sacred mountains. As he looked at this woman, he knew that she alone held the power to entice Hunter away from his people.

"Hunter desires to live here among his people, and I wish only to be at his side."

"I remember another white woman who spoke similar words. I opened my heart to her because of my son's great love for her. For many winters Hinhan Ska lived among us. The people loved her well. But then one day the white eyes came to our mountains to reclaim that which belonged to them. The army soldier coats came and took away my daughter-in-law and her two boys. They did not take only Hinhan Ska, Hunter, and Trapper, they also took my son's soul, and eventually his life."

"I do not want to see such pain on my grandson's face, Star-Of-Fire. Do you understand this old man's words when I tell you that my heart has been wounded and is now healed? I do not want it to be torn apart again."

Shannon did understand his words, but there were no promises in this life that anyone would not suffer from the loss of a loved one. "I too have lost people that I love, Two Owls. I know what it means to feel such pain of the heart. But life has chances that one must take in order to find happiness. I cannot promise you what tomorrow will bring, but I can promise that I will love Hunter until the hour that I take my very last breath."

There was no more she could say to relieve his fears. He would either accept her, or he wouldn't. For Hunter's sake, she hoped to win this old man over. But she was determined that she and Hunter would be happy together with or without Two Owls's blessing.

"And if the white eyes come to take you back to your own people?" Two Owls would hear her words. As he watched her features closely, he picked up his pipe and lit the Indian tobacco within the bowl with an ignited braid of sweet grass.

"I would not go. Hunter is my family now."

Two Owls softly sighed out a wreath of smoke that swirled around his head. "Then the people would have to fight the soldier coats. There would be many deaths among the Lakota."

"That would not be necessary." Shannon was shocked by his cold assessment of a situation that might never come to pass. "I have friends in Last Chance that I would go to until the situation could be straightened out.

Two Owls slowly nodded his head. Star-Of-Fire had a sharp mind. Perhaps enough winters had passed since Hinhan Ska had been taken from their village. Perhaps a similar situation could be handled differently today.

"I wish for my grandson to know happiness. I had hoped he would find it with a woman from our tribe."

Shannon could not help the small smile that came to her lips. "Hunter will have no other."

She sounded sure of herself. Two Owls smiled, too. "Even as a young boy my grandson knew what he wanted. You are right, Star-Of-Fire, he will have no other." Two

Owls's eyes twinkled as he allowed his gaze to fully appreciate her rare beauty.

"Then you approve?" Shannon could hardly believe she had been able to convince Two Owls so quickly that she was the right woman for his grandson.

"I do not wish to lose my grandson, Star-Of-Fire. I believe that you and I understand each other. If the day comes in the future when the *wasichu* come into our mountains to claim you back among them, you will know what must be done."

He was telling her without the words being spoken that if that day ever came, she was to seek the aid of her friends to straighten the problem out. He loved his grandson, but he also loved his people, and did not wish to see bloodshed in his beautiful valley.

Before Shannon left the lodge, Two Owls reached across the glowing coals of his center fire and clasped her hand within his own. "I will call you granddaughter from this day forth. When a warrior takes a woman to his lodge, in the eyes of the people the two are joined as man and wife."

Tears came swiftly to Shannon's eyes. "And I will call you grandfather."

That evening after dinner Spotted Eagle came to Hunter's lodge, and the two men companionably sat before the lodge fire. Shannon spent her time going through the basket of colorful beads Hunter had presented her that afternoon. She had watched the women sewing such beads in intricate design upon pieces of hide, and she was eager to try her own hand at doing such beadwork.

As the men spoke in low tones, Hunter's gaze often went over to the sleeping couch where Shannon sat. The conversation was serious, and twice after Hunter looked toward the sleeping pallet, Spotted Eagle nodded his head in agreement.

When Spotted Eagle left the lodge, for a while longer Hunter studied her from where he sat next to his lodge fire. She had appeared childishly pleased with his gift of beads that afternoon, and a soft smile lingered over his lips now as he watched her run her fingers through the little basket.

"I will get you cloth and hides to sew your beads upon," he softly announced, drawing her attention.

Shannon smiled warmly, only now realizing that they were once again alone. "I enjoyed sewing when I lived with my father. I am sure I have not forgotten."

"Come over here closer to me, my heart." Hunter extended his hand in her direction, and stretching his legs upon the beaded mat, waited for her to join him.

"I went and spoke to your grandfather this afternoon when you left with your friends." Shannon sat down between his legs, as always enjoying the feeling of him surrounding her with his large body.

Hunter had expected the two of them to come together and talk, but he had assumed that it would have been his grandfather to first approach her. "And how did your talk go?"

He was curious, but his voice remained even. His grandfather could be hard upon occasion, Hunter knew well, but Shannon did not appear upset, and he didn't wish to stir up trouble for no reason.

"I wasn't sure at first if Two Owls would be willing to give me a chance, but before I left his lodge, he called me granddaughter."

Hunter's breath released in his chest. Though he didn't wish to admit that his grandfather's approval meant so much to him, he was pleased with her words. "He is a wise man, and could see into your heart, Little Flame."

"I told him that you and I would have no other."

Husky laughter floated around the lodge as Hunter drew her tight against his chest. "I see your wisdom. He had no choice but to accept you." He could well imagine his grandfather's surprise in coming up against such a strong-willed woman.

"I think by the end of our conversation he was pleased that we had reached an agreement."

"An agreement?" Hunter was curious about her meaning.

"I told him that if the white men come to take me back to live among them, I would leave the valley for a time." She could feel the tightening of Hunter's entire body reacting to her confession.

"I will go to the Five Star until everything can be worked out," Shannon hurriedly explained.

"You will never leave my side, Little Flame." Hunter's words were a promise.

"I'm sure that no one will ever come here for me." Shannon turned in his arms, and her fingers caressed the tightening muscle in his jaw in a soothing fashion. "I told Two Owls this only to lessen his worry over you. He doesn't want to see you hurting as he watched your father, Hunter."

"You have a kind heart, Little Flame, but I will never let anyone take you from me." Hunter remembered the day as a child when the soldier coats came and took him, his mother, and brother away from the valley. The people had been powerless to protect Hinhan Ska and her children. His father had been wounded in the attack.

He silently swore that this would not happen a second time. If the soldier coats came again into the valley, they would not find his Little Flame. Even at this hour he had lookouts watching for anyone entering the Lakota lands.

"I don't want to think about being taken away from you, Hunter." Shannon pressed her head against his chest, her ear filling with the sound of his strong heartbeat.

"What is it that you wish to think about, Little Flame?"

"About this." Shannon's fingers trailed down his midriff, to his breechcloth, and settled over the bulge of his manhood.

"Your thoughts are much to my liking."

Shannon rose from the mat of the backrest, and standing next to the warmth of the fire, she lifted the hide dress over her head.

For a full minute she stood silently before Hunter's regard. His pleasure came from watching her . . . her pleasure was in knowing that he watched.

"Come, Little Flame, help me take off my breechcloth." His silver eyes never left her as she moved toward him, and he stretched back somewhat against the backrest.

Silently, her hands reached down, and with a simple movement the leather ties were unlaced. With the shifting of his hips, the breechcloth fell aside. Hunter's hard, blood-filled lance jutted upward with passionate need. His hungry gaze watched as her eyes turned to roam down the length of his body, and she inhaled a deep, ragged breath.

Shannon felt the intense heat ignite deep within her woman's depths, and then flame upward as she feasted her eyes upon his large, magnificent body. She swallowed hard as the bold display of his swollen shaft appeared to lengthen before her regard. Her gaze rose and locked with his, and captured within the sensual spell, she bent to her knees between his powerful thighs.

The tantalizing caress of her fire curls brushed softly against his groin and over his muscular thighs; the contact intimate and breathtaking. Even as such heightened passion gripped his senses, Hunter forced himself to remain still before her, not allowing himself the pleasure of reaching out and drawing her down upon his body.

Shannon felt the inner trembling of her body's needs as her slender fingers reached out to lightly brush against Hunter's erection.

With her slightest touch upon him, she felt her woman's power as she never had before. A long-held breath left her lips as her fingers gently enclosed the heated shaft. The blood pulsing thickness of him began filling her hand with a velvet hardness. She explored with her hand that which brought her so much pleasure, and as though it were a most natural thing, her head bent, lips pressing softly upon the sculpted head, moist tongue swirling around the heart-shaped apex.

A small moan rose up from the back of her throat and mingled with the groan that escaped Hunter's lips. His masculine scent ensnared her senses, the allure of the moment potently seductive as she lavished attention over the velvet-soft tip.

The fine strands of her copper hair flowed across the lower portion of Hunter's body, one hand resting against his inner thigh, the other encircling the base of his shaft as her heated tongue slowly wound a copious pattern of titillation down the vein-ridged edge, and as ravishingly enticing, she sampled the thick, pulsing length of him; her tongue irresistibly roaming back up the length of his lance in a manner that held the power to hold Hunter breathless upon the mat of his backrest.

Unable to endure more of this exquisite torture, Hunter reached downward, fingers gently encircling her chin. As her turquoise eyes looked upon his of heated silver, there was no need for words.

She read within their depths his searing desire; his need to join with her. A passion-filled gasp escaped her as her body moved, hips rising, buttocks lowering until she felt the throbbing heat of his manroot as the swollen head brushed against the moist entrance of her passion's heat.

With gazes locked, her slender hands splayed over his broad chest, her hair a fine-spun curtain shrouding them in a private world, the lower portion of her body slowly leveled down upon the branding heat of his turgid lance.

Inch by slow, tormenting inch, her velvet-warm sheath captured the pulsing thickness of his manhood, her breath escaping in small, ragged gasps. As his powerful size pressed against her womb, an inner tremor caught deep within her depths and a convulsive trembling took hold; her inner sanctum quivered, tightened around his massive length.

As his hands reached out and settled over her hips, he set the pace, his body moving beneath her to a tempo of sensuous undulation as he lifted her up and down; her moist velvet haven tightening, then releasing in a motion of consuming pleasure.

Incredible satisfaction flared and expanded as Shannon's head was thrown back, her body riding fully the wave of flourishing passion.

Hunter's upper body rose to meet her, his mouth capturing a fully ripe breast, savoring the tempting rose-crested peak, he sucked greedily, his shaft pressing an inch deeper.

Shannon lost all reason as molten heat traveled from her breasts to her womanhood. As Hunter moved with a sensuous rhythm beneath her, her entire body shook with the power of her climax.

Consuming . . . flaming . . . all-alluring satisfaction ingrained itself in every portion of Hunter's body. Her passion was his passion, her satisfaction his own. His manhood surged, pulsating as Shannon reached the peak of fulfillment, the heated liquid of satisfaction showering upon him, and at last he gave vent to the powerful urge of his own release.

An animallike groan escaped his lips and filled the lodge as the liquid fire of pure gratification rushed upward through the length of his manhood and erupted into her woman's depths. Shannon clung to him as she rode out the tempest of his raging pleasure.

Sometime later, Hunter carried Shannon to their bed of furs, and as the fire in the shallow pit dimmed fully, she sleepily murmured before falling to sleep, "Your grandfather said that we are now married."

Drawing her close, Hunter responded, "You are my wife, my life, my very heart."

EIGHTEEN

Shannon awoke finding herself alone upon the pallet of soft furs. For a few minutes she dreamily reflected over what she and Hunter had shared the night before upon the mat of his backrest.

She could not imagine sharing such feelings with any other man. Hunter had changed her world by bringing her into his life. All those things that she had deemed important in her life had now been placed in proper prospective.

She and Hunter were happy here in his people's mountain valley. All the trappings of a rich life had never brought her the happiness she was now experiencing.

Hunter's lodge was a safe haven from the outside world. Within this shelter they could fully explore the feelings they harbored for each other. As well, the lodge was a home, wherein one day they would raise their family.

Thoughts of that day when she would hold Hunter's child close to her heart brought a tender smile over Shannon's lips. He would be an adoring father. Their child would know an abundance of love, and always have a gentle hand guiding the way.

A slight chill stirred within the lodge, the center fire having long died out. As traces of sunlight filtered through the smoke hole at the top of the tepee, Shannon wondered where Hunter could have gone.

She supposed he had left the lodge to spend a few minutes alone to greet the morning star. Awakening that first morning alone in Hunter's lodge, she had left the warmth of the sleeping couch to go in search of him, and had found him near the river, his arms raised in prayer as he greeted the new day.

Since that first day, each morning after speaking his prayers to the One Above, Hunter returned to the lodge and climbed beneath the furs at her side. The feel of his hard body, and his searching mouth, were a pleasurable beginning to the start of a new day.

For a while longer Shannon waited in anticipation for Hunter's return. Perhaps he had been delayed by Spotted Eagle or one of the other village braves while at the river.

But as more minutes stretched past and still Hunter had not returned, Shannon decided to get up and dress. That morning she would build up the center fire and begin their breakfast.

More time passed, and by the time Shannon had completed heating water for tea, and cooking pieces of meat in a trade pot, she was beginning to worry about Hunter's whereabouts.

Perhaps he had gone to his grandfather's lodge, she told herself, but the thought did not relieve her anxiety. Setting the food to the side of the coals, she left the lodge.

Two Owls was not surprised to hear Shannon's call for entry as she stood outside the entrance flap of his lodge. "Come inside, Granddaughter," he called from where he sat beside his fire."

Glimpsing the old man alone, Shannon hastily apologized for. disturbing him at such an early hour.

"It is not early for me, Granddaughter. There is little enough for an old warrior to do with himself. I find I need less and less sleep as the winters pass. Now that I no longer have a woman in my lodge, I wake early and build my fire."

Shannon smiled warmly at Two Owls. "Hunter and I would love you to spend some time with us, in our lodge, when you find yourself with nothing to do. Hunter told me that you are a master at telling stories. I would love to hear some of them."

"You are a good granddaughter to welcome such an old man into the lives of the young." Two Owls grinned widely. He would take her up on her offer. There was nothing more in life that he would rather do than spend time with the only remaining family he had.

"I was hoping that I would find Hunter here with you. I awoke to find him gone from our lodge."

"He will return."

"You know where he went?" Shannon was surprised by the old man's reply.

"Come and sit by my fire, Granddaughter. Already I feel the chill in the morning air. It will be time soon for the people to move down from the mountains."

Shannon sensed that she wasn't going to get anything out of Two Owls unless she complied with his wishes. Sitting down across from him, she waited for him to explain his meaning.

"Are you hungry?"

"No . . . I fixed food for me and Hunter in our lodge." As he reached for his pipe, Shannon reminded him, "You were going to tell me where Hunter went?"

Two Owls's gaze held steady on her as he pressed Indian tobacco into the pipe bowl with his thumb and then lit it with a piece of braided sweet grass. "My grandson asked me to watch over Star-Of-Fire until his return."

"He asked you to watch over me?" A flush of cold dread washed over Shannon. "Where did he go?" She knew already the answer, but had to ask.

"He leaves to finish his work. Once he is done, he will return to the people and remain here in the mountains. He wishes for you to be waiting here for him."

"Oh, he does, does he? And did he tell you that I already told him that I wouldn't stay here without him?"

"He said you might be angry at first that he left without telling you." The old man admired the flash of anger that filled her beautiful eyes.

"I intend to follow him." Shannon's statement hung within the lodge for a full minute.

"You will get lost. You do not know the mountain trails." Two Owls found this young woman very interesting. He wished to hear what she would say next.

"I'll find my way if I have to back-trail all the way down these damn mountains." Her worry over Hunter was increasing by the minute. He was stubborn and muleheaded in believing that he could face off Rufus Murdock, Billy Snyder, and the men from the Bar-K alone. He would need help, and she intended on giving him hers whether he wanted it or not!

"I could make you stay here until Hunter's return."

Shannon looked wearily at the old man. Was he implying that he would keep her a prisoner in the village? Maybe she had made a mistake by coming to his lodge. Something in his manner told her that he did not mean the words he spoke. "You can, if you want your grandson to get killed!"

His dark eyes sparkled keenly at her response. "You will help him?"

"I don't know if he told you, but he has already been shot by these men he's after. I found him wounded, and helped him to recover." Now that she thought about Hunter's wound, she realized that he hadn't been as badly wounded as she had first believed. In fact, since the night he had entered her chamber window at the Five Star, there had been nothing else said about the shoulder wound. He had healed quickly, and appeared not bothered in the slightest.

"These men are dangerous?"

"Yes. Very dangerous. That's why I have to find Hunter before he runs into them again."

"He goes to confront them at their meeting place." Two Owls was pleased that this woman with the fire in her hair loved his grandson so much. He had been sitting before his fire all morning, trying to form a plan in which he could help his grandson. Star-Of-Fire had placed the plan in his hand.

"He knows where Billy Snyder and his thugs are meeting?" Shannon began to rise to her feet. She had to hurry if she was to catch Hunter before he confronted those outlaws.

"He told me of the meeting that will take place tomorrow when the sun is full up in the sky. These bad men will meet Cut Finger's band of Crow, and they will trade with them their gold, for the soldier coats' rifles, and ammunition."

"Hunter told you where this meeting place is?" When she caught up with Hunter, she was going to strangle him! He should have told her, not his grandfather. She could have helped him face these bandits!

The old man slowly nodded his head, plainly viewing her distress.

"You have to tell me where this meeting place is, Two Owls. I have to go there and somehow help Hunter. There is no one else!"

"My grandson has sent word to a man that he reports to from the agency where he works."

"But what if this man doesn't get Hunter the help he'll need in time?" Shannon was becoming more agitated as she stood and looked down at Two Owls. She wanted to scream at him that he had to tell her, but she knew that such action would do no good. The old warrior was taking his time, and wouldn't be rushed.

I have been thinking these same thoughts, Granddaughter."

At last he was beginning to speak with reason. "Tell me where the meeting place is." Shannon felt the sting of tears in her eyes but ignored their presence.

"I will call together some of the warriors of the village. They will travel with you to this meeting place. My grandson is stubborn and would have rejected such an offer, not wanting to endanger his people. But if the bad men sell

Cut Finger's people weapons, they will use them against my people."

Relief washed over Shannon with his words. She wanted to hug the old warrior, but she wasn't sure what he would make of such a show of affection. Instead, she dashed away the tears that were freely flowing down her cheek as she thanked him from her heart.

"Go and ready yourself for the ride, Granddaughter. The warriors will be eager to leave the village."

A half hour later Shannon exited Hunter's lodge wearing jeans, a plaid shirt, her boots, hat, and her six-gun belted over her hip.

Spotted Eagle was among the warriors that Two Owls had called together to aid his grandson. Looking at Hunter's woman, he smiled at the impression she made. She was a beauty no matter her dress, her copper hair had been pulled back and braided into a plump length that rested in the center of her back. Her hat was not yet placed upon her head, but was riding between her shoulders by the leather tie around her throat.

"Are you ready?" Shannon questioned Spotted Eagle when she returned before Two Owls's lodge and saw the group of at least thirty warriors.

"We are ready, Star-Of-Fire," Spotted Eagle replied, and brought forth the horse that Two Owls had ordered readied for her to ride.

The pony was sound and surefooted, and with one look Shannon fell in love with him. He was a paint, his red spots the exact color of her hair.

"He is called Eagle Wing, Granddaughter. He is my gift to you, for the love you hold in your heart for my grandson." Two Owls gave Shannon a leg-up in order for her to seat herself upon Eagle Wing's back.

"Thank you, Two Owls. I appreciate everything you are doing." She knew that Hunter's grandfather was risking much by sending the warriors of the village down the mountains toward Last Chance.

Their very presence close to a town could be considered to be aggressive. The townspeople and even the army could send forces against the party.

"Bring my grandson back to his people safe." The old man's glance went from Star-Of-Fire to Spotted Eagle.

The warriors set their horses into motion. Shannon, at the head of the group, was encircled by her escort as they rode out of the village.

Two Owls had talked for a long time to Spotted Eagle, giving careful instructions on how best to help Hunter. He had told him where the meeting was to take place tomorrow, and the time of day.

Spotted Eagle wisely knew that surprise would be their best advantage, and with this in mind, he kept the small band of warriors at a steady pace, not rushing their progress, but ensuring they arrive at this meeting place around the same time Hunter would.

Shannon would have pushed the riders at a harder pace. Each time they halted to rest and water their mounts for a few minutes, she nagged at Spotted Eagle, trying to impart to him the importance of catching up with Hunter before he walked into a situation he couldn't handle. Her worst fears were that Hunter would be caught unaware, as he had been that day by the bushwhackers near the stream.

Spotted Eagle listened to Star-Of-Fire patiently, but all her complaining did not make him change the set pace for the trek down the mountains.

By the time the sun lowered, Shannon was beginning to truly experience panic. The pace was even slower, Spotted Eagle insisting that it was safer for the horses that they walk them over the trails during the night hours, even though there was a full moon riding high in the velvet sky.

"We will reach Hunter in time, Star-Of-Fire." Spotted Eagle spoke a little harder than the other times he had stated this same assurance. But after the fourth time of her asking, "Can't they go a little faster," he found himself losing some of his patience.

"How can you be so sure we will get there in time? What if we're too late, and Hunter has to face these bandits alone?" She didn't want to imagine the harm that would be done to the man she loved if Billy Snyder and his boys caught him alone. And even a worse thought was Hunter coming upon the band of Crow Indians outlaws were to meet in the canyon. The Crow were sworn enemies of the Sioux.

"Two Owls and I talked this over, and I have set our pace so we will arrive in the canyon where the meeting is to take place around the same time these white men you call bandits and Cut Finger's band will arrive. "You should try to have more *wowicala;* faith, Star-Of-Fire. Hunter is a strong warrior, he will come to no harm."

Faith. The word was just sounding brass in her mind. She cared not to lay her faith in another's hands. She wanted to see Hunter with her own eyes and know that he was safe. She wouldn't know a moment's peace until they reached the canyon.

Hunter had ridden hard from the village to reach the scheduled meeting place before Murdock, and Snyder, and Cut Finger's warriors arrived and began their parlaying. It was still early morning when he arrived at Moccasin Wallow Canyon.

Securing his horse a distance from the ravine, Hunter found himself a hiding place up in the rocks. From his vantage point he could watch both ends of the gulch, and was protected well enough from any attack.

He knew that once all parties arrived, he wouldn't be able to hold the outlaws off for long unless reinforcements arrived. He was placing a lot of trust in Applebaum's having received his message and being able to round up enough boys to come to his rescue before he got his stupid head blown off.

Hunter knew it was a had plan, but there was no other way to see the job finished. This was the first bit of information he had gained about Snyder and Murdock having the rifles in their position, and he wasn't about to let it slip out of his hands.

Settling back against a large sandstone rock, and chewing on a piece of buffalo jerky, he allowed his thoughts to fill with the image of Little Flame as he had seen her last—sleeping peacefully upon his couch.

He could imagine the fury that had beset her when his grandfather told her he had left the mountains to go and finish his job.

A small smile tugged back the corners of Hunter's lips as he remembered the sight of her when she was in one of her tempers. She was as passionate when she was angry as when he was making love to her. But this time he was glad he wasn't anywhere around when the old man broke the news to her that he had left the village without her.

The only peace of mind he had had when he left the village was Two Owls's assurance that he would not allow Star-Of-Fire to make any hasty attempts to follow him.

As the sun rose higher, Hunter caught a glimpse of the reflection of sunlight hitting on a piece of glass. Cut Finger's scouts had arrived early to make sure that there wasn't any kind of trap set up in the canyon, Hunter clarified, and placed his hat on the ground as he ducked lower behind the rocks.

The Crow scouts wouldn't pick up his sign. He had backtracked and brushed away any evidence of his boot prints. The Crow would be expecting a trap, if there was one set up, to come from Snyder and Murdock. Finding the canyon empty, they would ride on in with their parfleches filled with gold, expecting to buy the wagon full of rifles and ammunition.

Again Hunter wondered if Applebaum had gotten his instructions. He hoped the Pinkerton man would be smart enough to let all parties enter the canyon before he and his men showed themselves.

Hunter knew he was placing his hope on a long shot by counting on Applebaum. There were too many ifs involved; if the Pinkerton man had gotten his message; if there was time for him to gather enough men and get to the canyon before Hunter was forced to play out his hand.

Hunter arranged the two rifles he had brought along, and both his six-guns, against the rock. Quietly, he made sure all were loaded, and set the boxes of ammunition on the ground next to him in order for him to reload fast.

In his mind was already formulated the plan that Murdock and the Snyder brothers would be the first he would sight in with his weapons once the fighting started. He would take care of those lowdown snakes at the first opportunity, he swore.

His main concern was the wagonload of rifles and ammunition. His people's very lives depended on the outcome of this day, and he had no intention of letting Cut Finger and his warriors drive out of this canyon with the wagon. He knew he had his work cut out for him, but he also knew, at least for a while, he would have the advantage.

As the minutes passed, Hunter's thoughts once more wandered to the woman of his heart. Hearing some noise below in the canyon, he sternly warned himself to focus all his attention on what was taking place here and now. It was foolhardy of him to think about anything at the moment except putting a halt to what was shortly to take place in the canyon.

Shannon's image fleetingly passed through Hunter's mind as he peered over the rocks and glimpsed Cut Finger and about a dozen Crow warriors, all armed with rifles.

The sun was full up by now, and it wasn't long after Cut Finger and his small band arrived in the canyon that Hunter could hear the sound of a wagon coming up the ravine.

Rufus Murdock and Billy Snyder rode out in front; a half dozen Bar-K boys rode in protective positions around the wagon.

"Hold up, boys." Looking directly up ahead at the group of Indians, Murdock held up his right hand, his left lightly settled upon the butt of his pistol in the holster on his left hip.

"Everything looks all right to me, Rufus," Billy verified as his blue eyes scanned the canyon for any sign of an ambush.

"Them red devils know better than to try something!" Mike Snyder barked out as he spat a stream of tobacco juice to the dust.

"Just keep your mouths shut, ya hear? Snyder, you better keep a tight rein on that brother of yours if you know what's good for you. I ain't about to ride away from here without that gold. He fouls up, and I'll put a bullet in his head!"

"He ain't going to mess anything up, Murdock," Billy assured. "Let's get this over with. I don't cotton to meeting here in this gulch anyway. I told you if there's a trap, we would have to make a run for it."

"There ain't going to be no trap. Them Injuns want our guns as much as we want their gold." With these words spoken aloud, Murdock kicked his horse into motion once again, and the wagon and men started up the canyon.

It was obvious that Rufus Murdock was the brains behind the group of outlaws. As they halted a few yards away from Cut Finger and his band, Murdock called loudly, "You got the gold, Cut Finger?"

"I have shiny rocks white men desire," Cut Finger called back as a packhorse was brought up next to his pony, the animals' packs loaded with gold. "You got rifles and ammunition, Murdock?"

"Throw back that cover, boys, and let these redskins see what their buying," Murdock instructed the two men sitting on the wagon seat.

Within minutes the canvas that had been stretched tight

over the back of the wagon was pushed aside, and crates bearing the imprint of the United States Army were revealed.

"Come on over here, and my boys will open a few boxes for you. You and your bucks can take a close-up look at the army's best. These here are brand-new repeating rifles, Cut Finger. You're going to be able to stand up to any white man, including the army. And me and my boys might just help you out if'n you can dig up any more of that gold in your mountains."

Hunter's informer had told him that Murdock had plans to help Cut Finger and his band attack settlers throughout the territory. He now knew the reason behind Murdock's offer of help.

White-hot anger rushed over Hunter as he listened to Murdock. These men were the lowest of the low. They were willing to kill men, women, and children for a payment of gold.

Fighting to keep a tight grip on his fury, Hunter told himself that he had to act before Murdock's men could open the crates. It would be too dangerous for him if Cut Finger and his braves got their hands on the repeating rifles.

Just as Hunter rose up from his position behind the rocks and leveled his rifle's sights on one of the men who had jumped off the seat onto the back of the wagon, all hell broke loose.

Hunter got off his shot, the man falling from the wagon to the dust, but as the confusion increased, the group in the canyon could not tell which direction the gunshots were coming.

From both ends of the canyon guns were being fired. Cut Finger's braves turned and began to fire upon the group of Sioux warriors heading straight for them. Murdock and his men were fending off the opposite end of the canyon as more Sioux warriors came from that direction.

Hunter wasted no time trying to figure out his good

fortune. Sighting in Mike Snyder, he squeezed the trigger of his Peacemaker. As the outlaw fell from his horse, he told himself one more down as he turned his sights on the brother.

"I'm getting out of here!" Billy shouted over the noise of the gunshots to Murdock, and with a shout he kicked his horse's sides and whipped him with the reins.

Snyder wounded two of the Sioux warriors as he exited the canyon. Murdock wasn't so lucky in his pursuit to follow his partner in crime. Spotted Eagle shot him in the shoulder as he passed him, but Murdock kept on riding hell for leather away from the canyon.

By then Hunter had jumped down from his position in the rocks and was firing at those of the Bar-K boys who deemed they had no recourse but to put up a fight. Most of Cut Finger's braves were fallen before the fierce fighting Sioux warriors.

For the first time during the fighting, Hunter recognized the copper-haired, slender figure at Spotted Eagle's side. "Little Flame." The name left his lips, and at the same time he saw Shannon shooting her six-gun and kicking out at her pony's sides.

Racing along with the warriors, and caught up in the excitement of the moment, Shannon had but one thought. That of reaching the wagonload of guns and making sure they didn't become the property of the Crow braves.

With a shout she called for her pony to fly like the wind, and as she came abreast of the wagon, she dove toward the seat. Without a second thought she grabbed up the reins and shouted for the pair of horses to set off at a run.

Hunter's heartbeat hammered fiercely in his chest as he watched her actions. As one of the Bar-K boys raised his gun to shoot at her, he fired without hesitation, the man flying backward to the ground.

What the hell did she think she was doing? Did she want to get herself killed? As a Crow brave came within a few feet of him, he leapt up and pulled him off his pony. Straddling the horse, and hitting the brave in the chin with the butt of his rifle, he was racing down the canyon after the wagon.

Three of Cut Finger's braves had also seen Shannon driving the wagon away from the fighting, and they were now giving chase. Hearing gunshots coming from behind her, Shannon turned and fired her six-gun. One of the Indians fell from his horse. She screamed for the team to race at a faster speed as she shot at the two who were closing in fast.

Thankfully, the pony Hunter was riding was swift, and in short moments he was within shooting distance of Shannon's pursuers. He hit one with a lucky shot. The other was near enough to the wagon to jump from his pony onto the crates of rifles and ammunition on back.

Shannon screamed as she turned and saw the fierce Indian only a few feet away from her. She lifted her six-shooter to fire, but found she was out of bullets.

Hunter pushed his mount harder, and as he gained the side of the wagon, he leapt just as the Indian was about to grab Shannon from the seat.

The struggle that ensued left Shannon sawing back on the reins as she attempted to halt the team. Her only thought was of somehow helping Hunter fight off the Crow Indian.

The team, though, was now too frightened to pay attention to the command given by the reins. They raced as though for their very lives as Hunter punched the brave square on the jaw, and he fell back on the crates.

Not giving a second to recapture his senses, Hunter was on the brave, punching and shoving, and with a burst of superior strength he punched him and sent him flying backward out of the wagon.

Jumping to the seat, Hunter grabbed the reins out of Shannon's hands. Allowing the team little head, he pulled with all his might. The animals began to slow, and at last they were brought to a halt.

"What the hell do you think you're doing?" Hunter

shouted, and throwing down the reins he grabbed Shannon by the shoulders and began to shake her.

"I was saving your ungrateful life!" Shannon screamed back.

NINETEEN

All Hunter had been able to think about as he raced after the wagon and the Indians who were giving chase was that he was going to lose everything in the world that held any meaning to him.

Now, his hands clutched over Shannon's shoulders, his relief was so great, he wanted to shake her to within an inch of her life for causing him such worry. "What are you doing here? How did you find out where Murdock was meeting Cut Finger's band?" He knew the answer to this question the minute it left his mouth. His grandfather had to have been the one behind Little Flame's and Spotted Eagle's arrival in the canyon.

Shannon attempted to jerk out of his reach, but her efforts were to no avail. His fingers continued to bite into her flesh as he clutched her. "You might not give a damn about your own stubborn hide, but there are people who care about you!"

"If you cared about me, you would have stayed in the village, where I would know you are safe!" Hunter eased his hold upon her but did not altogether release her. With the contact of her flesh beneath his hands, he was able to assure himself that she was all right.

"And if I had stayed behind, you would be in a sorry fix right this minute, Hunter. I saw where you were pinned in behind those rocks. Without Spotted Eagle and the braves' help, you would have been unable to hold off those outlaws for long." Shannon's anger was as explosive as his. He was the most foolish, stubborn, bullheaded man she had ever known!

Knowing she was right did not lessen Hunter's initial fury as he recalled his surprise and then shock as he had watched her ride into the canyon at Spotted Eagle's side. And when she had jumped from her pony onto the wagon seat, he had thought for a second that his heart would still its beating.

"You can't imagine the fear I felt when I saw you jump onto that wagon seat and ride down the canyon." Hunter's words softened, his hands now stroking her upper arms, his silver eyes drinking in her beauty as though he would burn her image into his mind.

"I'm sure you experienced the same fear that I did when I awoke yesterday morning to find that you had left the village and were coming after Murdock, and Snyder, and the Bar-K boys by yourself." Shannon's anger was not as easy in diminishing as Hunter's.

"I wanted to keep you safe."

"I told you I wouldn't stay behind."

"The next time I'll pay closer attention to your statements." Hunter pulled her into his embrace, savoring the feel of her in his arms.

"There won't be a next time." Shannon slowly began to feel her anger slipping away, and as Hunter's gaze held upon her, she clarified. "You promised you would give up your work with the Pinkerton Agency as soon as this job is finished."

Bending his head, Hunter sampled the sweet taste of her, assuring himself that she had not been harmed, but was well and alive in his arms.

Raising his head, he stated in a determined tone, "I'm afraid my job's not finished yet. Snyder and Murdock got away."

"I know. I watched them heading south. They must be riding toward Last Chance. Murdock's wounded, I saw him clutching his arm."

"More than likely he'll ride for Doc Martin to patch him up." Hunter pulled Shannon to her feet. "I guess if I told you to ride back to the village with Spotted Eagle and the warriors, you wouldn't listen to me?"

Adamantly displaying her refusal by the shaking of her head, Shannon was determined that he wouldn't leave her again. If he was riding into Last Chance Gulch to confront Snyder and Murdock, she would be around in case he needed her.

By the time the couple drove the wagon back down the canyon, they found Silas Applebaum and his boys had arrived and were helping Spotted Eagle and his braves round up the remaining Bar-K boys. Cut Finger and the few Crow braves who had fought their way out of the canyon had escaped.

Applebaum took charge of the wagon of rifles and ammunition, assuring Hunter that they would be directed back to the U.S. Army along with their prisoners.

Hunter and Shannon remounted their horses, and after thanking Spotted Eagle for his help, and sending word back for his grandfather that he and Little Flame would return to the mountains as soon as his job was finished, the couple started off in the direction of Last Chance Gulch.

Silas Applebaum called out that he and his boys would be heading toward Last Chance Gulch as soon as they finished up their work in the canyon, and he set a detail to take the wagon and prisoners to the nearest army fort.

"I want you to do exactly as I tell you." Hunter reached out and grabbed hold of Shannon's horse's reins when they arrived on the outskirts of Last Chance. "I don't want to have to worry about you when I confront these vermin!" Hunter relented as he witnessed the swift heat of anger surface to her cheeks.

"I won't get in the way."

"I want to hear you say that you will do what I tell you."

Hunter wasn't going anywhere until she gave the promise he wanted to hear.

"I'll stay behind you if that's what you're after, but I won't promise that I'll stand back and watch those outlaws shoot you without pulling my six-gun out to help!"

Hunter knew that he wouldn't get any more out of her than this assurance that she wouldn't rush headlong into a fight with Murdock and Snyder. "When this is over, I am going to keep you in the mountains out of harm's way." The thought of her even riding into Last Chance Gulch at his side rankled deep, but other than tying her up and leaving her in a safe place until he finished with Murdock and Snyder, he knew gaining her agreement to stay behind him was all the peace of mind he would get.

The main street of Last Chance Gulch was as busy as Shannon remembered. Hunter appeared not to notice anyone as he directed his horse toward the Red Dog Saloon. Shannon followed a few feet distant, but unlike the man before her, her turquoise eyes roamed over those standing in the streets and along the wood plank sidewalks as she sought out any sign of the men they were looking for.

As Hunter dismounted and tied his horse off at the hitching post before the Red Dog Saloon, Chantey, the town drunk, hurried up to his side. "If'n you're looking fer Snyder, he's in the Red Dog boasting how's he's going to kill ya on sight. Ya better go easy if'n yer looking to see the day out."

Hunter tossed the little man a silver coin for the information. Turning toward Shannon, he lifted her from her pony and set her to her feet. "I want you to go over to Beamford's store and stay put until I take care of Snyder. Murdock's probably seeing to the wound in his arm, so there won't be but one for me to face," he added as she began to protest his plans.

Shannon silently nodded her head. She held no intention of hiding out in the mercantile while Hunter faced the two men alone. But knowing that Hunter would only have her to worry about, besides trying to protect himself, she gave him the assurance he was needing.

Hunter pulled her against him and kissed her gently upon the forehead before he roughly pushed her down the sidewalk in the direction of the dry goods store.

For a few seconds he watched her take the steps that led her in front of the store before he turned and started toward the saloon.

Snyder had already been told that Hunter had arrived in Last Chance. Clutching the neck of the whiskey bottle sitting on the long bar in front of him, he tilted the bottle to his lips, and drank deeply. With a thud he slammed the bottle down. Wiping his mouth with the back of his hand, he turned and faced the swinging doors.

"The stinking breed killed my brother!" he mumbled aloud to no one in particular. He was already on his way to being drunk, having ridden directly to Last Chance Gulch and dismounted in front of the Red Dog Saloon. He had had a good half hour of drinking before Hunter's arrival in town.

Bolstered by strong drink, and the discouraging events of the day, Billy Snyder had his gun already drawn as he made his way to the double doors.

Hunter stood outside in the middle of the street, waiting for the bandit to face him. He held no doubt that the outlaw would meet his challenge. He and his brother both, if nothing else, had always thought too highly of their abilities with weapons. Most of their accomplishments had been gained through double-dealing and bushwhacking their opponents, but this time Billy Snyder would find himself facing someone who was more than eager for a gunfight.

Snyder swung open the double doors and rushed out, shooting. Hunter fell to the ground, his weapon slipping into his hand and firing with a sure aim.

Billy Snyder fell dead to the sidewalk in front of the saloon.

Shannon stood along the sidewalk, her six-gun drawn.

She had had time only to get her gun in her hand before Hunter fell to the ground and shot Snyder between the eyes. A deep, ragged breath escaped her as her eyes turned back to Hunter.

Pulling himself to his feet, Hunter noticed Shannon for the first time standing on the sidewalk with her gun in hand. An exasperated sigh escaped him. "I thought I told you to stay in the dry goods store until I finished this!" His words left his lips in a snarl.

Shannon paid no heed to his temperament. Her gaze rushed over him, making sure he hadn't been shot. "I was going to, but then I heard a shot, and turned around to see you in the dirt, and Snyder rushing out the doors."

This woman is driving me mad! Reaching the sidewalk, he stepped over Snyder's body, and grabbed her by the wrist. "You'd better stay near me so I can keep an eye on you."

Just as he was about to pull her into the Red Dog Saloon with him, a call from down the sidewalk halted him, and the five owners of the Five Star hurriedly made their way in Shannon's direction.

"This is all I need now." Hunter sighed, dragging Shannon into the saloon and going to the bar to order a glass and a bottle of whiskey.

He wasn't a drinking man, but at the moment he thought a stiff drink was in order. He still had Murdock to take care of, but, more important, Shannon to protect. He would attempt to soothe over the ranchers as soon as possible. He only hoped they weren't in a mood to give him a hard time about taking Shannon away from the ranch.

By then the saloon was beginning to fill up with townspeople. Marshal Taylor and his deputy had been informed of the gunfight, and were among the first to arrive. While Hunter began to relate the events of the day to the marshal, Shannon was surrounded by the ranchers, and a battery of questions were being put to her.

"Hunter and I will explain everything after Murdock is arrested," she assured Lucas.

"But, Honey darlin', for two days we didn't know where you were, or if you were dead or alive." Cookie's relief at seeing her was evident on his face.

"I'm fine, Cookie. Hunter and I are married now." She hoped this announcement would soothe the way for them later, when they went out to the Five Star and tried to explain to the ranchers how much they were in love.

Feeling a hand at her elbow, Shannon noticed Nancy Inverness for the first time.

Nancy pulled Shannon off to the side as the men were all talking. "I am so glad that you are all right, Honey." She smiled warmly, her husky voice low.

The usual unease that Shannon experienced when she was in the other woman's presence quickly asserted itself, and she would have stepped back to Hunter's side, except for the fact that he was now surrounded by the marshal and the ranchers, who were all talking at the same time.

"I'm fine, Nancy. I see that you are no longer staying out at the ranch?"

"Oh, no. Lucas and the ranchers were wonderful to me, but I couldn't impose for long upon their hospitality. They were worried, though, about you. When we found that you had disappeared from the ranch, I can tell you, all the men were in an uproar. Hunter's message soothed them somewhat, but they were still worried."

"I'll have to tell them how I met Hunter, and we fell in love. As soon as Hunter is finished with his business here in Last Chance, we'll go out to the ranch and explain everything." Shannon noticed that the marshal was sending his deputy over to Doc Martin's to see if Murdock was there having his arm patched up. Hunter and the marshal were making plans to capture the outlaw, and seemed intent upon their conversation.

"Why don't you come on up to my room while the men tend to their business, Honey?" Nancy suggested.

Hunter's dark head swung around, his pale eyes searching for Shannon. He had heard the other woman's invitation, and seeing Little Flame's hesitation, he nodded at her to go along with Nancy.

Even though the ranchers were now in the Red Dog, and he knew he could count on them to keep her out of trouble, he worried that something might go wrong if he had to confront Murdock. The safest place for Little Flame at the moment, he told himself, was out of sight.

The last thing Shannon wanted to do was go someplace with Nancy Inverness, but with the other woman's hand still clutching her elbow, and Hunter watching her intently, she felt as though she had no choice in the matter.

Reluctantly, she nodded her head and followed the woman up the stairs and down the hallway that looked over the saloon.

Hunter was more than a little relieved that Shannon was taken out of harm's way. Now he would be able to finish his job without worrying about her safety.

The minute Shannon stepped into the chamber, the door was slammed from behind and locked. In stunned dismay, Graylin Stone stepped in front of her.

"It was easier than I expected to get the bitch up here." Nancy Inverness pulled the blond wig off her head and slung it over on the bed.

Shannon thought she was going to faint as she looked at Nancy Inverness turn into a dark-haired man who was wearing makeup on his face and wearing women's clothing.

It took Graylin Stone a few seconds to recover his own composure at the sight of Nathaniel Ivey shedding his disguise. He had to admit, though, that the man was a master at his craft.

Recovering sufficiently enough to address his niece, he lashed out, "You thought to run away from me, did you? You should have known that I wouldn't give up. If I had to pay for every woman in this damn town to be murdered, I would see this thing to its finish!"

Slowly Shannon was beginning to grasp the meaning of witnessing Nancy Inverness turning into a man before her very eyes, and her uncle Graylin here in her chamber. "You had Bonny and Abigail Primer murdered? But why? Why kill them? They never did anything to you. My God, they didn't even know my real name!"

"Because they rode on the stagecoach into Last Chance Gulch with you." Nathaniel Ivey supplied the answer for her.

"And you killed them for that?" Shannon couldn't believe that anyone could be so cold-blooded.

"The three of you arrived the same day. You each had red hair in common, but none of you had the name I was looking for. I had no choice but to kill all three of you, and I would have finished the job the night I arrived at Five Star except for the fact that you disappeared from your chamber the same evening."

Shannon's life had been spared that evening only because Hunter had come for her. Looking around in desperation, her hand slipped to the butt of her gun.

Graylin Stone was quicker. He grabbed the six-gun, and without a thought to the consequences struck her against the cheek with the weapon before slinging it away from him onto the bed.

Shannon fell to the carpet with the force of the hit. Shaking her head, she attempted to clear her senses as she glared up at her uncle.

"You have been nothing but trouble in my life from the moment my brother died." Graylin glared. "Now at last I will have finish with my burden."

"Hunter won't let you get away with this. I swear he'll track you down and kill you if you harm me."

Ivey was already wiping the makeup off his face and pulling off the women's apparel. Graylin looked to the killer in concern at her words.

"Don't pay any attention to her. No one knows you in this town, and as soon as I change clothes, no one will know me. They'll find her body up here, and be looking for the woman she left the saloon with, not you or me."

Graylin appeared to relax with this assurance. "In truth,

I hate to have a part of this. She is my brother's child, after all."

Shannon's simmering eyes held her loathing in their depths as they stared up at Graylin where he stood over her prone form.

"Then leave the chamber. I can take care of her. You paid me well enough. Go on back to St. Louis and live your rich life, and forget you ever even came here to Last Chance Gulch."

Nathaniel Ivey could not help letting some of his true feelings be heard in his tone. Men like Graylin Stone sickened him, even though he admitted that this type of man was the reason he could afford the best that life had to offer.

Graylin also heard the contempt, but he ignored it. He was relieved to have an out at the moment. He held no desire to witness his niece's murder. All he wanted was to make sure the deed was done.

"I think I will go downstairs and have a drink, then. When you get back to St. Louis, contact Armstrong. There will be a sizable bonus waiting you. I can afford to be generous, after all, I will be spending her inheritance." With this said, Graylin Stone turned and left the chamber, holding every intention of having a drink of brandy before going to the livery, renting a horse, and heading out of town.

Graylin found the saloon crowded. The townspeople were all talking about a shootout, and another man found wounded and unconscious in the local doctor's office. The marshal had apprehended the outlaw without a struggle.

Hunter was standing at the bar, talking to the marshal's deputy and the Five Star ranchers, when he glanced up to the second-floor landing and noticed the gray-haired gentleman leaving the same chamber which, a few minutes earlier, he had watched Shannon enter with Nancy Inverness.

Instantly, the fine hair on the back of his neck stood on end. He eyed the man as he walked down the stairs and ordered a drink at the bar. He appeared somewhat nervous; his glance kept rising from the bar and back up the stairs.

Hunter knew something wasn't right. Deputy Seth Duley was getting the rest of the information that the marshal had instructed him to get from Hunter about the incident at the canyon, when Hunter interrupted him.

"Do you know who that gentleman is over there at the bar, Duley?"

It took the deputy a few seconds to reorganize his train of thought and look over in the direction Hunter indicated. "Came into town a couple of days ago. He's been hanging around here in the Red Dog a lot. I think he's sweet on the blonde that works here, Nancy."

"I'm going to go upstairs and get my, wife. Why don't you keep on eye on him for a while, until I come back down." Hunter didn't like the idea of leaving the stranger unwatched. If his feelings of disquiet proved to be true, he wanted the stranger to be occupied.

Without waiting for Deputy Duley's agreement, Hunter began to make his way across the saloon and up the stairs. He halted outside the same chamber door he had seen Shannon enter earlier, and as he reached for the knob, he glanced down toward the bar.

The gray-haired man was looking directly up at him. There was panic in his gaze as he gulped the last of his drink and hurriedly turned to leave the saloon. Hunter watched the deputy halt him with a hand placed on his arm.

The minute Graylin Stone left the upstairs chamber, Shannon leapt to her feet and made a dash toward the unlocked door.

Ivey was quick for a man preoccupied with dressing. His long legs carried him across the room in a matter of seconds, and he was pulling Shannon away from the portal.

He clasped her tightly in his embrace, his warm breath brushing against her cheek as he dragged her back across the room. "Ah, dove, I'm afraid I can't let you flee." His one hand twisted in her hair, the other was wrapped around her throat.

"Please, let me go!" Shannon begged, knowing that she was totally at this madman's mercy. There would be no help forthcoming from outside the chamber. Hunter was busy trying to capture Murdock, the ranchers as well were caught up in all the excitement, and no one cared that she had left the saloon with the woman everyone in Last Chance Gulch believed to be Nancy Inverness.

"I can pay you whatever money you want. You heard my uncle, I will inherit a fortune in only a few months. I will give it all to you, whatever you want!"

"The game's too far gone to change the stakes now," Ivey purred against her ear, his slender fingers caressing the soft texture of her skin against her throat.

"I won't tell anyone about you if you let me go!" Shannon was too stricken with terror to notice the tears that filled her eyes.

As she felt Ivey's hand around her throat, all she could think about was Hunter and the happiness she had shared with him. Though what had passed between them had been brief, they were the happiest moments of her life, and she was loath to know that they would soon be over.

Dragging her over to the bureau, Ivey pulled a silk stocking from a drawer and tightened the sheer material around Shannon's neck. "I admit it is a pity that such beauty must be wasted, but there is nothing else to do."

"Please," Shannon whispered, feeling the strain at having to attempt to draw air into her lungs.

"My mother would have loved your touch, dove. I remember as a child she would dress me in her sheer negligees and stroke my body. She never seemed quite pleased enough with me, complaining that my skin was too rough to her touch.

"My efforts to please were always wasted, but there is one thing for sure, without dear Mother, I never would have been so successful in my career. Because of her, I acquired a love for satin and silk caressing my flesh. And because of this love of dressing as a woman, I am the best in my field of employment."

Shannon knew the man was insane. His fingers roamed over her flesh in adoration, but at the same time the opposite hand was gently twisting the stocking and cutting off necessary oxygen.

Shannon felt her body sagging against him, and heard a buzzing in her head as she gasped aloud for air.

"Don't fight it, dove. Allow fate to claim you."

The husky words came to her from a far distance as Shannon slipped down to the carpeted floor.

Wishing only to assure himself that Shannon was all right, Hunter did not knock upon the outside chamber door, but instead pushed the portal wide. The scene that met his gaze filled him with horror.

Shannon lay slumped on the floor. A man with makeup smeared over his face, and wearing a woman's petticoat, was over her, his fist twisting a stocking that was wrapped around her throat. As the man looked up at the sound of the opening of the door, his mad gaze locked with the rage that filled Hunter's regard.

As Hunter ran across the room, his gun was already out of his holster and pointed at the man. "Get away from her!" His words were a demand that would brook no delay.

As the chamber door was pushed open and Ivey looked in the direction to see the large man entering the room, some of the madness that always washed over him when he killed began to slip away. Looking down at Shannon as he heard the man's order, he let the stocking fall in a silken heap upon her chest.

She appeared lifeless. Hunter's anguish was overpowering as he stood a few feet away, his gun pointed at the killer, his eyes set upon the woman on the floor.

With the release of Ivey's hand from the stocking, a small bit of air was allowed to go down Shannon's throat. She gagged, gasping for more air as her hands reached up, her fingers raking at the stocking.

At that moment Hunter forgot about the killer. He knelt

at Shannon's side and pulled the sheer stocking from around her throat.

To Ivey, everything now hinged on the survival of the quickest. He did not hesitate, but grabbed up the six-gun on the bed that earlier Graylin Stone had taken away from Shannon.

He would have to kill both of them and get out of this room if he were to have a chance of getting out of Last Chance Gulch without being caught. Pulling the hammer back, he directed the weapon at the man's back and squeezed the trigger.

Hunter's sharp ears heard the clicking sound of the hammer being pulled back. With a single swift motion he turned and fired his Peacemaker.

Nathaniel Ivey fell to the floor, the expression on his face revealing his surprise in at last being handed his final justice. His mother had told him the last time he had seen her, right before he had placed a satin pillow over her face and snuffed the life out of her body, that he would go in a bad way; with a moment's reflection left him, he guessed she had been right.

Gasping loudly, Shannon drew large gulps of air into her tortured throat, and as Hunter gathered her up into his arms, she wept upon his shoulder. "He was going to kill me. He killed Bonny and Abigail Primer. I was to be his next victim!"

"You are all right now, my love. He is dead, he can't hurt anyone ever again." Hunter soothed her as he brushed the copper curls away from her face. As he held her in his arms, he felt her trembling, and knew how close to losing her he had come.

It was painful for Shannon to talk, but she knew that she had to ask about her uncle before he got out of town. "My uncle, Hunter. We have to find him before he gets away and goes back to St. Louis." She knew that if he returned to St. Louis, where he wielded so much power, no one would believe her accusations that he was a murder and had paid a hit man to follow her all the way to Montana Territory.

"Your uncle? The man who left this chamber was your uncle?" Hunter was stunned by this new revelation. "Did he know what this man was going to do to you?"

"Yes . . . yes. He hired him to follow me to Last Chance Gulch and to murder me."

This was all Hunter needed to hear. With Shannon still clutched in his arms, he exited the chamber and started down the stairs.

Marshal Taylor joined Deputy Duley in detaining the stranger in the Red Dog Saloon. As the two lawmen stood on either side of Graylin, and he glimpsed his niece, still alive, being carried down the stairs by the tall man, his immediate thoughts were of getting out of the saloon and as far away as possible from Last Chance Gulch.

"Listen, gentlemen, as much as I have enjoyed talking with you, I have to be somewhere in just a few minutes." Graylin hurriedly pulled out his pocket watch, looked rapidly at the time, and then over toward the stairs once again.

"And where would you have to be going, mister?" Duley asked, his suspicion increasing by the man's agitated manner.

"I . . . I . . . there's someone I have to meet." The large man and his niece were making their way through the crowd and quickly approaching in his direction.

Marshal John Taylor also thought the stranger's actions rather peculiar, and laying his hand against his arm, he inquired, "Why don't you tell me who it is you are to meet? Perhaps I know the gentleman."

"I don't have the time, Marshal." Graylin jerked his arm away and started quickly toward the door.

"Hold that man, Marshal Taylor," Hunter shouted across the room, catching hold of everyone's attention. All eyes in the saloon looked in the direction of the gentleman trying to rush through the double doors.

Taylor and Duley leapt into action, each lawman grabbing Graylin Stone by an arm.

"Unhand me this minute," Graylin Stone declared in his haughtiest tone; the same tone that in the past had gotten him almost everything he wanted.

"Well, let's see here, mister. You can be on your way in no time at all once we see what Hunter has to say." Marshal Taylor spoke in a cool, easy tone.

Stepping before the lawmen and the one they were holding on to, Hunter questioned Shannon. "Is he the man, Little Flame? Is this your uncle, the same man who sent a man to kill you?"

Tears rolled down Shannon's cheeks as she nodded. "He sent him to kill me, but instead he killed Bonny and Abigail Primer, only because they rode into Last Chance Gulch on the same stage as I did, and both women had red hair."

"I don't know what she's talking about," Graylin Stone declared in a firm tone, his hatred for his niece evident in his glaring stare.

"I saw him kill a man, that's why I fled St. Louis and came here to Last Chance Gulch." Shannon's voice was pitiful, no one in the saloon doubted her for a minute.

The five ranchers stepped to her side as though they would protect her from any farther harm.

"She's insane. She's my niece all right, but she's as crazy as my brother was. That's why I'm here in Last Chance Gulch. I was looking for her, to take her back to St. Louis, where I can get some help for her willful imagination."

"I guess the best we can do, then," Marshal Taylor stated, "is to see what Hanging Harry thinks of this matter. He's the circuit judge in the area, and is due to arrive in Last Chance Gulch tomorrow morning."

Graylin Stone's face paled, his voice, stammering out the declarations of injustice being handed out to him. "You can't keep me! I demand to see my lawyer! She's mad, I tell you. You can't keep me on her word alone!"

"No, Marshal, you can keep him jailed on the scene that you will find upstairs. The man he hired is dead. I killed him as he was trying to strangle my wife." At the moment

Hunter would have enjoyed nothing more than to do harm to Shannon's uncle, and seeing the fury on his face, Graylin tried to stay behind Deputy Duley.

"That's enough for me," Marshal Taylor stated-in firm conviction. Hanging Harry can decide his fate."

Graylin Stone visibly cringed at mention of the judge's name, and at the angry faces glaring at him as the patrons of the saloon gathered closer, and the five angry men standing protectively close to Shannon.

Deputy Duley escorted the prisoner across the street to the jail while Marshal Taylor and Hunter set Shannon down in a chair in a corner of the saloon.

Attentively, Hunter hovered over her, wanting to make sure she was all right. The ranchers stood only a foot away. "Should I send for the doctor to see to your throat?" There were purple bruises on the tender flesh, and with the sight of them, Hunter's anger surfaced again.

"No . . . no, Hunter. I am only glad that it is at last over." Though minutes earlier Shannon's very life had been in jeopardy, she was relieved that her past had finally found her and everything was now out in the open.

"Do you want to tell us everything now?" Marshal Taylor took her hand within his own, lending her the security that he knew she was in need of at the moment.

Shannon slowly nodded her head. "I saw my uncle kill a man outside his study one evening. I had been living with him since the death of my father, and fearing what he would do to me, I ran."

No one interrupted as Shannon drew in a small sigh. "I was so frightened that night. I was all alone in St. Louis. I wound up in a house that I know now was not the respectable establishment I believed it to be."

"This is where I met Honey Belle."

"But I thought you were Honey Belle?" Marshal Taylor interjected here, and the ranchers listened closer, but with Hunter's stare directed at the marshal, he sat back in his chair.

"No, Marshal. Honey Belle worked in Madame Lilly's

establishment. She was dying the night I met her, and she told me that she had answered an ad for a mail-order bride, and was to leave St. Louis the following morning and head for Montana Territory."

Shannon's turquoise eyes looked up at the ranchers, and glimpsing Alex, she softly stated, "I'm sorry I deceived you all, but I was frightened that my uncle would find me. My real name is Shannon Stone."

Her gaze went back to Hunter. As she hoped he did not think her too horrible, she continued. "I switched identities with Honey Belle and came here to lose myself until such time as I could return to St. Louis and confront my uncle."

"I guess that you can forget all about that now, ma'am. Hanging Harry will take care of your uncle when he arrives tomorrow." Marshal Taylor rose from the chair he was sitting in, having gotten all the information he needed for the time being.

Reaching across the table, Hunter took Shannon's hand into his own. "I love you, Little Flame."

"You're not angry that I didn't tell you about my past before now?"

"I am only glad that you met this woman called Honey Belle and were able to get away from a man such as your uncle." Hunter spoke his feelings, not able to imagine how Shannon could have survived if she had not fled Graylin Stone's cruelty.

"We are all of the same mind, my dear Honey . . . I mean Shannon." Lucas, as usual, spoke for the group of ranchers.

"I would like you all to meet Honey Belle." Shannon clasped Hunter's hand tightly within her own as she turned to look across the bar at the painting of the beautiful young woman reclining naked upon a gilt-edged sofa.

"There she is. Honey Belle. The most famous artist in all of St. Louis sought her out and painted her." Shannon's tone turned sad, and Hunter wrapped his arm around her shoulder.

"Because of her I found you, Hunter, and I know what real happiness means. She was right. I was able to lose myself in Montana Territory and find a life that can be filled with joy."

"I thank this woman in this painting, Little Flame. She sent me my heart."

EPILOGUE

As Hunter approached Shannon where she lay upon their bed of soft furs, his eyes lingered upon the gentle swell of her abdomen before drawing upward to hold upon her questioning regard.

"Are you troubled this evening, husband?" Shannon made room for Hunter to settle next to her.

As Hunter stretched his large frame down next to her, he lovingly gathered her within his embrace. "My only worry is over you, Little Flame."

"And why would you have cause for worry, Hunter? Our child grows strong beneath my heart." She caressed her stomach in a loving gesture. "I have never been so happy." To Shannon, her world was complete. Hunter was the type of man every woman wished for as a husband, and soon they would have their first child.

"I worry that tomorrow, when the ranchers arrive in the village, you will tire yourself by tending to their needs."

Shannon's laughter filled his ears as she considered the humor of his remark. There was no fear of her wearing herself out as far as Lucas, Logan, Jackson, Alex, and Cookie were concerned. The last time they paid her a visit she had been only a couple of months gone with her pregnancy, and at every hand she found one of the ranchers in her way as they attempted to help her with some small chore.

Now that she was showing so well with. the babe, she

held little doubt that the five men would be stumbling over themselves with their attempts to pamper her.

"Don't worry, Hunter." Knowing her husband saw little humor in the prospect of the ranchers paying a visit, she soothed him. "I promise this time I won't allow them to monopolize as much of my time as they did on their last visit. Summer Rose and Spotted Eagle have promised to entertain them. As well, your grandfather assures me that he has some fine stories to amuse them with."

Hunter's hand possessively covered hers where it lay upon her belly, and as he inhaled her sweet scent, his heated breath caressed her throat. "I thought with time that the feelings I hold for you would settle into the same easy structure as does the rest of my life. I fear, though, that with each day's passing, the love in my heart for you blooms and grows beyond the limits of my simple control. I am a man who willingly admits that your slightest frown holds the power to bring me to my knees."

Shannon loved these moments when Hunter spoke his heart to her. Turning and pressing her body tightly up against him, she sighed softly as the security of his love surrounded her, "I love you, Hunter."

"Forever, my heart," he whispered right before his lips found hers.

ROMANCE FROM JO BEVERLY

DANGEROUS JOY   (0-8217-5129-8, $5.99)

FORBIDDEN   (0-8217-4488-7, $4.99)

THE SHATTERED ROSE   (0-8217-5310-X, $5.99)

TEMPTING FORTUNE   (0-8217-4858-0, $4.99)

ROMANCE FROM JANELLE TAYLOR

ANYTHING FOR LOVE   (0-8217-4992-7, $5.99)

DESTINY MINE   (0-8217-5185-9, $5.99)

CHASE THE WIND   (0-8217-4740-1, $5.99)

MIDNIGHT SECRETS   (0-8217-5280-4, $5.99)

MOONBEAMS AND MAGIC   (0-8217-0184-4, $5.99)

SWEET SAVAGE HEART   (0-8217-5276-6, $5.99)

ROMANCE FROM FERN MICHAELS

DEAR EMILY   (0-8217-4952-8, $5.99)

WISH LIST   (0-8217-5228-6, $6.99)

AND IN HARDCOVER:

VEGAS RICH   (1-57566-057-1, $25.00)

LOOK FOR THESE REGENCY ROMANCES